A LITTLE GAME

"Spider! Big spider!"

Sarah spun and buried her face in Hawk's shoulder. She clutched him tightly, clinging to fistfuls of his shirt and vest. She felt his arm flinch as he flicked the horrid creature off the end of his knife and into the jungle and wiped the blade clean on his pant leg.

He shifted his stance and wrapped both arms around her, catching her more fully in his embrace. "That's it, honey. You're gonna be all right." Hawk heard the endearment slip out and questioned the wisdom of his actions. He'd never had a woman melt into him with such guileless abandonment before. She fit him just right, with the crown of her hair nestling beneath his chin and her long legs placing her hips just at the juncture of his thighs.

And then she looked at him with those big eyes, golden pools flecked with green that revealed raw, uncontrolled emotion, and he nearly lost all perspective. She wanted to be kissed. Even if he couldn't read the desire swirling about her face in a fiery halo, he could see it in the breathless parting of her lips. And man, was he tempted to give her what she asked. Tempted to forget decorum and missions and taking care of business, and sample what she unconsciously offered him.

He could just tilt her chin up and slide his mouth over hers. Play a little game with her, teach her and tease her with his lips and tongue. . . .

Other *Love Spell* books by Julie Miller:
IMMORTAL HEART

Shadow of the Hawk

Julie Miller

LOVE SPELL BOOKS NEW YORK CITY

LOVE SPELL®

June 1999

Published by

Dorchester Publishing Co., Inc.
276 Fifth Avenue
New York, NY 10001

ISBN 0-505-52322-1

Printed in the United States of America.

For my family.

With special thanks to my ace critique partner, Sherry Siwinski, and my friends and supporters in Prairieland Romance Writers, especially Kristin Gabriel, Mary Ann McQuillan, Sue Riggins Lessor, Sue Baumann, Brad Roberts, Kathleen Pieper, Connie Morgan, Karen Beilke, and Victoria France Lipovsky.

Thanks also to fellow teacher Carol Noel, for helping with the Spanish.

I'd like to thank all the teachers who influenced my life, in the classroom and as a colleague, in particular Jane Boursaw, Jane Furkin, Sally Williams, Doug Allbritton, Nancy Gilmer, George Lake, and Dr. Ben Nelms.

And I'd like to thank the students who have made teaching so special for me, including that rare 1997 Speech Team of five ladies—fine young women and heroines all.

You may contact the author by writing to:
P.O. Box 5162, Grand Island, NE 68802-5162

Prologue

"Shadow Man."

Hawk ignored the static interruption from his radio, closed his eyes and stood perfectly still. He tilted his nose to the sky and tested the scent of the jungle. His breath moved in and out in sync with the hot, oppressive breeze on the humid air.

He sifted through the exotic perfumes of lush green vegetation, animal spoor, rotting underbrush and rare flowers. He recognized the fresh kill of a predator. He tilted his head and reassured himself that the acrid odor of recently fired gunpowder still whispered through the air.

But no man.

He should pick up the scent of man.

"Dammit, Hawk! Are you there? Report in! Over."

His eyes flashed open; dark pools of midnight sank into the angles of his camouflage-streaked face. He beat down a surge of panic that could obliterate his powers and scanned the perimeter of the trampled foliage one more time.

He flexed his white-knuckled grip around the barrel and trigger of his AK-47. Where was his calm? Where were his guides?

"Hawk! Either you get a trail or you get the hell out of there! I can hold this chopper on the ground another two minutes, tops. The Chameleon's men are closing in on our position."

Hawk flipped the switch on his radio. "Shadow Man here. Shut up already, Major. I read you."

Relief tempered the authoritative clip in Major Murphy's voice. "Del Rio's got this thing jerry-rigged to fly us out of here, but she won't take another hit." A two-second pause echoed like thunder in Hawk's ears. "Any sign of the colonel?"

"Nothing." Hawk backed over his own path, not wanting to disturb a single clue. "There ought to be some track. I've got a firefight. Two men. I've got a U.S.-issue boot print and the Russian guy's sweat. But it goes nowhere. I can't find him."

But he'd been here. Hawk knew it in his bones that Colonel Ramsey had taken the hit in this man-made clearing. He'd followed the trail easily enough. One military man in pursuit of a civilian, both stripped of heavy gear to travel fast.

The evidence of their fight was here. Crushed greenery. Impacted earth. Blood on a leaf.

But there was no track out.

Neither man had left this place.

And yet they were gone.

"Head out, man. That's an order." The heavy sigh across the static plunged into the hollowness of Hawk's soul.

He'd never failed before.

* * *

"Peace, my son." The ancient voice spoke the words in his native tongue. "Look into yourself and find your peace."

Hawk threw the blanket off his shoulders and inhaled deeply. The tangy spice of the burning offering filled the sweat lodge. In his mind, he named the scents one by one . . . tansy, hickory bark. . . . He squeezed his eyes shut, fighting off the demon that threatened to lead him astray from his destiny. Dampness coated his naked skin. Heat moved through his pores like the wings of the spirit he sought, and cleansed his mind of troubling thoughts.

Otis Peace Hands's wizened voice guided him back to his quest. "Seek the light, son. The past is the past. Seek the light."

Blackness swirled into a kaleidoscope of color. Shapeless at first. Then the fuzzy images began to take form.

A gray-winged hawk, flecked with black points, soared from the center of the maelstrom. His spirit guide.

Hawk joined the bird and flew high above the swirling mass, then plunged with him down into the color. As they descended, the hues around him took shape. Leaves. In greens of every shade from the newest grass to the most ancient of firs. Trees. Golds and browns and tints of black defined the trunks and branches.

The jungle.

His guide had returned him to the jungle.

Hawk struggled against the image. He sought the future. He sought the answer to the dreams that plagued his lucid nights.

Ancient words chanted in his brain. Otis was calling the power. The old man was calling forth the power within Hawk.

Hawk's lungs constricted. He gasped for air and collapsed to the floor. His body spasmed in one strong seizure that compressed every fiber in him.

And then he was free.

Not the jungle.

The wooded glade of his Alaskan home where he'd lived as a child. His favorite among his sixteen homes in eighteen years as a third-generation military brat.

The hawk sailed above the treetops, following a ribbon of crystal blue water that twisted down the mountain to the ocean.

The air around Hawk cooled. He relaxed and fell into the dream.

The hawk glided down to the water and snatched a fish in its talons. The triumphant hunter settled on the shore and thanked God for the kill, in the tradition of the old ones. He thanked God for the bounty of this day and the strength it would provide.

Then the raptor turned its head and Hawk's vision became one with the great bird's. A flat rock jutted out into the water. Two bear cubs frolicked in and out of the glacial stream, batting at fish, teaching themselves the way it had always been, learning their strengths, honing their skills. Nature continued its balanced cycle of life.

A hoarse bellow trumpeted from the woods, the warning bark of the cubs' mother. Hawk watched the massive Kodiak lumber out from the trees onto the rock shelf. She sniffed and nuzzled her cubs, bonding them with her scent.

Then she turned toward the hawk, toward Hawk himself, and reared up on her hind legs, crying out a warning to him. She raised her snout and bellowed again, and as she took the defensive stance, Hawk could see the blood matting the fur on the left side of her chest.

The brave maternal warrior's heart had been ripped out.

And then Hawk sensed the darkness behind him. He felt a chilly rush of air wrap a dank cloak about his shoulders. The trees around him blurred, then popped, exploding into utter blackness.

The water crashed against the rock, splashing blue, then gray, then freezing into black tendrils of ice that reached out toward the cubs.

The Kodiak howled. She dropped to all four legs and circled her cubs, placing herself between them and the darkness that closed in around them.

The encroaching void swept Hawk up in its clutches and carried him toward the rock. Then the ground itself shattered beneath his feet and fell away into a nothingness darker than the darkness itself.

The bear turned her tawny eyes to him. Sad eyes. Pleading eyes. Empty eyes.

And then it was gone.

Hawk jerked again and knew himself once more. The sweat lodge. His father's uncle, Otis. The vision quest.

Damp with sweat, gritty with smoke and dirt, he flattened his palms on the floor of the lodge

13

and pushed himself up to a sitting position. His father's blanket lay twisted about his hips. A mystic warmth hung in the air, but Hawk felt cold. He felt a lingering chill all the way to his bones, and shivered.

The only warmth he knew radiated from the oblong piece of black obsidian—his sicun, or spirit stone—that hung from a leather strap around his neck. He clutched the stone in his fist, feeling the heat of spirit magic coursing through it, ebbing from it into his hand.

"What does it mean, Otis?" he asked, explaining in brief detail the vision that had come to him. "The mother? The encroaching darkness? What is she telling me?"

Otis rubbed a thumb and forefinger back and forth across the tip of one of his silvery braids. Hawk knew no one could truly understand a vision except the recipient. But he also valued the wisdom of his elders, and respected their knowledge of secrets that even one with his gift did not yet comprehend.

"I do not know, son," the old man finally said. "I can only tell you this: You must save her. Or *you* will die."

Chapter One

Hawk slipped into the town meeting almost thirty minutes after it had started and wondered what he had missed. The verbal fireworks spouting from one side of the room to the other were threatening to turn these normally dull, endless monthly proceedings into a riot.

"They're heathens down there!" A plump Anglo woman with a shrill voice pointed an accusing finger at a gray-suited man across the aisle. "It simply isn't safe for them to go."

The man adjusted his wire-rimmed spectacles on the bridge of his nose in an irritated gesture. "I say it's a matter of money. With budget freezes on the horizon, the school system simply can't afford this trip or the insurance liability it would create."

Hawk folded his arms across his chest and leaned against the back wall. Allowing the debate to fade into a meaningless buzz of white noise, he used his unobtrusive position to study the packed high school auditorium.

He attended these town hall meetings as a matter of course, an unofficial representative of the Native American citizens who populated the town and two reservations on the outskirts of Marysville, Kansas. His main concern had always been to see that tribal lands were maintained for tribal use, at the discretion of the council of elders. His own Pawnee ancestors came from a different region of the country, but many traditions were the same across Indian cultures—a respect for the land, honor and respect for one's ancestors, and an inviolate sense of community.

Since retiring from the Marine Corps and settling in Marysville almost four years ago, Hawk had established a counseling practice that catered to the various needs of the tiny rural town in northwest Kansas. He'd just come from a session with a young couple dealing with the grief of losing an infant son to SIDS.

One didn't have to live in the big city to face tragedy. The crazy, inexplicable problems of the world could touch down anywhere.

Hawk had discovered that living in a sparsely populated rural area sometimes meant those problems were secreted away and left to fester, either from lack of knowledge and resources to combat them, or because of town gossip. He'd seen a lot in his forty years, but one thing he'd learned at a young age was how damaging and demoralizing a few misspoken rumors could be to a person's character and spirit. Judging by the number of people in the audience springing to their feet to voice their two cents' worth on the issue at hand, little Marysville was no different.

The mayor pounded his gavel on the table, trying to maintain order. The auditorium quieted briefly, and even Hawk gave the man his full attention.

"I think the council should table the discussion for now." He gestured to the four men and one woman on either side of him on the stage. "We'll look at this in executive session and address your concerns next month at the May meeting."

"But you can't wait that long!" A dried-up string bean of a woman stood up next to the plump one who'd spoken earlier. "This field trip is scheduled for the end of the school year. We have to stop it now!"

"Stop what?" A new voice entered the fray. A younger woman in the very front row, who'd been hidden from Hawk's view by all the bodies in between them, stood up and spun around to face the audience. "Stop their education?"

Every eye in the now-silent room focused on her. Her wide-flung arms slowly dropped to her sides. Her tongue darted out to lick her lips, and her fingers crept together and clenched tightly in front of her.

The poor thing had a sudden case of stage fright. Hawk stood up straight, his intuition immediately kicking in when he sensed someone in trouble. Though too far away to read her facial expression clearly, he could see her head moving from side to side as though scanning the audience for a friendly face and finding no one.

Hawk knew Sarah McCormick by reputation only. She taught at the high school. He didn't socialize much with the townsfolk, but he recognized the McCormick name as one of the old guard. Her family had been one of the first to settle in Marysville. A street and park were named after one of her pioneering ancestors. Her family's name seemed to have captured the attention of the crowd, but it didn't appear to be giving her much confidence right now.

Almost unbidden, he let his powers of perception slide over her. A coppery glow of fear surrounded her plain oval face, but the paleness in the halo he perceived revealed she was more self-conscious than afraid.

She was a thirtyish woman of average height who hid the details of her figure beneath a drab printed dress that fit her like a sack. She had tamed unruly strands of toffee-colored hair into a restraining clip at the nape of her neck.

Her suddenly timid, undecorated appearance called to mind the unflattering phrase *spinster schoolmarm*. Hawk swallowed the sour taste in his mouth. Nicknames were labels. And labels could be cruel things.

He'd heard plenty of them himself. *New boy. Weirdo. Crazy man.*

He beat down the old memories and concentrated his power on Miss McCormick. Besides her coppery aura of fear, he detected something else. An indefinable determination about her slender shoulders. He saw courage in a rich azure light that darkened and gathered strength around her. In a few seconds of interminable silence, Hawk picked up more valor from her lone figure than from anybody else in the room.

He wondered if she had any idea just how much spirit she carried inside her.

"Sarah, sit down. You're embarrassing your-self." Walter Kensit, sitting to the right of the mayor, whispered the warning in a voice that was painfully loud enough for anyone without a hearing aid to catch.

Hawk spared a piercing glance for the newly reelected councilman. Miss McCormick turned and looked at him, too, revealing thick waves of hair that fell to her waist. It seemed so old-fashioned to wear hair that long, hair that probably hadn't seen more than a trim since she'd graduated from high school.

But there was nothing old-fashioned about the steely set of her posture. The schoolmarm pulled back her shoulders and lifted her chin, defying Kensit's thoughtless interruption. Her courage eased Hawk's flare of concern and transformed it into respect.

When she turned around to face the crowd, her fear had receded. He tamped down on his sixth sense and listened to what she had to say.

"Education isn't limited to the classroom," she began quietly, moving to the center aisle so everyone could see her. "It isn't limited to books or computers or equations."

The thread of steel mixing with the soft silk of her voice captured Hawk's attention along with the rest of the audience.

"The opportunity to learn is all around us. If we limit ourselves, we limit our children's futures."

The woman had very expressive hands, thought Hawk. She moved her hands and arms with a precision and grace he'd attribute to a ballet dancer or artist. She used them now to emphasize her point.

"This is no different from taking our elemen-

19

tary students to the zoo. It's no different from taking our ag students to the fish hatchery. The only
difference is in distance."

"A thousand miles is a lot of distance." Walter
Kensit broke the hushed spell Miss McCormick
had temporarily woven about the room. Muffled
conversations broke out among several in atten-
dance.

Mayor Webber struck the table with his gavel
and regained silence. "Miss McCormick, no one is
questioning your insight as a teacher, but we are
concerned about your judgment in arranging this
field trip for these students."

"There's more to the world than Kansas, your
honor."

"Yes. But some island we've never heard of in
the Caribbean?"

Her hands closed into fists and pounded the
air. "We're visiting a cradle of civilization. His-
toric ruins. We're not sunning on the beach picking up Latin lotharios. We'll learn about where
we come from. What we can become if—"

Councilman Kensit interrupted her impas-
sioned plea. "Sarah. Have you ever been outside
of the country? Outside of Kansas?"

Hawk bristled at the condescension in his tone
right along with Miss McCormick. He sensed
some personal connection between the two, and
Kensit's words conveyed a subtle dig that was
meant to put her in her place.

He half expected her to give up the battle. She
stood there, center stage, staring at the floor for
almost a minute of utter silence. Hawk acknowl-
edged a little voice in his head, secretly rooting
for her to fight back.

He shrugged with a twinge of disappointment

when she walked back to her seat. But in that instant before she sat down, her chin came up again as something galvanized her into action. She stood up straight and pointed to various areas in the audience.

"Lyndsay, Denise, all of you—stand up." The crowd murmured again. Heads spun around to see five girls, about sixteen or seventeen years of age, rise to their feet. Hawk recognized one of them: Colleen Walks-a-Deer, the daughter of a friend of his who farmed outside of town.

With a wave of her hands, Miss McCormick quieted the room. "These five young women have earned the right to go. They wrote a winning essay about the role of women in society. The contributions women have made, and that they hope to make to create and nurture a civilized world."

Hawk couldn't tell if this was feminist diatribe or a throwback to the traditional values of women keeping hearth and home. Either way, Miss McCormick was slowly wooing some of the audience to her side.

"There's more to this world than Marysville or Kansas or even the United States." The woman was right. Hawk had seen a lot more of the world than he ever wanted to, but he recognized the value in her argument.

"It's arrogant to think that this is the only way to live. That we can't learn from other cultures. Just because I've never been to Isla Tenebrosa doesn't mean their culture has no value."

Isla Tenebrosa?

Hawk's mild amusement at the evening's entertainment vanished in a heartbeat. Tenebrosa was his worst nightmare.

21

His shock at the mention of the island's name kept him from picking up the tense undercurrents between Sarah McCormick and Walter Kensit when she turned and walked toward the stage. "Just because you've never been married, Walter, doesn't mean that that institution has no value."

Hawk reeled at the implication of what this woman was proposing. He tried to sort out the thoughts skidding through his mind. What was history. What was real. What was unexplainable.

What was certain.

Meanwhile, Miss McCormick crossed down the aisle to the man in the gray suit. "Mr. Hammond. Through these essays, my students were awarded a grant that will fund the entire week, including transportation, lodging and food." She turned toward the missuses Plumpy and String Bean. "Their parents have signed release forms entrusting them to my care. We're traveling with a reputable guide on an expedition he's led several times before. We'll carry a two-way radio to call in a medevac helicopter in case we need serious medical support."

A medevac chopper in the jungle? Hawk squelched the surge of mad laughter in his throat. She was so naive. She had no idea.

"Besides, we'll be gone only a week," said Miss McCormick. "What could happen in seven days?"

A lot. A hell of a lot. Hawk had seen jungle missions go bad in less than seven hours. He'd lost friends and comrades in less than seven minutes' time.

He'd lost himself on Isla Tenebrosa.

Hawk shook the thoughts aside and breathed in deeply, seeking his calm center. This was only a school field trip, after all, not a covert military mission.

And yet that was exactly what propelled him out of the anonymity of the crowd and down the center aisle to face Miss Sarah McCormick.

"You can't go." He said it flatly, plainly, and all eyes turned to face him. Including hers.

She had big round hazel eyes that blazed more gold than green as she vented her frustration on him. "Excuse me?"

Her fists rode to her hips and she moved toward him, a slender package of righteous anger and determination. "Mr. Echohawk, right? I don't see how a field trip with my students concerns you. You don't have children. You don't work for the school. . . . "

Tawny eyes.

"I've been to Isla Tenebrosa, Miss McCormick. And I know from personal experience that one hell of a lot can go wrong in seven days."

Sarah escaped outside into the night and breathed deeply. A light rain had cooled the April air, giving her some relief from her pounding headache caused by the heat and stubborn opposition in the auditorium.

Her mouth felt parched and her throat ached. She must have talked to every single pillar of the community—and even in a town the size of Marysville, there were plenty. That . . . that . . . Echohawk person had nearly destroyed all the headway she'd made in securing community approval for her field trip to the ruins outside El Espanto.

Not that she needed their approval.

This opportunity was a geography teacher's

dream. A chance to actually see and touch a piece of history, to learn about a culture by experiencing it, not just reading about it.

She'd learned too much in her life by just reading about it. *Good grief.* She was thirty-four years old. It was high time she seized an opportunity and lived a little. Experienced life on the front lines.

Not that she didn't love teaching.

Her students were her life. Her work was more than just a job. She was an expedition leader, a tour guide who led her students through life, helping them discover knowledge and learn to love history and geography along the way.

So when the flyer came from the Sinclair Geographic Foundation, offering female students a Windjammer-type adventure in archeology, Sarah jumped at the chance. She had a particularly bright group of girls in her sophomore geography and junior world history classes this year. She submitted their group essay and they won the Sinclair competition.

Couldn't the town see the honor they'd earned? Not allowing those girls to go would be a slap in the face to their accomplishment. Too many times in Sarah's career, she'd seen girls' programs overshadowed by boys', and sports programs emphasized over academics. This was their chance to shine.

It was *her* chance.

And no big, taciturn Indian growling dire warnings in a voice so soft and low it made her nerve endings tingle was going to spoil that chance for her.

She lifted her shoulders in another deep breath and started across the emptying parking lot, keys in hand. She'd dreamed herself out of Kansas so many times, she'd lost count. Every time she'd had the chance to make those dreams a reality, fate stepped in and forced her to stay.

First it was her mother's terminal illness. Then her father's death. As an only child in her generation of the family, the care of her maiden aunts, Millie and Doris, had become her responsibility. And as they aged, their demands on Sarah's time increased.

Soon she'd be trapped in this town forever.

She'd put her desires and goals aside for others her entire adult life, escaping only through her books. She thought Walter Kensit had offered her a way out, a chance to see the world firsthand. But that, too, had been only a dream. Not a dream, she corrected herself. An all-too-painful reality lesson.

Reason enough to forgo ladylike acquiesence and publicly speak out in support of the trip. More than enough reason to defy Millie and Doris. To turn her back on Walter. To ignore that . . . that . . . Mr. Echohawk.

"Sarah."

She stopped in her tracks and cringed at the sight of Walter leaning against the side of her car. He unfolded his arms and straightened, approaching her when she refused to come any closer. Six feet of Ivy League grooming, from the ruffled waves of his wheat blond hair to the polished tips of his leather penny loafers.

He was a handsome man, she thought absently. Chiseled features, trim body. A well-established insurance man with the ability to charm money out of the pocket of a miser. His natural grace and intelligence had charmed her easily enough.

She'd been such a fool. Such a stupid, gullible fool to have risked her heart on him.

"Walter." She crossed her arms in a defensive posture and sidled away when he touched her elbow. He spread his hands, palms-up, in mock surrender.

"Sarah, sweetie, I'm sorry tonight was so rough on you." He flashed her a boyish smile. "I did try to warn you, though. Folks just don't think what you're planning is safe or proper."

How could she ever have been taken in by that slick used-car-salesman expression on his face? Walter didn't exactly lie. But he knew how to skew the truth in such a way that a lie would be preferable.

"We're going, Walter," she said, dismissing him. She scooted around him toward her car. When his fingers closed around her elbow, she jerked her arm away, hating herself for betraying how easily he could make her lose her cool. "You had no right to put a school issue up for a community vote like that. Nonetheless, the people sided with me."

"By a narrow margin."

"It doesn't matter. We're going." She inserted her key into the door lock, but Walter grabbed her wrist and spun her around, backing her up against the door and pinning her there with his body.

"You're playing a dangerous game, Sarah. Stay here and let me take care of you. I can make a few phone calls and this whole thing will be forgotten. Think of your reputation. You may even have put your job on the line with this reckless behavior. You don't want to be known as a rabble-rouser."

"A rabble-rouser?" Sarah flashed back over her

thirty-four years and tried to think of one instance when good manners and her natural shyness hadn't kept her from causing trouble. She drew a bland, sterile blank. She didn't know whether to be proud of or embarrassed by such an unremarkable, pristine history.

Shaking aside the internal debate, she argued, "I'm trying to enrich my students' education. I hardly deserve to be branded with a scarlet letter!"

"I know that, sweetie. But your family's good name . . . " He let the implication hang in the air like a humiliating fact. Walter traced her cheekbone with his index finger, a gesture meant to be tender.

His line was as smooth as his caress. But it was too practiced, she realized now. A show of light and mirrors without any substance to make it real.

How could he think she'd want this now? She'd been so curious when they'd first started dating. So embarrassingly eager to have him teach her about things a man and woman could share. But now . . .

Sarah slapped his hand away and pushed against his chest. He leaned back, but the angle only thrust his lower body closer to hers. He smiled down at her as if he knew the self-conscious discomfort this intimacy caused her.

But Sarah wouldn't show him that satisfaction. Since physical force hadn't worked, she resorted to a useful old standby: her tart sarcasm.

"How can you stand to even touch me, Wally?" She performed her best bimbo impersonation before getting seriously annoyed with him. "I thought I wasn't woman enough for you."

"I could make you that way. I can teach you

everything you need to know to make me happy."
Walter rocked his hips against hers in a mocking
display of male prowess that disgusted rather
than frightened her. "Get over your prudishness
and come back to me."

Sarah tilted her chin up in defiance of his
mocking seduction. "I'm not leaving to get even
with you. Don't make this personal."

"Those ancient civilizations you keep harping
about. They used to make virgin sacrifices, didn't
they?" He leaned in and nuzzled her ear with an
intimate whisper. "Are you sure you'll be safe
there?"

"Damn it, Walter!" She swung her hand up,
aiming for his face.

But he caught her wrist before the slap connected and laughed. "That's what I like to see. A
little fire."

With that outlet thwarted, she twisted her body,
battling to get away from him. "That's it, sweetie.
You fight me. One on one."

Then the charm bled from his voice, stilling her
struggles with an unmistakable threat. "But not
in public."

He returned his attention to her ear, running his
damp tongue around its outer shell. An uncontrol-
lable rush of panic replaced her frustrated irrita-
tion. "Walter . . . " Her voice dropped to a husky
plea.

"Miss McCormick, are you all right?" A shadow
materialized out of the darkness.

A big shadow.

Walter released her, but retreated only a few
inches to glance over his shoulder at the intrusion. Sarah held herself flush against the door,
paralyzed by the flood of relief washing through

her. That relief was tempered by wariness as the shadow took shape in the pool of light cast by the street lamp next to her car.

Darkness from darkness, she thought.

Mr. Echohawk's voice was polite, conversational, but incredibly deep. More than a low-pitched baritone. The timbre of his voice rang clear and true from the hollows of his deep chest and broad face. Defined by high cheekbones and a powerful jaw, his craggy face revealed no expression beyond casual curiosity.

Yet his presence kept Walter at bay, and for that she was grateful. She brushed at a strand of hair that wasn't really out of place and offered a shaky smile. "Mr. Kensit and I were discussing my field trip to the Caribbean."

Mr. Echohawk looked down the straight line of his nose at her. Sarah squinted, trying to return his gaze. Maybe it was a trick of the light, but his eyes seemed unnaturally dark. Midnight. Obsidian. Coal. None of those seemed to fit the absolute darkness there. It was as if his eyes absorbed the light instead of reflecting it.

Before her staring became rude, she blinked and turned her head. When she glanced up again, he was looking at Walter.

"There's no trouble, Echohawk." Walter flashed a cool smile and inclined his head toward Sarah. "We had a slight disagreement, but I think we worked it out."

The Indian made no comment. He made no reaction whatsoever to Walter's timeless man-to-man I-can-handle-my-woman wink.

And as much as Echohawk's strange demeanor intrigued her, it infuriated Walter. His smile eroded into a sneering curl of his upper lip. Walter wasn't used to making a concession, but the unbudging presence of her rescuer left him with little choice but to make a graceful exit.

"I'll call you in the morning," said Walter. She turned her head away when he leaned in to kiss her, and, after hovering a brief moment, he settled for a peck on her cheek.

When Walter had pulled back to a respectful distance, he smiled at the Indian again. "Nice try in there. But I'm afraid even your firsthand account of life on Isla Tenebrosa isn't enough to sway Miss Prim and Proper here. Maybe you can talk some sense into her. See if you can keep her home, where she belongs."

Walter sauntered off toward his car. Sarah didn't breathe easily until she heard an engine turn over and saw his black Seville drive out of the parking lot. Only then did she take in a complete lungful of air.

"Thank you, Mr. Echohawk," she said as graciously as she could with a delayed set of nerves sweeping through her and making her jittery. "That was a bit awkward, wasn't it?"

He shifted on his feet, and the tiny movement seemed to break the tension in the air. He waited until she had unlocked the door, and then he held it open for her. "You have to tell a man like that straight out if you don't want him to be forward with you, Miss McCormick."

Sarah walked into the vee formed by the open door of the car and tossed her purse onto the passenger seat. "Walter is a gentleman. He wouldn't do anything to hurt me."

"A gentleman doesn't lie in wait and then trap a woman against her car."

Sarah froze before climbing in. *Lie in wait?*

How did he know Walter had been waiting for her? Just how long had Mr. Echohawk been lurking in the shadows? How much had he heard?

A shiver of realization trickled down her spine. Maybe her relief had been premature.

The man on the opposite side of the door from her stood three or four inches taller than Walter. And judging by the thickness of his arms and the width of his chest, he outweighed the smaller man by a good fifty pounds. His jeans and chambray shirt lacked the polish of Walter's Brooks Brothers suit, giving a rough edge to his wild appearance.

No. *Wild* wasn't right. Despite the inky waterfall of black hair that flowed past his shoulders, and the exotic coloring and angles of his face, there was nothing out-of-control with this man. The very atmosphere around him seemed to bend to his will, as if he could somehow draw the protons from the atoms, leaving the air charged with his own electrical energy.

Like those darker-than-midnight eyes that absorbed the light.

Sarah blinked and shook her head, discouraging her fanciful imagination. Mr. Echohawk's comment was nothing more than an observation. With his counseling practice, he must have become very adept at reading people's emotions. Heck, it wouldn't require a Ph.D. to figure out that she'd been frightened by Walter's behavior. Anyone happening by could have interpreted the situation just as he had.

"I appreciate your concern." It struck her then that even though this man was bigger, darker, more enigmatic than Walter, she felt less threatened by him. Whereas Walter had used his size and sex to intimidate her, Mr. Echohawk used his masculinity to offer her a shield of gentle protection.

She hadn't dated much. Her male friends were truly that—friends. Walter had been the only "love" of her life, and that had turned out to be a pitiful lesson in just how different she was—how totally unfeminine, unsexy, unfun and unattractive she was to the opposite sex.

To have a man, especially a mature man with the coiled strength and exotic appeal of Mr. Echohawk, go out of his way to make sure she was safe gave her fragile ego a delicate little stroke of courage. And it reminded her of her manners.

"I don't think we've been formally introduced, Mr. . . . " What was his first name? She tried to recall. Had she ever actually heard it before? *Curious.* " . . . Echohawk." She extended her arm over the top of the door to shake his hand. "I'm Sarah McCormick."

He studied her hand as if he wasn't sure what the gesture meant. Or didn't trust her sincerity. At the moment she thought he had rejected her overture of friendship and started to withdraw her hand, he captured her fingers in his. He had the callused grip of a working-class man. His touch was firm, warm.

She was mesmerized by the contrast between him and Walter. Her hand looked small and delicate wrapped in his. And creamy white as a daylily next to the coppery hue of his skin.

"Call me Hawk," he murmured in that deep, soft voice before releasing her.

A nickname, she noted. He was a man of many secrets. She wondered what, if anything, ever rattled that composure of his. Certainly not any feminine wiles she could conjure up. Sarah laughed at herself over her fascination with the man. She should accept this brief encounter for what it was, a polite gentleman doing what he thought was right to protect a woman in trouble, and nothing more.

She had other, bigger problems to attend to than her own lonely heart.

"I'm glad to see that chivalry isn't dead." Sarah climbed in and Hawk closed the door for her. She almost regretted arguing down his objections to the field trip earlier. He seemed like such a kind, patient man. She rolled down her window to wish him good night.

Instead of moving away from the car, he surprised her by squatting down beside her window. "It's a mistake to go to Isla Tenebrosa, Sarah."

The gentle reverence he gave her name almost made her overlook the challenge in his words. But the sly way he'd gotten around her defenses, with his gallantry and sexy voice, triggered the frayed strands of her temper. "You have no say in this," she said. "Tenebrosa's revolution is over. It's not a drug trafficway. They welcome tourists and their money." She pounded the steering wheel with her fist, punctuating each word. "I am going to the ruins at Las Lagumas, and you can't stop me!"

A flash fire sparked in the depths of his eyes. It was the first glimmer of emotion she'd seen there. "You're a fool, schoolmarm. Tenebrosa isn't the place to prove your independence or show that bleached-blond bureaucrat of yours how strong a woman you are. It isn't safe. Anyone as naive and idealistic as you has no business taking a bunch of girls into the middle of that jungle."

"I am thirty-four years old. I work with teenagers, for gosh sakes. I am hardly naive!"

A muscle jerked in the side of his jaw, another outward sign that he, too, possessed a temper. "If I hadn't stepped in when I did, Kensit would have had his hands on you. He would have had his mouth on you. You wouldn't have liked it, and you couldn't have stopped him."

Sarah's mouth opened in shocked protest at his vile words, but he never let her speak.

"So, lady, if you insist on being so pigheaded and foolhardy that you won't change your mind, then I insist on one thing."

"What's that, Mr. Echohawk?"

"I'm going with you to Tenebrosa."

Chapter Two

May 25 rolled around with astonishing speed, yet for Sarah, the departure date couldn't have come soon enough. She hurried down the concourse at Kansas City International Airport, trying to keep her five teenage charges in sight. They, too, were bursting with anticipation to get their trip under way.

But for Sarah, the adventure had already begun. With her aunts safely ensconced at their home with promises from neighbors to check on them daily, the school year over with her grades and requisitions turned in, and her bags packed, she'd been ready for three whole days.

Correction. She'd been ready for this her whole life.

Denise Adams's parents had volunteered to drive the group from Marysville to the airport across the state line in Kansas City. The other parents, Sarah's principal, and a handful of interested townsfolk saw them off at the high school early that morning.

Sarah had nervously scanned the group of well-wishers and doubting gossips, looking for Hawk Echohawk to step forward, suitcase in hand, and climb into the van with them. When he didn't show, she breathed a huge sigh of relief and settled on the middle seat along with Andrea and Lynnette.

She'd made it. They were going. They were finally going.

For some reason, Hawk's threat to accompany them on the field trip had done more to make her question the wisdom of going than any of Walter's weekly attempts to dissuade her had. On the surface, both men appeared to have her best interests at heart.

But she sensed a more personal motive behind each man's determination to have her stay put. With Walter, the motive seemed fairly obvious. She'd challenged his judgment in public. With an ego like his, he couldn't afford to back down from anyone who didn't give him what he wanted. And after discovering his true character—and hearing those humiliating reassurances that stripped her self-confidence down to her very soul—she wasn't about to give him anything he wanted.

Sarah laughed inside, a wry sensation that twisted her stomach into knots. So much for not making this personal.

Sarah gave herself a mental shake and stared out the window, watching the flat plains of northern Kansas turn into the rolling hills of the Missouri River valley. This trip was about rewarding *herself*, not punishing Walter. She had always wanted to see something of the world. With her inheritance, she had the means to travel as she wanted, but she'd never had the opportunity to leave for any extended period of time.

Until now.

And even Hawk's mysterious ways and secretive warnings couldn't stop her.

Once she held her boarding pass in hand, she felt like a student playing hooky, slipping past the principal without getting caught. She was glad Hawk had decided to stay home. His threat to go with them to Tenebrosa must have been spoken in the heat of the moment. Except that she had the vague impression that he didn't say or do anything without first giving it careful thought.

All the same, when the departure gate came into view, she dared to feel triumphant. She walked through the metal detector and felt like Alice entering a whole new Wonderland.

"Ma'am?"

The bored request lifted her from her dreamworld. Only then did Sarah realize that she'd set off the metal detector. At the uniformed gatekeeper's request, she removed her watch and the heavy metal barrette that held her hair back. Shaking loose the kinky waves, she walked through again. Silently this time.

She retrieved her leather shoulder tote and watch, then stuck the barrette in a side pocket. She decided to plait her hair into one long braid and secure it with a rubber band once they got on the plane. There'd be metal detectors when they transferred in Mexico City, too.

See how adaptable I am? she thought proudly. Walter and the townspeople had nothing to worry about. She was an intelligent woman, a quick learner. Just because she'd never flown on a plane before, just because she'd never been out of the country, didn't mean she couldn't handle herself responsibly on such a trip.

"Miss Mack." Lynnette Stevens's bright young voice interrupted her self-praise. "Look who's here."

Sarah turned and knew she'd been sentenced to detention. Her worst fear unfolded as he lifted his big, rangy frame from a row of connected seats. Hawk. A man who kept his promises.

Damn.

"Miss McCormick."

The muscles of her face tightened into a frown. She gawked rudely at him, without acknowledging his greeting. He'd cut his hair so that it barely brushed his shoulders now, catching it off his forehead with a black cloth headband. A black T-shirt clung to his broad shoulders and powerful arms, and he wore a pair of thigh-hugging jeans over the tops of black ostrich-skin boots.

"You cut your hair." As far as telling him off went, her response bordered on the asinine. When she should be sending him packing, she found herself secretly mourning the subtle changes in his appearance.

The man who rescued her in the parking lot had been a gentle hero. This man looked hard. Distant. All business. And he was quite possibly the most potently attractive male she had ever spoken to in person. Ever imagined speaking to. Ever . . . *Oh, double damn.*

"What are you doing here?" She crossed her arms in front of her, tilted her chin and gave him her sternest look, which she usually saved for recalcitrant pupils.

"You should cut your hair, too," he said, ignoring her question.

"I beg your pardon?"

Without asking permission, he reached out and captured a lock of her hair between his thumb and fingers. "Yours is so long and thick that once you wash it, it'll be damp for a week in the tropical humidity. It's a pretty heavy weight to carry around in the heat of the jungle. Might give you a headache."

Self-conscious, Sarah pulled the rest of her hair together at her nape and shook it down behind her back. His eyes flickered with the movement, flaring to life in a moment of recognition.

"What?" she prodded, curious to know what he saw.

Still holding the lock of her hair, he pulled his fingers down it, smoothing it as he went. Sarah knew full well there were no nerve endings in strands of hair, yet the delicate inspection of his gaze and fingertips whispered through her with the intimacy of a caress.

A slow friction sparked stirrings in parts of her that had never known a man's touch. She caught her breath, wondering what he might be thinking. Wondering if he knew what he was doing to her. Wondering if his mouth might be a little too dry to speak at that moment, too.

Wondering if he might be evaluating her as Walter had, rating her no higher than a D plus. For just an instant, she imagined he saw her with different eyes, viewed her with different results. For just an instant, she felt pretty.

But he blinked once and the light went out in his eyes.

"Mr. Echohawk, are you going with us?" Lynnette's curious question sounded right beside her ear, and woke Sarah from her adolescent stupor. *Good grief!* Hawk was offering travel advice, not a proposal. She snatched her hair from his fingers and tucked it behind her shoulder, safely beyond his reach.

"Yes."

"No!"

Her negative answer released him from whatever had snagged his attention. His mouth narrowed into a thin-lipped frown directed at Sarah an instant before he turned and smiled at Lynnette.

"I'm an unofficial chaperon. I've been to Tenebrosa before. I know the language and some of the customs."

"Cool." Lynnette beamed under Hawk's attention. "Lyndsay and Colleen have had three years of Spanish. I just hope I know enough to order the right stuff off the menu."

The devil! His smile broadened to reveal straight white teeth that gleamed against the contrast of his skin. "Well, I'll make sure you don't end up with fish-head soup."

"Ooh." Lynnette squealed on three different pitches. Sarah cringed. The last thing she needed was for the girls to develop a crush on Hawk. Judging by Lynnette's reaction, he could easily charm their loyalty away from her.

She already had most of Marysville to fight. She didn't need to defend her actions to a self-appointed bodyguard who was subtly eroding what little authority she had left.

Sarah touched the young brunette's arm. "We'll be boarding in about ten minutes. Why don't you tell the others to get their stuff together and wait by the gate."

"Will do, Miss Mack."

After Lynnette scooted off to relay the message, Sarah turned on Hawk. "These are not your students. They're not your children. *I* didn't even know you a month ago. . . . "

"I'm going."

His clipped words left no room for argument—and triggered her temper, all the same. "What is with you and that island? The Sinclair Foundation is a reputable organization. I would never take those girls someplace that wasn't safe."

"Strange things happen on Tenebrosa." There was no evidence of the smile he had given Lynnette when he looked down at Sarah. "Go to Machu Picchu or El Tajín if you want to see the sights, lady."

His soft, spine-tingling voice dropped to a pitch that chilled her to the bone. "If you want to get yourself killed, if you want to go to hell . . . then you vacation outside El Espanto. There's no revolution. No disease. But it'll kill you just the same."

Sarah stared at him in mute shock. The blood seemed to drain from her body, and then a wave of righteous anger surged in to take its place. "How dare you speak to me like that! You're deliberately trying to frighten me because of something that happened to you. You don't say what. You just step out of a crowd and start spouting threats and portents like you're some kind of fortune-teller."

She thumped him on the chest with her index finger, ignoring the potential danger of taunting someone much bigger and stronger than she. "You're a man, Mr. Echohawk. Apparently a very disturbed, single-minded man who's obsessed with some little island that nobody else cares about."

Suddenly the air around them stilled. It filled with an invisible tension that radiated from Hawk and surrounded her in its suffocating embrace. As much as his touch had electrified her earlier, this eerie calm terrified her.

And reminded Sarah that she was supposed to be shy. Her hand trembled and fell to her side. She dropped her gaze to the slight puckering in the cotton material on his chest where she'd struck him. Vulnerable and exposed, she floundered as helplessly as a newborn chick.

"I'm sorry." Her apology came out on a breathy whisper. She struggled to make her gaze meet his, struggled to make him understand how desperately she needed to do this without his interference or the town's censure. "I don't usually hit. . . . Please . . ."

She never got any higher than the unforgiving line of his jaw. Before she could explain herself, before she could mend the inexcusable damage she'd done, a shadow loomed up behind her.

Glancing over her shoulder, she did a wide-eyed double take and spun around. The man closing in on her was a giant. Hawk was a good-sized man, but this guy was even bigger. And broader. And the icy gray color of his eyes only heightened the air of threat that surrounded him.

Without conscious thought, she backed up next to Hawk. Ridiculous, she thought, as if he would shelter her after the rude things she'd said to him. She'd been treating him like some sort of demented stalker.

Still, the gentle protectiveness she'd sensed in him a month ago in that parking lot had haunted her unguarded moments. It had been nothing more than the impersonal gesture of a concerned citizen, and yet she'd felt more cherished, more important at that moment than she had since she was a little girl.

She sought that shelter once more.

The big man's hand reached out. Sarah backed away. Hawk extended his hand, and the two men clasped each other in a grip like brothers. A clash of titans, she thought. Who would be the victor?

"Hawk," the big man said, his voice rumbling deep in his chest. "Glad we didn't miss you. We had to stop and find the bathroom."

The bathroom? Warriors didn't talk about such things, did they?

Then a woman waddled up to the big man's side. *Waddled* wasn't a very flattering description, but the woman was pregnant. Extremely pregnant. Sarah experienced a brief pang of envy. She'd given up on her own biological clock. She was too old, too plain, too proper to find a man who'd give her a son or daughter. She'd accepted long ago that her students would be her children. But she couldn't help the wanting. Not when the beauty of love and impending motherhood shone out of the woman's face.

The big man dropped his arm around the pregnant woman's shoulders and pulled her close. Hindered by her full belly, she still managed to wrap her arms around his waist and snuggle. Sarah's initial rush of concern that he would hurt the woman or the baby shifted into astonishment. Everything about the big man softened when he touched her: his imposing stance, his grim expression, his cold eyes. They clearly adored each other, and Sarah was ashamed of her initial fear of the man.

Her gaze dropped to the floor, which she

wished would swallow her up. She'd been raised with manners. Were her nerves too tightly drawn to remember anything she'd been taught?

Hawk leaned forward and kissed the woman on the cheek. She laughed at something he whispered in her ear. Sarah felt like an outsider. Tension fluttered in her stomach, and she couldn't get the apology in her head past the constriction in her throat.

Obviously these were friends of Hawk's who'd come to see him off at the airport. There was nothing to protect her from here. Because of her anxiety over the trip, she'd panicked when there was no need to. No wonder half the population of northeast Kansas wanted her to stay put.

In an effort to preserve what was left of her battered self-esteem, she quietly stepped away, escaping while the other three adults caught up on shared history.

But five long fingers closed around her arm in a deceptively light grip, like steel sheathed in velvet. Her gaze flew up to Hawk's as he pulled her back to his side. The faintest light glowed around his dark irises, silently calling to her, connecting to the cold, frightened part of her that had battled enough for one day.

How does he do that? He didn't look *at* her. He looked into her. Looked deep into her heart and saw secrets that even she couldn't remember keeping. How could a man of such darkness radiate such a light?

Sarah frowned, questioning her own perception. It was just a trick, she thought. A trick of her tired mind and overactive imagination.

"Sarah." Hawk was speaking now, and she made herself concentrate on his words. "I'd like you to meet Brodie Maxwell, an old friend of mine. And his wife, BJ."

"Hi." BJ shook hands first, and Sarah could tell this woman had a magic about her that drew people out and made them feel like a friend.

Sarah succumbed easily enough and smiled in return. "Nice to meet you."

"Ma'am."

She hesitated only an instant before accepting Brodie's hand. "Mr. Maxwell."

And then in a move as natural as if he had done it a hundred times, Hawk shifted and slipped his hand around her back and rested it at the small of her waist beneath her hair. The connection he'd made through his eyes now seared into her skin through the gauzy cotton of her dress. His light touch provided a warmth that instilled its strength into her. Miraculously, her tongue untied itself, and the backbone she'd discovered when her trip was threatened returned.

She didn't know why he'd reached out to her, but she appreciated the support in his touch. As if he'd read her mind. As if he knew right when she needed a hand.

"Brodie and I served in the corps together."

"Marines?" she asked, thinking a military background explained a lot about his warriorlike demeanor this morning.

BJ took over the conversation. "These two go way back. I didn't meet Hawk until last year, when he helped me with . . . when he counseled me on . . . "

BJ paused and looked up at her husband. Sarah saw Brodie squeeze BJ's shoulder before she continued. "He helped us with a personal situation before we got married." Then BJ smiled again as though the dark moment had passed. She nudged a playful fist at Hawk's stomach. "We can't get this guy to the big city often enough to visit us."

So Hawk was a rescuer by nature. *Curious.* Just what was it about Sarah that he thought needed rescuing? And why did he insist on volunteering for the job when she'd made it clear she didn't want him to?

Sarah surprised herself by joining the conversation as if her alarm at first meeting them had never happened. BJ's polite inquiries and Hawk's broad hand flattened against her spine made her feel included. BJ and Brodie worked at LadyTech, a software company whose products Sarah used on the school computers. She had just asked BJ about a suggested update to a tutorial program when the flight attendant announced the boarding of their plane.

An immediate change came over the two men. Smiles evaporated and Hawk let go of her, leaving Sarah with a chilled sense of abandonment.

"Sorry I can't go with you," said Brodie.

Hawk shook his head and bent down to pick up a duffel bag and sling it over his shoulder. "You can't leave BJ now. She's due any day."

Brodie nodded. He clapped Hawk on the shoulder and turned him away from the two women. Whatever they were about to discuss concerned her, she was sure of it. She inclined her ear to eavesdrop on their private conversation.

"Kel Murphy has alerted his contacts in Tenebrosa. And I got a hold of Del Rio. He claims he's a little out of practice, but if you need anything, give him a call. He'll be there." Brodie handed Hawk a business card and the Indian laughed.

"I've never known Rafe to miss a party."

"Yeah."

A soft touch on Sarah's arm distracted her. "Ignore them. They're always a bit overprotective. It's just their nature."

BJ smiled indulgently, as if she thought having someone else take charge of her life was a good thing. Sarah felt trapped. All she wanted to do was see something of the world. All she wanted was to have some kind of adventure to fill her heart before she returned home and was resigned to small-town spinsterhood like Doris and Millie.

Hawk seemed determined to take that chance away from her.

"Last call for flight number two seventeen to Mexico City," the intercom announced.

Everyone said their good-byes. Sarah adjusted her tote bag over her shoulder. When she straightened, she found Hawk looking down at her with that unreadable expression of his. She tried to plead her case one last time. "You have to go?"

"I have to go."

She nodded, accepting her fate, but not liking it. "Okay. But let's get one thing straight. *I* am in charge of this expedition. As far as I'm concerned, it's just a freaky coincidence that you ended up on the same flight and tour that we did. If you interfere with those girls' education in any way, if you so much as scare them, or if you—"

"I won't spoil this trip for you, schoolmarm." He finished her sentence with deadpan accuracy. Before she could register any kind of protest, he grabbed her by the elbow and ushered her toward the departure gate. When he bent to whisper in her ear, the most delicious sensations

47

danced down her spine, along with an unnerving rush of fear.

"But make no mistake. If anything happens down there, we go. And when I say to get your pretty little butt in gear, your ladies better hustle it into overtime."

Pretty little butt?

Sarah felt her backside grow warm. Was it possible to blush down there? It must be the residual effects of him touching her. And looking at her. As if he really could see . . . As if he really might think . . .

But no, it was just a figure of speech. A warning to let her know he meant business by going with them. Hawk was a rescuer by nature. BJ had practically said so. He meant nothing personal by his remarks. Nothing personal in the way he'd drawn her to his side and included her in the meeting with his friends.

Besides, Walter had said—

Sarah stamped out the memory without acknowledging the damage it had done to her. She stiffened her resolve and pulled away from Hawk's grip. She rushed on ahead of him, putting the five girls between them as they boarded.

She'd fought hard for this little shot at independence. She wasn't about to let some dark, enigmatic stranger dictate how she should live her life.

And yet Hawk made it so easy to depend on him, to believe in his word. He made her think she could trust him.

Thank God they had five teenagers along on the trip to keep her busy and knock that kind of sentimental nonsense right out of her head.

* * *

Colleen, Lynnette and the other girls swarmed around Sarah, hanging on every word their teacher said as she showed them a map and talked through their itinerary. They bombarded her with questions, and she patiently listened to and answered each one. The girls practically idolized their precious Miss Mack. Did that mean they shared the same foolish tendency to rush headlong into situations for which they were totally unprepared?

Man, *that* was a sobering thought.

Hawk settled down in his seat a few rows back and tried to find a comfortable position for his legs, which were invariably cramped in the tight confines of an airplane. He closed his eyes and feigned sleep so no one would disturb him as he tried to tap into the inner wisdom that guided him.

Returning to Tenebrosa wasn't something he'd want to risk with a crack team of soldiers like the operatives he'd been with the last time he was there. But to go in with a self-righteous school-marm and five bubbly, eager, moody teenage girls was like contemplating suicide.

Not smart. Not smart at all.

Hawk breathed in deeply through his nose and expelled the air quietly through his mouth, seeking his calm center. Five years ago, he'd sensed an evil on Tenebrosa. An evil that could turn a man's soul and destroy a good friend without leaving a trace.

Even with his powers, he hadn't seen it coming. By the time he realized unnatural forces were at work, it was too late. Jonathan Ramsey was gone. Vanished.

And he couldn't even find the body to take home to his grieving widow and daughter.

Some power. Some soldier.

Hawk rolled his neck, fighting to relieve the tension there. He needed to meditate. He needed to silence the drone of the plane's engines and the self-doubting mantra that blocked him from finding peace. He drew on the advice of his spiritual mentor, Otis Peace Hands, and tried to picture a totally different scene in his mind.

The flat, treeless plains of Kansas were about as far from the dense tropical jungles of Tenebrosa as he could get. Mentally, he put himself there. A man standing alone in a barren cornfield, with nothing but miles of faded brown cornstalks and clear autumn sunshine in every direction. No place for the enemy to hide.

Hawk breathed again, more relaxed this time. He imagined filling his senses with the dry, clean air of the vast prairie. Thoughts of Tenebrosa slipped away. The notion that he was setting himself up for doomsday again receded into a hidden part of his mind.

He tapped into the resurgent strength of his spirit brother, the hawk, and soared high above the ground, looking for symbols to give him peace and courage. But other images, not of the spirit world, but of this earth, slipped into his dreams.

Tawny eyes. The golden-brown bear of his vision blinked, and he saw Sarah's eyes. Hazel, really. But he'd seen enough gold amongst the green to remind him of his vision. Fine, beautiful eyes set in her pale oval face.

She was of average height, yet she seemed like such a tiny thing. From the smooth span of her back he'd felt beneath her cotton dress to the slim, sinewy strength of her arms, she was a finely boned woman. Everything about her seemed slender, fragile, delicate.

Everything but her mouth and her spirit, that was. The muscles at the corners of his lips twitched as he controlled the urge to smile. She could cut a man to ribbons with that tongue of hers. She was so prim and proper, with high-and-mighty ways that compensated for her natural shyness. Yet she didn't back down from a fight.

On the surface she was feisty, and about as effective as a kitten spitting at a bobcat. But he'd glimpsed the woman beneath that shyness. He'd seen her stand up to Kensit. Stand up to a whole town. Stand up to him.

She had more in common with that she-bear of his dreams than prim, proper Miss Sarah McCormick could possibly know. Even the color of her hair, cascades of golden brown toffee, reminded him of the Kodiak.

Half dozing, Hawk felt the recognition tug at him, creating a ripple of unease in his meditative state. He wondered just how repellent it would be to Miss McCormick if she knew he was comparing her to a bear.

And appreciating the comparison.

Not to worry. He'd never tell her. She'd never be interested in his opinion of her anyway. Not just because she saw him as the bad guy in all this. Women didn't appreciate men like him, who could read beneath the surface of their secrets.

He was revered among his own people for his mystical gifts, and native women maintained a respectful distance, as if he were some kind of demigod. And Anglo women . . . if they could see beyond the color of his skin that made him some sort of exotic plaything, they resented his gifts. *Creepy. Uncomfortable. No privacy. Not right.*

He'd heard all the excuses. He could find and give pleasure with his body, but let his spirit get involved, let them see the inner man—and he was history. He could lie about who and what he was. Or he could be alone.

He chose to be alone.

With the peace he had sought completely disrupted, Hawk shifted in his seat again. He kept his eyes closed so that the flight attendants and other passengers wouldn't disturb him, but instead of meditating, he focused on the days ahead.

Tenebrosa was the last place he wanted to go. But he had to. Whether she knew it or not, Sarah needed his help. The resemblance between her and his vision was too strong to ignore.

He just wished he didn't feel as if he'd have to go to hell and back before he got Sarah and the girls safely home.

Chapter Three

"You see, Hawk?" Sarah's smile turned into a gloat of satisfaction as she watched the girls sitting around the campfire, enthralled with Luis Salazar's tales about the legend of Las Lagumas. "And you were worried."

Hawk grunted in response without looking at her. His gaze continued its slow survey, a seemingly endless sweep back and forth that he'd started when they left El Espanto that morning and maintained even now when they were settling into camp for the night. She couldn't tell if he was studying the people on the expedition, or the myriad plays of shadows and light in the dense vegetation of the jungle surrounding them.

Every now and then he stared into space, as though he relied on unseen eyes in the back of his head to give him input. When his dark eyes glazed over like that, Sarah looked around, too, spooked by his preternatural awareness. She tried to see what he was seeing, tried to feel what he felt. Yet she never saw anything unusual beyond a conversation among their guides or the darting movement of leaves in the undergrowth when an unseen animal passed.

All day, she'd bumped along in silence beside Hawk as their caravan of three trucks jostled over a rutted excuse for a road on their overnight journey to the ruins of Las Lagumas. Mosquitoes the size of hummingbirds raised itchy welts on the side of her neck and on her bare forearms. When she tried to make a joke about her discomfort, Hawk dug inside his duffel bag without comment and handed her a stinky salve that she suspected would deter people and small animals, as well as keep the bugs away. The salve took care of the itching, but even her sincere gratitude couldn't put a dent in Hawk's stone-faced silence.

By nightfall tomorrow, they'd be camped outside the excavation site. But her growing anticipation at touring the uncovered catacombs and pyramid and maybe even discovering an artifact herself was tempered by Hawk's strange behavior.

She'd volunteered to ride on the last truck with him, since none of Salazar's men seemed comfortable around him. She didn't blame them. Hawk towered over them in stature. And today, in addition to his ever-present Apache-style headband, he'd dressed in lightweight jungle fatigues tucked into black military boots. He needed only a couple of swatches of greasepaint across his cheekbones to look like a guerilla soldier who'd just emerged from jungle combat.

"And now I turn the details of the legend over to Antonio." Luis Salazar excused himself and slipped outside the center of the circle. His cousin, Antonio Robles, continued the story of the long-dead king with a lot of gusto and very little fact.

"King Meczaquatl was a second-born son," said Antonio. Sarah tried to ignore Hawk's disturbing presence and concentrate on Antonio's version of history. "Because he could not inherit his father's wealth, he sailed across the sea to Tenebrosa, conquered the pitiful native resistance, and created his own kingdom."

Sarah shook her head. Tomorrow morning she'd have to remind the girls to reread their textbooks and not rely on Antonio's romanticized view of history to learn about ancient cultures.

"Señorita McCormick." She heard her name an instant before she felt the warm grip on her shoulder. She spun her head around, startled, but quickly smiled when she recognized Luis Salazar. "If I could talk to you for a moment?"

Sarah forced her breathing back to its normal rate and stood, glancing over her shoulder at Hawk. "If you don't mind, I'm going for a short walk with . . . "

There was no need for polite excuses. An unnamed shadow deep in the jungle had captured Hawk's attention. Feelings of hurt warred with her temper. She'd been overlooked and taken for granted a number of times in her life. But today she'd fought past her natural reserve and gone out of her way to include Hawk as part of the group. She'd endured his silence and defended his right to be there with her presence.

And now he rewarded her with . . . with . . . *Damn the man, anyway, for ruining this trip!*

Furious with herself for caring one way or the

other what Hawk thought of her efforts, she linked her arm through Luis's and even allowed the older gentleman to pat her hand possessively with his own. Though his face had been weathered by the elements, Luis was nonetheless an attractive man, made more so by his old-world charm and deference to her as a lady. He guided Sarah outside their encampment, inquiring about her impressions of the journey thus far and going over the next day's schedule.

After they'd left the reach of the campfire's illumination, the thick canopy of jungle vegetation shut out the remaining twilight. Luis switched on a high-beam flashlight and escorted her along a hacked-out path to a tributary several yards beyond where she'd last seen their tents. Once in the clearing beside the water, he turned off the light and allowed her several moments to soak in the untamed beauty of greens and golds adorned by bright shots of red and orange where exotic flowers bloomed. A symphony of tree frogs and wild birds and animals she couldn't name enriched the sensory overload. She shut her eyes and imprinted the images in her mind, storing them away to savor over and over again.

"It is beautiful, no?" Luis asked, pride in his homeland evident in his voice.

Sarah looked at him and smiled. "Beautiful and unspoiled."

He tucked the flashlight under his arm, took both of her hands in his and bowed, brushing his lips across her knuckles. "We are glad to have such charming guests to share this with."

"The girls and I are glad to be here." Sarah clenched the muscles in her arms, torn between the desire to pull away from his unexpected familiarity and her schooling in good manners. The man was, after all, following the customs of his own country, not putting the moves on her.

Luis smiled down at her, the lines in his face crinkling all the way back to the silver-streaked black hair at his temples. "This man who is with you. Señor Hawk. He is not a teacher?"

This time Sarah did pull away. So this little evening walk had nothing to do with her. When would she learn? She would never be anything more than a means to an end with men. One of these days she would have to wise up, or give up and just accept her fate.

She stuck her hands in the pockets of her khaki shorts and told the story she had come up with to explain Hawk's presence. "He's a chaperon." Luis had asked that everyone speak in English to help his men improve their language skills. But he frowned as though the term was unfamiliar to him. "He's another adult, a parent figure, to help watch the girls."

"Colleen is his daughter?"

"No." Black hair and dark eyes formed the only resemblance between Hawk and Colleen. Sarah tried again. "He's helping *me.*"

"I see." Luis grinned broadly and nodded. "He is *your* man."

"My man?" Understanding dawned and she hastened to correct him. "You mean my boyfriend? Oh, no. No."

The very idea was ludicrous! The idea that a man as worldly and mysterious as Hawk could be attracted to a plain brown mouse like her made her laugh. "He's not with me. He's just . . . " Sarah stopped in midsentence. Exactly why was Hawk there? She couldn't explain that herself. But judging by the expectant look on Luis's face, she'd better come up with a darn good answer. She couldn't. "He's been here before. He wanted to come back."

"I see," he said simply. "Then Hawk is nothing to you?"

A distraction. A fascination. An unexplained mystery that frustrated her like an itch she couldn't reach.

"Nothing personal."

Luis's gaze shot back toward the path. Curious, Sarah looked, too, but saw nothing. Her guide's whole demeanor had changed in the space of a heartbeat. The easygoing charm of a man who enjoyed his siesta had been replaced by the alertness of a sharp-eyed animal, cornered and looking for options to escape. The elegant leisure of his movements took on a nervous edginess as he worked his jaw and curled and uncurled his fists at his sides.

"Is something wrong, señor?" she asked.

He went still at her question, staring at her as though her voice was intruding on his thoughts. In her next breath, the old Luis returned, save for the wariness that stayed in his cool brown eyes. He pressed his hand to her shoulder and squeezed her with a solicitous apology.

"Forgive me. I was fearful for a moment. You see, I imagined Señor Hawk to have a personal interest in you and the girls. I assumed he was protecting you."

"From what?"

Luis patted her arm and shook his head gravely. "Your girls are very pretty, no?"

Sarah nodded.

"One of my men, Martín de Vega, he is a skilled driver and knows his way through the jungle."

And his point was?

"Martín is also very much a ladies' man."

Sarah didn't bother to add that Luis also seemed to consider himself a ladies' man. She didn't like the implied threat in his words. "What exactly are you saying?"

"I will speak to him at once, remind him of his place. But you must be sure to keep your girls together. Do not let them stray alone. Ask Señor Hawk to help you keep them safe."

Stunned by the implication, Sarah made no comment.

"You can follow the path?" he asked, handing her his flashlight before moving toward camp.

Sarah nodded mutely and watched the leaves of the jungle swallow him up. She seethed with anger, unable to move, unable to find any scapegoat except herself. Luis might knowingly have hired some lecherous pedophile or rapist or God knew what kind of creep to work on his crew, but it was her fault they were there. Her fault the girls might be in danger. Her fault she didn't know how to read men. Her fault.

Hawk was right. She had no business coming to Tenebrosa. She should be grateful to Luis for at least giving her a concrete reason to stay away from the place. Hawk had yet to prove so helpful. She didn't want to alarm the girls, but she had better get back and make sure they understood the need to stay together with her or a friend at all times.

As she followed the trail of hand-cut leaves and branches along the jungle floor, she lifted her long braid from the natural valley between her breasts. With an annoying realization, she conceded that Hawk was right on at least one point. Wherever the weight of her hair touched her, she broke out in beads of sweat.

The unaccustomed heat only added to her aggravation with him. Silently cursing him with each step, she stalked back toward camp until a movement caught her attention from the corner of her eye. She froze in her tracks and swung the light to her right, catching the end of a green tail scurrying away into the underbrush.

And then, while she waited for her heart to settle back down out of her throat, she became aware of another sensation. A featherlight cloak of awareness settled over her shoulders. Gentle as a caress, the unseen touch nevertheless chilled her with its unwavering intensity.

Drawn by some untapped sixth sense, Sarah slowly turned and shined her light over her shoulder. Hawk stood there, several paces behind her, looking at her. Looking into her. His dark eyes blazed with that unearthly light she'd seen back at the airport, and she was struck by the sensation that he knew what she'd been thinking. Knew how damning her thoughts had been.

"You shouldn't be out here alone." His voice vibrated across the distance, a bare whisper in the encroaching night.

"How did you get here? Are you following me?" He advanced on her, and Sarah involuntarily backed away as he quickly closed the distance with his long strides.

"Sarah!"

She jumped back from his hoarse command. The flashlight clattered to the ground, and her hair snagged on something behind her. She reached back to free her braid from its entanglement, and Hawk lunged forward.

"No!"

He grabbed her wrist and yanked her toward him. At the same instant, he reached into a pocket of his vest and pulled out a knife. Not a knife. A sword! A wicked, twelve-inch killing thing that glinted in the twilight.

He raised it above his head and swung it down with deadly force. Sarah screamed. She jerked her shoulder away from the sure blow and rammed into the brick wall of his chest. His arm trapped her there like a steel vise and lifted her clear off the ground. She pounded with her fists and kicked with her legs, pummeling for all she was worth, frantic with the knowledge that he would attack her, desperately frightened to realize how much bigger and stronger and unyielding he was than she.

"Sarah! It's over now. It's okay." Her feet touched the ground and his shoulders curved over her, blocking out the rest of the night.

His chest muffled her screams. Through her daze of panic she heard low-pitched reassurances crooning in her ear. The arm that had cinched her to him still held her just as tightly but he splayed his fingers and stroked up and down the side of her rib cage, soothing her like a frightened animal.

As the hazy grip of panic began to clear, she realized that she felt no pain. He hadn't stabbed her after all.

"What?" She gasped, gathering her composure as much as her breath. "Why?" Her senses returned and she remembered the knife. The big knife. She angled her head back because she could move no further and slapped at his shoulder. "What are you doing with a weapon like that here? It's stupid and dangerous—"

"That's better. I'd rather see you spitting mad than afraid." She wanted to stay angry with him. She wanted to vent her frustrations, but his unexpectedly boyish teasing undid her. She stopped her tirade and noticed his mouth, mere inches from hers. Smiling.

She caught her breath at the sheer masculine beauty of it. Straight white teeth framed by firm, thin lips. They were close enough that she could feel his warm breath fanning across her face. She inhaled the soapy, clean, masculine scent of him, tinged by the faint pungency of the insect salve he, too, wore.

Sarah's stomach flip-flopped. An unusual heat sparked there and curled lower as a whole new set of sensations vibrated through her, every bit as powerful as her anger, but much more pleasurable. His chest was so hard, his hold so unbreakable yet gentle, his mouth so tempting.

She stared at that temptation and discovered she couldn't speak. Her throat tightened with a customary clench of shyness. She damned her cursed inability to voice her desires. She wanted to savor the rush of adrenaline coursing through her. She wanted to channel it in a way a woman and man could share together. She wanted him to kiss her. She wanted him to *want* to kiss her. And yet she knew he wouldn't. All she could do was lecture him. All he could do was put up with her.

"You were backing into a web." As if sensing her clouded ability to speak, Hawk took over the duties for her. Grateful for the change of topic that doused both her desire and her embarrassment, she relaxed and followed the inclination of his head.

He twisted his right wrist and lifted his knife to eye level. Skewered at the end was a brown, hairy spider the size of two Ping-Pong balls stuck together.

"Spider! Big spider!" she shrieked.

She spun and buried her face in his shoulder. As hard as she had hit him before, she now clutched him tightly, clinging to fistfuls of his shirt and vest. She felt his arm flinch as he flicked the horrid creature into the jungle and wiped the blade clean on his pant leg.

He shifted his stance and wrapped both arms around her, catching her more fully in his embrace. He tugged at her braid, picking out the sticky white residue that had caught her hair. He bent his head and cooed into her ear, calming her with whispers in a language she didn't understand. The ups and downs of the day caught up with her and she sagged against him, weary with emotional fatigue, grateful for his gentle, steadying strength.

"That's it, honey. You're gonna be all right. You'll beat this like you beat those bureaucrats back home."

Hawk heard the endearment slip out and questioned the wisdom of his actions. He'd never had a woman melt into him with such guileless abandon before. She fit him just right, with the crown of her hair nestling beneath his chin and her long legs placing her hips just at the juncture of his thighs. He doubted she had any idea how provocative it could be to empower a man with that kind of trust.

What could be the harm in just holding her? he reasoned weakly. She'd been through a real scare. First him, then the knife, then the spider. Any decent man would comfort her. And he liked to think of himself as a decent man.

She sighed and burrowed into him, unwittingly rubbing her thighs against the one place she shouldn't, and all thoughts of decency popped out of his brain. Prim and proper Miss McCormick wasn't a shapeless bag of fragile female as he had first envisioned. Even in the trim knee-length shorts and sensible blouse she was wearing he could feel the shape of her. Her hips flared, full and womanly, hinting at an earth-mother fertility he loved, but which most women tried to diet away or camouflage. Her breasts were small but unexpectedly sassy, like their owner. Having them flattened against him like this, he couldn't help but notice their proud tips.

And when she looked at him with those big eyes, golden pools flecked with green that revealed raw, uncontrolled emotion, he nearly lost all perspective. She wanted to be kissed. Even if he couldn't read the desire swirling about her face in a fiery halo, he could see it in the breathless parting of her lips. And man, was he tempted to give her what she asked. Tempted to forget decorum and missions and taking care of business, and sample what she unconsciously offered him.

He could just tilt her chin up and slide his mouth over hers. Play a little game with her, teach her and tease her with his lips and tongue.

He knew instinctively that this was a woman who would respond to a man's touch, a sensual woman made all the more appealing because she wasn't aware of her sensuality. She didn't flaunt her assets or make coy come-ons to a man.

It was that ladylike reticence that brought him to his senses at last. He eased his hold on her, but didn't pull away because she had yet to let up her death grip on the front of his clothes. As base as his own thoughts had been, he couldn't leave her without the support she needed until she could summon her own strength.

Now was the time that he should reassure her. He should explain that the spider's bite wasn't poisonous, though its size alone could leave a nasty wound that would need medical treatment to prevent infection. He should tell her that all of Salazar's men carried big hunting knives, too, that it was standard equipment for jungle travel.

But he didn't want to talk. He didn't want to say anything that might break the spell that anchored Sarah to him.

Because the wishful part of him that he guarded so carefully didn't want her to leave. He might be a god to some, a freak of nature to others, but he was still a man. And like a man, he relished the joy of simply holding a woman. He found a rare contentment in savoring the fresh, unperfumed scent of her. His hormones churned with renewed vigor as his thoughts wandered into the realm of fantasy.

The soldier in him knew he should move on. He should separate himself from irrelevant complications like discovering a sexy side to Madame Schoolmarm, and get back to the business of seeing her safely back to camp. But he didn't listen to the mystic or the soldier. He listened to the man.

He leaned back and sheathed his knife in the

leather casing inside his vest. As expected, her eyes lit with a spark of nervousness, but still she clutched at him. He brushed his fingertips along her cheek, quieting her as he'd soothe a skittish colt. And then he slipped his fingers beneath her chin and tipped her face toward his. The unpainted angles of her cheeks and forehead were flushed with the colors of fear and anticipation.

He studied her mouth. Asymmetrical in shape, it was precisely drawn on top and full on the bottom. It had blossomed like a flower when she smiled. Would it do the same if he kissed her? He touched her bottom lip with the pad of his thumb. Just as he imagined, it was soft as a petal beneath his callused touch, pink as a rosebud against his bronzed skin. The contrasts alone aroused him, lured him. He bent his head, seeking just a taste, a crumb to feed his lonely soul. But before their lips met, she trembled beneath his touch, ever so slightly, stroking him with an unintentional caress.

He felt the tiny tug all the way down to the soles of his boots.

The electric jolt snapped him back to reality.

Hawk cursed himself for dropping his guard like that. What was he thinking? The last thing he needed was to turn his curiosity about a prim and proper virgin into some kind of mystical experience. She had to be an innocent. She was too damn naive and trusting for her own good. She had no idea what she'd been asking of him. No idea how he wanted to answer her!

Hawk released her, holding his hands out to either side as if she had scorched him. "Not tonight, schoolmarm."

Her gaze snapped at him at the intentional use

of the nickname. He braced himself, waiting for her to go all prissy on him. Waiting and deserving to hear her chew him out good for playing with her like that.

She shoved her fists against him and he willingly stepped back, putting much-needed breathing space between them. But she didn't yell at him. She didn't lecture him for putting his hands on her. She didn't accuse him of forgetting his place. She didn't do anything to him.

Instead, she closed herself off. The aura he read so easily vanished as if she'd flipped a switch. She folded her arms across her stomach, protecting herself. Not from him, but from something hidden within. A memory. A secret. A forgotten fear or disappointment that he'd stirred up accidentally.

"Sarah, I'm sorry. I couldn't believe Salazar left you out here alone. I didn't mean to—"

"Of course you didn't mean to. No one ever does." She shuddered, shaking off whatever unwanted feelings he'd roused in her. She squared her shoulders and lifted her chin. Hawk waited for the onslaught.

The fact that it never came bothered him more than he cared to admit. Being shy and inexperienced was one thing; he found her natural timidity endearing. The way she got tongue-tied at times made her human, vulnerable. But her shutting everything off inside worried him. At the very least she should slap his face for holding on to her like that, for flirting like a man when she needed an impersonal bodyguard. It was wrong for her to accept blame or embarrassment or whatever it was that shut down that tart tongue of hers.

"Sarah?"

"I'd better get back. I don't like what Luis said. I should be with the girls now." Impersonal and efficient as an automaton, she picked up the flashlight and started off. She halted after two steps into the darkness. "Darn it."

She turned around and held out the flashlight. "I think I broke it."

He could be coldly efficient, too. Hell, nobody, not even Miss Priss, was better at that game than him. He snatched the flashlight and inspected its metal casing. He tightened the cap, then slapped the butt of it twice in his palm. The light snapped on, canceling out the shadows surrounding them.

He ignored her outstretched hand, reminding himself of the reason he'd come to Tenebrosa in the first place. Evil was a dark thing. And the shadows of the jungle gave evil plenty of places to hide. Sarah and her band of teenagers were innocent lights. He'd come here to make sure their light didn't go out.

He'd come to reclaim a lost part of himself from the shadows.

His mind clear to its purpose once more, he handed her the flashlight, but kept hold of his end, binding them together for a brief moment of understanding.

"I heard what Salazar said. Martín won't hurt the girls. I promise."

She dropped her aloofness once the topic turned to someone other than herself. "How do you know that?"

Should he tell her he could read the black-tipped auras of deceit surrounding Martín and Antonio? Should he tell her how much it concerned him that he couldn't get a clear impression of Salazar himself? That he'd spent all day looking for nonmystical clues to either confirm or deny his suspicions of the man?

He answered by pulling himself up to his full six feet, four inches of height and turning his face into her light, purposely enhancing the angles and shadows of his face. "Do I look like somebody they'd want to mess with?"

She smiled at him then, not the least bit intimidated by his show of force. "I guess not."

Caught off-guard by her unanticipated reaction, Hawk thought her generously curved mouth was the most incredible thing he had ever seen. Stunned by the surprising revelation of beauty, he released the flashlight and murmured a response to her good-night.

"Hawk? What's your real name?"

Preoccupied as he was, the query came out of left field. But not since a painful day on the playground back in second grade had he let that one slip. "Un-uh." He shook his head. "Family secret."

Her smile remained fixed in place, and Hawk basked in the glorious gift that pierced the darkness around his heart. "I'm a smart woman, you know. I enjoy figuring out puzzles."

"Believe me, you'll never figure me out."

Her mouth flattened into a serious line. "I believe you when you say you'll protect us. I hope it doesn't come to that, though."

Accepting her trust was a dangerous responsibility, one he couldn't guarantee living up to. But for his own sake, he had to try. "It won't."

"I'll see you in the morning, then. Save a seat on that last truck for me."

Hawk followed the sweet little sway of her tush all the way back into camp, torturing himself with thoughts that were sure to shock Sarah. Talk about puzzles. No one, not once since he'd lost his father late in the Vietnam War and his great-uncle Otis had stepped in to teach him how to be a man and how to use and respect his special gifts, had ever been curious enough to figure him out. No one except Otis and his mother, Lily, had ever cared enough to try.

But the schoolmarm wanted to. He didn't mistake her curiosity for caring. He'd known a couple of women in his time who were intrigued enough to peel away a few layers of the mystique he'd carefully built around himself for protection and survival. But once they got to the weird stuff, they fled, repulsed by the unnatural powers of the man beneath the facade.

The difference this time was that he felt equally intrigued. What made the men of Marysville ignorant of Sarah McCormick's quiet beauty and amazing courage? What made her cling to him like a bee on a flower, then force him into battle mode to defend himself against that wicked, preachy mouth of hers?

The prim and proper schoolmarm was a puzzle he wanted to solve. But he couldn't allow himself that pleasure. He was here on a mission, determined to keep history from repeating itself.

Forgetting that might turn Sarah into another victim of Tenebrosa's evil history.

And he had yet to forgive himself for the last victim he'd lost.

"Hey, Miss Mack! Come take a look at this!"

Sarah glanced up from the marker she'd been reading and hiked up the next twenty steps to the opening in the black basalt pyramid where Lyndsay and Andrea stood. Her stiff muscles relished the exertion after a second nearly full day of riding in the back of the truck to Las Lagumas.

Upon their arrival, a lesson in the gentle digging procedures they'd use to help uncover more of the ongoing excavation had whet her appetite to unearth the archaeological treasures buried inside and around the tomb. But she tempered her own eagerness to embark on this adventure in order to set an example for the girls. If they had to wait until first light to begin the hands-on part of this cultural geography lesson, then so could she. In the meantime, they could review what they had learned about the site thus far.

Andrea held out her worn, dog-eared handbook and pointed to a picture. The primitive sunburst nestled in the cupped palms of two open hands was the same as the picture carved above the doorway where they stood. "This must be where the queen is buried. That's her symbol," said Andrea, her quiet features wreathed with excitement. "According to my book, all the jewelry and treasures Meczaquatl gave her are engraved with it."

At his uncle's urging, Raul Salazar had escorted Sarah, Hawk and the girls up to the ruins to get their first glimpse before nightfall while his crew stayed behind to set up camp.

Raul was a delightful young man of eighteen or so, patiently content to answer any and all of the girls' questions. His sparkling brown eyes and lilting voice had already captured Lyndsay's interest, and he lapped up their attention, adding his own amiable flirtations to his lecture about the hazards and highlights of working on an archaeological dig.

He had already shown them the ground-level entrance to the tomb. Tomorrow they'd explore the catacombs there, including Meczaquatl's sealed burial chamber and the many hidden passageways and niches where his treasure had been stored for centuries.

"It is too dark to go in now," said Raul, his accented tenor voice full of a young man's bravado. "Even in the morning we will need torches to explore."

"Why isn't the queen buried with her husband?" asked Denise.

"Their marriage wasn't sanctioned by his people. Prini, as she was called, was not a native Aztec. Although she was the daughter of a village chieftain, she was originally taken as a slave," explained Raul. "She willingly sacrificed herself upon her husband's death to be buried with him, but his people refused to give her that honor. They buried her in the same tomb among the gifts he ordered for her, but they would not lay her by his side."

"Yuck." Lynnette's assessment of the story reflected her modern tastes. "I wouldn't die just to be buried with my guy. That's worse than *Romeo and Juliet*."

"I think it's tragic." Lyndsay's dreamy voice matched the sadness in her bright green eyes. "Did they really love each other?"

"I suppose," answered Raul. "That is why Meczaquatl cursed his people. Soon after his death, they were decimated by a smallpox virus."

Sarah enjoyed the story of romantic tragedy, but as an adult, she felt obligated to add an element of fact to their discussion. "European explorers brought the new illness to the island."

"Perhaps. But for generations since their demise, it has been acceptable to the citizens of Tenebrosa to raid Prini's chamber and sell those artifacts to help our economy. No one has yet violated Meczaquatl's chamber in such a way. The artifacts uncovered in his antechamber are kept in El Espanto as national treasures."

Talk about a double standard. Out loud, Sarah made note of the lengthening shadows. "Luis said we had only about an hour. It's been longer than that now. We'd better get back to camp so we can eat dinner and get a good night's sleep. Tomorrow we become archaeologists."

"Yes!" A chorus of enthusiastic cheers followed Sarah down the steep stone steps. She noticed that the attraction between Lyndsay and Raul seemed to be mutual. Of all the girls, he took her by the hand and guided her down the treacherous descent.

Sarah smiled to herself, recapturing some of the eagerness that had led her to apply for this trip in the first place. She was finally seeing something of the world. And, for a few short days, she would actually be a part of living history.

At the base of the pyramid she stepped to one side and mentally tallied off the girls as she had done countless times that day. Martín de Vega had flirted with them at lunch, but he had yet to make any alarming overt gestures. Just the same, even with Hawk looking over her shoulder, she planned to follow Luis's advice and keep the girls together and away from the potential threat.

Her class of bright young women paraded past: Denise leading the way; Lyndsay hand in hand with Raul; Colleen and Andrea discussing the merits of burying treasured keepsakes with departed loved ones; and Lynnette, looking this way and that, taking stock of every single detail to record in her journal.

But where was Hawk?

Sarah had gradually gotten used to his unnerving company hovering in the background, much like the omnipresent heat she couldn't avoid. She had logically decided to make him her friend, since she'd had no luck in making him stay at home. After the way she'd thrown herself all over him the night before because of that stupid spider and her own timorous fears, and after the way he'd held her so tenderly—so politely, when he could have easily told her to get over herself— it became imperative that she reach some kind of truce with him, or the rest of the week would be hell, as he had once promised.

The poor man. She was a mercy date waiting to happen. He'd only been trying to protect her from her own carelessness, and she had turned to him as if he were some kind of knight in shining armor—molding herself to him like a wanton, thinking with her heart and hormones instead of really thinking. She'd had a lot of years to polish her self-sufficiency, and she prided herself on staying cool in a crisis and not giving in to her fears.

But last night she'd forgotten all that and hatched a one-sided fantasy with Hawk. Not since her parents' deaths had anyone else offered to be strong for her. And he hadn't even offered; she'd forced him to be her rescuer. God, how she must have embarrassed him. Like a gentleman, he had tried to comfort her, and she had thanked him by putting him in the awkward position of having to turn down her unwanted, unskilled advances.

But those humiliating circumstances wouldn't happen again. They couldn't happen again if she turned her dark knight into a buddy like the other men in her life. And the first thing she would do for any friend would be to ensure his safety. If he hadn't gone up the pyramid with them, then he must have gone inside the entrance down below.

Pulling a pocket flashlight from her shorts, she entered the squared-off archway and walked down the long hallway leading to the center of the tomb.

"Hawk? You in here?" Turning on her light, she rounded the corner to the antechamber that led to Meczaquatl's tomb. The eight-foot-square room featured walls built of sandstone blocks, and was painted with frescoes detailing the king's achievements in life.

But the bronze and umber drawings, highlighted with bits of paint containing actual gold dust, didn't catch her attention. The man at the center of the empty chamber drew her entire focus.

Standing still as the corpse sealed inside, with his feet braced apart and fingers splayed at his sides, Hawk tipped his face up toward the juncture where the top stone of the wall met the ceiling. His nostrils flared, but his breathing was almost undetectable.

"Hawk?" She called to him again, shining her light on the wall, trying to see what picture in particular fascinated him so. Frowning, she looked at him again. The only thing on the top of that wall was a shallow crevice where the mortar between the stones had disintegrated into dust.

She could almost hear a hum of tension radiating from his body like the fallout of a controlled chemical reaction. It thrummed and rippled through the air, as tangible as heat rising from hot pavement. But the air inside the perpetual twilight of the tomb remained chilly in its gloom, pricking her skin with goose bumps.

Her light flickered to his face, and Sarah gasped at the unblinking intensity of his eyes. His pupils had dilated, forming bottomless pits in the reflecting pools of endless night. The stifling air sucked at her breath, making her light-headed.

She tried to call his name again.

He didn't hear her.

Chapter Four

Sarah shook her head, trying to clear her ears of the heavy air. Dropping the flashlight, she raked her fingers into her hair at either temple, squeezing out the haze that clouded her mind.

Her breath came in shallow pants. Blindly she reached out, squinting to find Hawk's shadowy, still frame silhouetted in the darkness.

Was he feeling this, too? Was there some leak of poisonous air, gone stale after eons bottled up in the tomb with a dead man? Could the excavations already in progress in other parts of the pyramid have tapped into a fissure beneath the earth, releasing gases from the dormant volcano that formed the island? Though they had barely begun exploring, Luis had warned them of the uncharted network of endless passages. Addicting, toxic air could travel along pathways a man might never find.

They had to get out of there. *Now!*

"Hawk?" Sarah leaned forward, battling an unseen force inside her head that made her feet feel like lead weights mired in a deep snowdrift. She pressed on, inches at a time, her progress hampered as if she were moving upwind into a blizzard.

The spinning vertigo in her head worsened the closer she got. Sucking in a fortifying breath, she reached out and touched his arm. "Hawk?"

He snapped his head around as if she'd given him an electric shock. Sarah jerked back, singed by the sudden violence roiling through him.

He stepped toward her, then took another step. Sarah stumbled backward, terrified by the unrecognizing glint in his eyes and the grim look of purpose on his wild, striking, sinister face. He advanced on her, a devilish wraith emerging from the night. Her back hit a wall, puffing up a cloud of ancient dust around her face and shoulders. She put her hands up in a futile attempt to ward off his overpowering strength, and still he kept coming.

"Hawk!" she cried out, desperate for him to recognize her and regain his senses. "It's me. Sarah. The schoolmarm!"

She bit out the awful name he'd dubbed her, just as his fingertips grazed her neck. His hand closed around her throat and she shrank against the wall. Dust sifted into her nostrils and clogged her throat. Her neck constricted against his hand and she coughed. Panicked in her need for air, she grasped at his bare forearm and dug in eight of her short nails, crying his name on a gasping breath.

Hawk squeezed his eyes shut and gritted his

teeth, dragging in a lungful of air. When his chest receded on the exhale she heard the barest whisper of a word. "Sch . . . school . . . "

"Hawk?" She tried again, her own voice a ragged little squeak. She repeated his name over and over as he struggled to find his way back to her.

Finally, when she had no voice of her own left to call to him, he loosened his grip on her. She breathed in deeply, sucking the dusty, rank air down her throat. The action triggered a spasm of coughing that inflamed the bruised and tender skin around her neck.

Maybe it was her hushed groan of pain, maybe it was the shaking of her body, but Hawk opened his eyes and glared at her with a fierce determination that she felt rather than saw. With her back literally against the wall, she was helpless when he reached for her again.

He crushed the collar of her shirt in his fist and tugged her forward. He ignored the beseeching gesture of her outstretched arms and spun her around, taking her by the shoulders and pushing her in front of him. He shoved her around the corner into the hallway, where she could see the lighter shadows of the night outside waiting several feet away, the literal light at the end of the tunnel.

He shoved her again, following behind her in heavy, staggering steps. "Out . . . " His voice sounded behind her like the strangled croak of a trapped animal. "Now."

Risking a glance over her shoulder, she saw Hawk stumble to his knees. His eyes were scarcely more than black slits cutting through the agony that clenched his features. Damning her foolishness and forgetting her fear, Sarah

79

stopped and reached out to him when she should have run.

He snatched her wrist, his painful grip cutting into her skin. He swung her arm aside and used the momentum to drag himself back up to his feet.

"Get out now!" he hollered in her face, and in one fluid motion he hauled her up into his arms. Ignoring her shriek of protest, he crushed her to his chest and lurched toward the opening.

Sarah slung her arms around his neck to shield herself from the jarring ride. His hands on her thigh and shoulder were fierce talons, gripping her in desperation as much as protection. As he neared the opening, his pace quickened. And when they reached the air outside, he lengthened his stride into a run, evening out his steps into a feral smoothness that carried them both deep into the jungle.

She tucked her head beneath Hawk's chin and curled into a ball to protect herself from the stinging slap of thick leaves and hanging vines as he ran. An eternity passed, though maybe only a minute of real time, before he stopped abruptly and released her. She sailed out of his arms, landing with a cushioned thud on a bed of giant ferns.

While she scrambled from her bottom to her knees, stiffly giving her body time to adjust from its human roller-coaster ride, Hawk bent over at the waist, grasping his knees for support and gulping in lungfuls of the reviving air. Though more humid than fresh, it was nonetheless clean, and Sarah knelt beside him, transfixed, while his chest heaved in and out with an exertion more emotional than physical.

Again drawn by his pain in a way she didn't understand, Sarah touched his side. He might not have noticed the shy touch through the layers of his vest and shirt, but when he didn't flinch away, she grew bolder. She rose up on her knees beside him, laying one hand at the small of his back and the other over his bicep, holding him in a gentle embrace. She patted and stroked him, silly gestures, really, for a man of his size, but she didn't know what else to do for him. She had no idea what to say that might help.

She had no idea what was wrong.

He slowly angled his head back to see her. Confusion banked in his eyes, a dullness that darkened and engulfed his gaze until it squeezed out a tiny rim of light that ringed his irises. He blinked, and when he looked at her again, recognition dawned.

"Sarah? Are you real?"

Held still by his gaze, Sarah barely nodded. Then, before she could utter a word, he was on his knees in front of her, crushing her in his arms. He palmed the back of her head and pressed it to his shoulder. He folded her into him, wrapping her up so tightly that breathing wasn't much of an option. Her hands settled at his waist as he rocked her back and forth. Sarah simply held on, sensing he needed the kind of comfort that holding on to another human being could provide.

Time seemed suspended in that nameless place in the tropical night. Hawk released her, and she felt suddenly bereft of his warmth, of his hardness and need. Walter had never clung to her like that. No man had ever held on to her as if she were a lifeline. It didn't matter that it could have been anybody that Hawk needed right then. What mattered was that he had needed someone. She was there. And he hadn't pushed her away.

Sarah pursed her lips together, trying to come up with a suitable excuse to move away from him. While the sounds hummed in her vocal cords, he cupped her jaw in his large hands and tipped her face up to his. His gaze roamed her features, searching, seeking answers to an unasked question. His fingers feathered across her ears, sending tremors of awareness through her. His gaze focused on her mouth, just as his thumbs pressed against her lips.

Her bottom lip throbbed with the memory of his touch the night before. Walter had kissed her on occasion. He had taught her how to open her mouth and touch his tongue with her own. At the time, she thought herself daring, on the verge of discovering passion. But the memory of that intimacy seemed a pale imitation of what this man did to her with just the brush of his fingertips and the power of his gaze.

He traced her lips with his thumbs. The callused tips abraded her sensitive skin, making her feel hot inside. Her pores opened to cool her from the oppressive humidity outside, but inside she felt breathless and trapped, with no way to assuage the rise in pressure and temperature swirling from all the points where he touched her with his hands and eyes. The heat spiraled downward, gathering deep in the heart of her.

How did she ask a man to kiss her? What could she say or do to make him understand what she wanted?

"Hawk." She breathed his name like a prayer. And shocking her right down to her feverish little toes, he answered her.

His fingers tightened around her face and his mouth came down on hers, hard, probing, taking what she was so willing to give. If he had taken the time to woo her, to speak soft words, she might have become aware of what she had asked, of what he offered. She would have locked up behind a wall of self-conscious doubt and screamed a protest or slunk away in shame. But he never gave her the chance.

He plunged his tongue through the barriers of her lips and teeth and she opened for him, inhaling his essence, absorbing his taste with her own mouth. His tongue mated with hers, stroked the sensitive walls of her mouth, streaked across the bruised arc of her lips. He was maddening. Hot. Primal. Man.

She was primed to a flash point already, and his kiss triggered a chain reaction inside her. The world spun wildly around her and she closed her eyes, overwhelmed by the assault on her senses, inside, outside, everywhere. She dug her fingers into his chest, clutching handfuls of vest and shirt and skin, and hung on for her life. His hands tangled in her hair, swept along her back, cupped her bottom and lifted.

When her knees left the ground, she fell against him, too dizzy to support herself. His arms closed around her as he caught her tightly, closing out the rest of the world with the bulk of his chest and broad shoulders surrounding her. She felt the indentation of his stomach, the hard columns of his thighs, and the jutting testimony of his male need between them.

She should have been shocked. She should have remembered her unspoiled reputation. She should have remembered her fear of the man.

But robbed of conscious thought by the marauding magic of his hands and mouth, she could only react. Desperate for something just out of her reach, aching to relieve the buffeting demands inside her own body, she stretched against him and freed her hands, beginning an exploration of her own.

She skimmed the prominent angle of his cheeks, rasped her palms along the unforgiving line of his jaw, then discovered the midnight waterfall of his hair. It was softer than silk, heavy like the molten weight at her feminine center; she sifted it through her fingers, catching and tugging, then drowning her hands in it again.

The woman was tinder in his hands!

Hawk angled his mouth and let her do as she willed. With every clutch of her fingers, Sarah kissed him. She pulled away, then tugged him back, pressing harder with her own lips, nibbling him with a hungry need that matched his own. Her breathing came short and deep like his own, hot little puffs of air that caressed his face. Soft, downy caresses contrasted with the driving abandon of her long, lithe fingers clawing at him.

He wasn't sure why he had kissed her in the first place, wasn't sure he was entirely himself when he first touched her. The shadow world had gotten so mixed up inside his head that he couldn't tell whether to believe what he saw with his eyes or what he saw with his mind.

Sarah brought him fully back to his senses, then took him beyond. Her eager, eloquent, needy hands took him to a plane of reality so sweet and hot and inviting, he never wanted to leave. She was soft and pliant, delicate and sweet, and the sexy curve of her derriere fit his hands as if he'd been made to hold her.

God, she was brave. He'd known grizzled soldiers to walk a wide berth around him once they caught him in one of his trances. But Sarah reached out to him, her concern greater than her fear. She'd stood by him. Opened herself to him in a way that triggered a volatile need.

A need to be accepted.

In all fairness, he hadn't given her much of a chance to refuse him. But if she had said something, if she had pushed away instead of pulling closer, he would have let her go. But her willingness to touch and be touched, to breathe one air, to mingle their spirits in matching heartbeats, filled him with a power that made him feel human. Not the power that separated him from others. But the power that bound him to another person in the real world. To Sarah.

It was a far-fetched dream that could never be his. But for now he took strength in the physical reactions of his body. He enjoyed the ache in his loins and the foolish hope in his soul.

He should stop this madness. *He* was the one with the experience. *He* was the one who knew where this was leading. *He* was the one who could hurt her.

Who might have already hurt her.

The thought washed over him like a cruel torture. He was Tantalus trapped in Hades, always hungry, always thirsty, with the fruit and water forever beyond his reach.

Drawing on the strength of his shaman forefathers, Hawk lifted his hands to Sarah's slim, strong shoulders and pushed her away. The few inches of air he put between them made the jungle feel cold.

Dazed by the same loss his own body protested,

she sank to her knees and latched on to him for balance. She blinked rapidly, as if trying to awaken, then focused on his chin. Her tongue darted out and licked the swollen curve of her lips. He'd been rough with his need, and the proof was in the pinkened skin around her mouth.

Hawk cursed himself. He had awakened her and left her wanting. But that regret didn't alarm him as much as the telltale evidence he saw when she lifted her face to his.

"He hurt you."

Too dazed to comprehend the self-loathing in his voice, Sarah misunderstood. "You didn't hurt me."

He pushed aside the collar of her gingham blouse and stared at the exposed skin. In chilling slow motion, he wrapped his right hand around the base of her throat. She stiffened at the contact and Hawk thought she must be remembering something he couldn't.

The red marks on her neck, just beginning to darken into bruises, fit the span of his hand like two pieces of a puzzle joining together.

Hawk jerked his hand away and swore viciously. He rolled to his feet and stalked away, ignoring the wounded look in Sarah's eyes.

What the hell kind of bastard was he? He could have killed her! And judging by the strangle marks on her gullet, he must have tried.

He whirled around to face her and felt her reaction like a punch in the gut when she scooted away from him. He quashed the urge to help her up, to scoop her into his arms and kiss her until she was too mindless to distrust him again. She crawled unsteadily to her feet and crossed her arms in front of her. The shielding action that shut him out was no more than he deserved.

"I'm sorry I hurt you, Sarah," he apologized. "You'll never know how deeply I regret that."

"It's okay." Green had become the dominant color in her huge eyes, and he wondered why he couldn't read her emotions just then. She had shut herself off again, shutting him out in that way, too.

Without another word she turned and pushed aside a fern as tall as she and walked away from him.

"Sarah," he called. Night came early beneath the dense canopy of the jungle. "Where are you going?"

"Back to camp." She stopped and gave a toneless answer. "The girls shouldn't be alone."

Hawk swallowed past the hard knot of remorse in his throat. "You're going the wrong way."

She turned and came back to him. With her hands balled into fists at her hips, she challenged him with the proud tilt of her chin. "How do you know?"

He wondered what this show of spirit cost her. He lobbed her emotional havoc on top of his growing mound of guilt. "I just know."

"Then take me back."

It wasn't an offer of trust so much as a deference to practicality. Nodding to her command, he held out his hand. She stared at it with repulsion in her eyes. Was she remembering the way he'd held her? His own palm itched with the memory of her womanly shape. Mentally, he closed off the memory. He needed to concentrate on his alternate senses to find their way back.

"I can't afford to lose you on the way," he said aloud, struggling to remain detached and use the same common sense she displayed.

Reluctantly, she placed her hand in his, but she didn't hold on. He had to squeeze his hand around hers to maintain the contact. Words were useless at this point. How could he explain what had happened to him in the tomb? How could he rationalize the way he'd kissed her a few moments ago? How could he ask forgiveness for pulling away so suddenly?

If he needed any further proof of his failures, he felt it in the chill of her hand. Hawk tipped his nose to the sky and waited for the scent of the campfire to reinforce his sense of direction. When he hiked out of the clearing, Sarah followed meekly behind.

She had turned to him to offer comfort, and he had taken advantage of that generosity and awakened her to passion. Her innocence had given him false hope; her hands had set him on fire. What kind of man did that to a woman?

What kind of freak?

He'd proven unreliable. His actions were unforgivable.

Again.

He couldn't blame the damn island this time.

Sarah buttoned her blouse, deferring to modesty over the heat. She paced her tent like a caged animal, trapped inside by the suffocating curtain of rain falling outside. Since their arrival on Tenebrosa, she'd quickly learned that these rainstorms lasted only a few short minutes, but the rain fell with such an awesome natural force and abandon that everything else in this tropical world stopped for that short period of time.

Much like Hawk's kiss.

Luis had warned them to stay inside their tents

during the blinding deluges, but she was tempted to run outside and let the rain pelt her body. Maybe if it rained long enough or hard enough, she could erase the memory of Hawk's hands on her skin or the taste of him on her mouth. Echoes of her foolish foray into passion still reverberated through her like tiny aftershocks from an earthquake.

Her concern for him had been justified. That weird gas inside the tomb had affected his mind somehow; otherwise, she knew, he never would have kissed her. She'd set herself up for his rejection. If she'd kept her wits about her, she wouldn't have subjected herself to that kind of humiliation. She'd very nearly succumbed to her attraction to him the night before. Tonight she hadn't been so lucky.

If she were more of a woman, she'd have seen what was coming. She'd have known that Hawk's reactions were beyond his control. She could have played some game, bantered her way out of there, given him the hug he needed and walked away.

But she had wanted him to kiss her so badly. Her single-minded fascination wasn't just with the act—if she was curious enough she could read a book about it—but with the man himself. She'd never experienced that overwhelming rush of desire with any other man; she'd never *needed* to be kissed by anyone else. She hadn't said the words, but somehow he'd known what she wanted. Where to put his hands, when to use his lips or tongue, how to angle his mouth.

Too bad she hadn't known how to do the same for him.

She forced herself out of those thoughts and realized she was rubbing her finger back and forth across her lips, remembering how Hawk had felt there. She stomped her foot on the wooden platform floor and dug her brush out of her tote bag. She resumed her pacing, dragging the bristles through her hair with the same frustrated, repetitive motion.

Hawk hadn't even known what he was doing, hadn't even known who she was, when he'd held her. As soon as he came to his senses, he pushed her away. And she still couldn't make herself forget him.

"Grow up already," she chastised herself. Walter had taught her that a man couldn't want *her*. She owned property and a reputation that would make her a suitable wife, but she had nothing more to offer a man, nothing to interest him in *her* instead of the family name or bank account. And it wasn't just Walter, though he'd been the only man generous enough to be honest with her.

Shyness and plain looks had kept her from dating when she was young and her friends had started. She'd thrown herself into her books in college, building self-esteem through academic accomplishments and hard work. Then, when she would have left home to take her place in the world, her mother fell ill. Two long, difficult years that demanded her full attention turned her into an adult with heavy responsibilities. Left alone with her father, she couldn't shirk those responsibilities, because he needed her then.

She was twenty-seven when she lost him, though she'd felt ages older. By the time she'd worked through her grief, Aunt Doris and Aunt Millie began to claim her time. They weren't invalids, but they were lonely. Loneliness was one sentiment she understood in spades, and she could hardly abandon them to such a fate. By the time she turned thirty, she was firmly entrenched in her role as an icon of the community: the spinster schoolmarm who lived in the big house on the hill all alone. When Walter began to court her, she gathered the courage to be young again, to try to catch up on everything she had missed over the years.

And then he made her realize it was already too late for her.

But when her students won the Sinclair grant, she began to hope there was a little bit of life left in her. And when Hawk materialized out of the crowd, out of the shadows, and out of the jungle, she began to wish. Her pulse raced and her words got stuck in her head and her spirit felt more alive than she could ever remember.

He was pure danger to her sheltered life. She was drawn to him like a moth to a flame, a foolish addiction that only guaranteed her destruction.

And Sarah was too smart a woman for that. At least, she hoped she was. She stopped at the foot of her cot and listened to the softening drumbeat of rain on her tent roof, a sure sign that the storm would end at any minute. Like a game-show contestant whose time was running out, she made a decision.

She had to have everything spelled out in black and white so that needy little well of wishing inside her wouldn't embarrass her again. She could at least retain her dignity and her common sense, and not lose the girls' respect for her.

When the rain stopped, she knew there was no turning back.

The hour was late, and as much as confrontations like this twisted her stomach into knots, she had to do it. She had to talk to Hawk. With her flashlight lost for the night in Meczaquatl's tomb, she picked up the camping lantern from her tent and went outside.

The clouds hadn't dissipated yet, and even in this clearing where the tents surrounded the fire pit, her lantern cut a meager yellow halo of light through the thick, moonless night.

She extended the lantern to arm's length and tried to get her bearings. Hawk had led her unerringly back to camp without aid of lantern or flashlight, but here she stood in the circle of six tents and had difficulty telling which marked path led to the ruins, the lagoon, or Hawk's tent.

Trusting her instincts as much as the flip of a coin, she chose the narrowest trail, assuming his path would show the least amount of use. Hawk's tent was a smaller structure that had been pitched directly on the ground outside the circle of the camp. Curious, she thought, as she picked her way over exposed tree roots and chopped vegetation, that Luis and his men hadn't asked Hawk to bunk with them. Hawk hadn't complained, but in Sarah's mind, the exclusion bordered on rudeness, in addition to the impracticality of doubling their time and effort to set up his quarters.

Though at this moment, she was glad for the relative seclusion. She didn't want to risk anyone else overhearing what she had to say, or it would defeat the whole point of the conversation.

The fates were with her, and within minutes she stood before the front flap of Hawk's darkened tent. He'd already gone to bed! Of course, he didn't have painful concerns to keep him up at night, the way she did. Sarah hovered outside, debating whether she should announce herself and wake him now, or come back early in the morning and catch him before breakfast. The rain had been only a temporary excuse. She couldn't be sure her shaky fortitude would last until sunup.

With her fist poised to knock, the tent flap was flung open. Startled, she snatched her hand to her chest and jumped back. In the space of a heartbeat, Hawk filled the opening. Naked to the waistband of a pair of khaki green boxer shorts, and bare from his thighs down his sleek, strong legs to his long, masculine toes, he stood before her, holding that twelve-inch knife in his fist, ready to pounce.

Rendered speechless by a sudden jolt of awareness, Sarah stared at his chest. Smooth and supple, and as coppery-dark as the rest of him, the broad planes tapered down across his rib cage to the healthy flatness of his stomach. Dusky brown male nipples perched like badges of honor on the sculpted rise of muscle, and she didn't dare wonder if the parts she couldn't see were as bare and hard and sinewed as the rest of him.

"Is something wrong?" he asked, his soft voice a dark, wary sound in the night.

Oh, God, what was she thinking, coming here in the middle of the night?

Big, big mistake. What did she think the man would sleep in? A more sensible woman would have guessed, and waited until he had dressed in the morning to have this discussion.

"Sarah?" he asked again, lowering his knife to his side.

"No, nothing's wrong." Her tongue felt dry and swollen in her mouth. She discovered a rip in the netting at the door of his tent and concentrated on that. "I just need to talk."

He stepped around her and scanned the surrounding trees before holding the flap open with his extended arm and ushering her inside. "All right."

She walked to the center of the tent and he followed her in, closing the flap behind him. This seemed so much smaller than her own quarters. There wasn't a stick of furniture except for his cot. On top of that lay a rumpled sleeping bag, a cord necklace with some kind of black stone tied at the end, and the black leather sheath for his knife. He must sleep with that thing. She'd alerted him by making some noise, and he'd jumped out of bed, armed and ready for battle.

"Just what kind of danger are you expecting to find here on Tenebrosa?"

She turned to speak and caught a glimpse of a light in his expression. But blackness shuttered his eyes so quickly, she wondered if she had imagined the intensity of his reaction. "Hawk?"

He shrugged his broad shoulders, an action that disturbed the atmosphere of the small tent like ripples spreading through water. While Sarah looked away, feeling that unaccustomed awareness heating her cheeks again, Hawk bent over the cot and sheathed the knife in its leather case. "If Salazar doesn't trust his own men, I don't see any reason we should."

When he straightened, he stood beside her, with his broad, smooth, beautiful chest positioned scant inches from the tip of her nose. Sarah blinked rapidly, temporarily forgetting her concerns and her reason for coming here in the first place.

An animal urge to nuzzle his chest, to lean into him and test the smell and dampness of his skin, sprung upon her unawares. With a monumental effort, she thought of Doris and Millie and their prim, ladylike ways. Grasping that slim straw of propriety, she turned away and crossed to the back of the tent.

"Would you put on a shirt? Please?" Was that husky little quaver part of her own voice?

Keeping her back turned, she blushed at the colorful oath that slipped from his lips, then listened to a rummaging sound as he sorted through items in his duffel bag. She heard a whispered rasp of material, and a few moments later his dark voice penetrated her mental image of him dressing behind her. "All right."

Breathing easier, Sarah turned around and could have kicked herself. Maybe the one thing more distracting than Hawk's naked chest was the sight of that chest encased in tight black cotton. The clinging softness of his T-shirt only accentuated what it covered, and instead of overlooking his sexy dimensions, she busied herself imagining and remembering what lay underneath.

Treating herself like a recalcitrant pupil who continued to stare out the window while the teacher lectured, she quickly chastised herself. She tipped her chin up and practically clicked her heels together, stiffening her posture to near attention. "Are you feeling better?"

"Better?" He'd also pulled on his military fatigues and was now in the process of tucking his shirt into the waistband.

His perfunctory movements eased her nervous awareness. He clearly felt no similar attraction to her, so mooning over his body was a wasted effort. Remembering that made it easier to talk to him. "Earlier this evening in the tomb, you weren't yourself. It was like you'd taken a drug. I thought there might be poisonous gas. Maybe the tomb isn't safe for the girls."

"It isn't safe." He tucked the knife behind his back and sat down to pull on his socks and boots. He did spare her one direct glance. "And no, I don't take drugs."

She felt the sting in his voice. She'd meant only to suggest a comparison for his behavior, not make an accusation. "I know you don't," she said by way of apology, believing him.

The tension in his shoulders eased a fraction. But his first warning still bothered her. Sarah frowned and set the lantern on the floor, hiding his face in otherworldly shadows. "Why isn't it safe?"

The silence that followed engulfed the tent, making it hard for Sarah to breathe. Then, in one swift movement, Hawk snatched her wrist and pulled her down on the cot beside him. He let go immediately, but the bottomless pool of night in his eyes pinned her there and kept her from moving away.

"I sense things." He released the words haltingly, as if saying them aloud created an unpleasant taste on his tongue. "I'm aware of things that other people often overlook."

Sarah looked at his face. On first meeting him, she might have described it as expressionless. But here in the shadows, after three days in his presence, after watching him with a fascination that bordered on obsession, she realized he revealed a great deal with his eyes. Right now they were pleading. Desperate. Wary. He wanted to share something with her, and yet she sensed he wasn't comfortable sharing this with anybody.

A thought struck her. "Are you telepathic? Can you read people's minds?"

His straight lips curved in the trace of a smile. Her intuition pleased him. "Not exactly. I read emotions. Histories. I can see past events that shape people's actions, and"—he hesitated—"I get impressions of future events."

"You read auras?"

"Yes." His smile broadened but didn't reach his eyes.

That explained the kiss. That explained why he showed up when Salazar had abandoned her. But that didn't explain . . . "So did you sense something in the tomb?"

He spread his hands across his knees and inhaled deeply, bracing himself for the next revelation. "I am what's called a shaman. A spirit master. Not only do I interpret the living spirits of the earth, but I can communicate with the spirits beyond."

"Ghosts?"

"More of an awareness rather than any physical manifestation. A temporary possession as a means of communication. There's a presence there in the tomb. Someone who's very unhappy. Very angry."

While she believed in psychic phenomena to some degree—after all, there were times when she'd thought her mother, deep in the throes of her cruelest pain, had communicated her subconscious needs to her. And occasionally she still felt the wise, comforting presence of her father. But there were limits to what explanations she could accept.

Sarah shot to her feet, angry with herself for listening and giving credence to Hawk's wild story. "An evil spirit possessed you? That's why you tried to strangle me? So it wasn't you who put his paws all over me, but some unhappy spirit?"

Hawk stood and closed his hands around her elbows. "I'm not sure when I snapped out of it, but I knew what I was doing when I kissed you. I'm sorry I didn't realize it sooner."

Sarah jerked away. "Keep your hands off me!"

The vehemence in her voice and the force of her movements froze him to the spot. Sarah grabbed the lantern and stomped to the door. He hadn't even turned when she spun around and jabbed a finger at him. "That will never happen again! Do you understand?"

She dropped her hand and ranted on in a softer, more cutting tone. "I have a reputation to consider. That kiss was a mistake. I wouldn't want the girls to think something was going on between us. That's hardly appropriate behavior for a chaperon."

"It won't happen again." If she weren't so angry, if she didn't feel so foolish for believing in him, she might have noticed the dead quality in his voice.

"It had better not." There. She'd made the point she wanted to. She should feel triumphant. Relieved. Instead she only felt miserable. But she couldn't back down now. Everyone expected her to fail on this trip, and with her wild fantasies about Hawk she'd nearly done so. "I don't want to hear any crazy talk around the girls, either. Luis has spooked them enough. They think you're some kind of hero who's going to protect them. But you're not, are you?"

Hawk faced her then, and the bleak look in his eyes nearly stopped her. The harsh edge seeped from her voice. "You're just some crazy man who carries a big knife and spouts nonsense about evil and dead spirits. And I was stupid enough to . . . "

To what? Believe in him? Care about him? Want him?

"I'm not crazy." He said it like a fact she should believe. She almost did. "And you're not stupid to be afraid of me."

Sarah laughed, a joyless sound that got sucked up by the tent's thick air. "I was more comfortable with the noxious-gas theory."

"I can't promise it won't happen again. Sometimes, even with my abilities, I can't control the will of the spirits." When she realized how hard he looked at her, she listened to the call of his eyes and met his gaze. "But I can promise to keep my hands to myself, if that's what you want."

"I . . . It's for the best." That was what she wanted, wasn't it? Sarah struggled to remember why it was so important to keep her distance from Hawk.

"It's not what I want." His soft voice caressed her with a promise that left her wanting. "I'm not sorry I kissed you. I'm only sorry I hurt you because of it."

I'm not sorry? Wasn't he embarrassed? Disappointed?

If he was an honest man—and crazy people spoke exactly what they felt, didn't they?—then the idea that he truly wanted to kiss her warmed her like a hug.

Don't worry, sweetie, I'll still make love to you. I want to have kids. Walter's voice intruded, a shameful reminder that overshadowed the healing kindness in Hawk's voice.

Seizing that reality, she managed a civil smile. "Then if we understand each other, I'll say good night."

"Sarah?" He moved a step closer, but he stopped when she put up a hand.

"Good night, Hawk."

She escaped from the oppressive confines of the tent into the oppressive humidity outside. Walking down the path, she considered her own foolishness. Her anger with Hawk had more to do with her own embarrassment than with any real suspicions about his character. She didn't really think he was crazy. He just had some crazy ideas. And she honestly believed he sensed people's emotions. Look how accurately he read her desire and anger and self-doubt.

Lord, she was a fool! A plain, uptight, inexperienced fool. She should learn from Walter's example and just give up on men. She didn't understand them. She didn't know how to handle them. Why the heck did she think she needed one?

Why did she think she needed Hawk?

The thought stopped her in her tracks. Somewhere along the line, her attraction to the man had deepened into some sort of emotional attachment. A hunger that went deeper than physical desire.

"Talk about crazy," she chided herself.

When she shook her head and stepped forward again, a figure materialized out of the shadows, blocking her path. Looking up, she saw that it was no spirit, but a man. A slick-haired, slitty-eyed, sweat-stained man with a leering smile.

Martín de Vega.

He reached out and touched her cheek with the tips of two grimy fingers.

"Tomorrow night, Señorita Sarah, you will visit *my* tent?"

Chapter Five

A prickle of unease touched Hawk's mind the way a cool breeze would raise the hairs on the back of his neck. It was the same awareness that had kept him and the men in his rescue/recon unit alive more than once in the past. He wasn't sure he trusted that instinct anymore. But a soldier's training had been ingrained in him since childhood, and, doubtful or not, he'd grown too used to listening to that keen sixth sense to ignore it.

He retied his boot, buttoned the fly of his khakis, and wondered why he'd gone to so much trouble getting dressed after midnight. He'd jumped from his cot earlier, fortified by only his underwear and his knife, braced to surprise the intruder who'd strayed so far from camp.

He'd known it was Sarah before he opened the tent flap. When her guard was down, she broadcast her spirit like a beacon, a connecting signal strengthened by her appearance in his vision. His mind had leaped to all sorts of conclusions— none of them very comforting. There'd been an accident. Martín had gone after the girls. That hateful, waking presence in the tomb had managed to escape and find a way to stalk Sarah.

But no, she had just wanted to talk.

Hawk sighed in utter frustration with the woman and closed his eyes, tuning his senses to the impression that had alerted him through the darkness.

She'd come to him, determined yet delicate, daring yet afraid, and said she just wanted to talk. Her hair fell freely in a caramel-colored cascade around her shoulders and back, with the ends of it drawing his eye to the sensuous earth-woman flare of her hips.

He still felt raw from fighting off that damned demon that tried to possess him, and she'd traipsed in, wide-eyed and vulnerable, spouting self-righteous nonsense about his inappropriate kiss while staring at his chest as if she wanted to devour him.

Her aura spoke of desire, but her words were all cold business. He tried to respect the conscious choice of the people he read when their words didn't match their emotions.

But it was damn hard to watch Sarah struggling to conquer an overwhelming physical need while she talked like a prude. Especially since he wanted to hold her again, to see if her response was as incendiary as he remembered, or if his memory of her untutored, unrestrained kiss was a feverish exaggeration of his demented mind.

She wanted him to maintain an impersonal distance. He knew it was the right thing to do.

She had a reputation to protect with her students, and he needed to concentrate on the potential danger at hand. But then she did that shy, stammering thing and triggered a protective urge to swallow her up in his arms and make whatever frightened her go away.

Except *he* was the thing that frightened her.

So instead of telling her to get lost, or touching her again, he put on all his clothes and tried to reassure her of his good intentions that way. But if she didn't learn to douse the hungry look in her eyes, he wouldn't be able to stay away from her.

"Damn." He offered the curse as barter for his tormented soul and left the tent.

Extraneous thoughts vanished when he saw the light through the trees. Unmoving. Sarah had stopped on the path not far from her tent. Was it another spider? A snake?

Or something equally loathsome?

He heard the raspy whisper of a man's voice. "Do not worry about the strange one. My friends and I, we will show you the hospitality of Tenebrosa."

Silent as a jaguar, Hawk crept closer. He felt Sarah shudder when Martín de Vega stroked his fingers across her cheek. An unexpected rush of possessive anger surged through him. He balled his hand into a fist, but relaxed it almost immediately.

Thus far, he'd shown himself to be paranoid and unable to control his own actions. Much as she cringed away from de Vega's flirtations, Hawk doubted Sarah would appreciate any more demonstrations of violence.

He was an able enough fighter, but his best skill lay in the element of surprise. His uncanny knowledge could spook an enemy into making a mistake, rendering Hawk an intimidating victor.

Materializing out of the shadows directly behind Sarah achieved the intended result. Startled, de Vega jerked his hand away from her face. Even Sarah jumped at his low-pitched voice.

"Go back to the pit you crawled out of and leave the lady alone."

De Vega spread his legs in the time-honored stance of a man expecting a fight. Not much taller than Sarah herself, he preened with all the false bravado of a bantam rooster. "Luis says she does not belong to you."

Hawk answered in Spanish, sparing Sarah the harsh words, though she could probably pick up the gist of his threat, judging by de Vega's response. With his bottom lip already curled in a perpetual snarl, Martín contorted his face with downturned lines of contempt. Hawk never so much as blinked. The lowlife quaked in his sandals, imparted his opinion of Hawk's parentage, then turned and scurried back toward the main camp.

Hawk didn't slacken his battle-ready pose until he saw Sarah's shoulders lift and sag with a gut-deep sigh. "Are you all right?" he asked.

Slowly she turned and tilted those big green-gold eyes up at him. "What did you say to him?"

"The most polite translation I'll give is that if he touches you again, I'll give him a taste of *my* hospitality."

He felt the premonition a split second before her words struck him. It was too late to brace himself for the brunt of her ingratitude. "Great. Now he'll hit on the girls."

105

"Excuse me?" He wasn't so full of himself as to expect a thank-you, but the thinly veiled reprimand took him by surprise. "You want me to ignore your fear of the man?"

"That doesn't matter. The girls' safety comes first. If he's occupied with me, then he's not bothering them."

"He'll bother them *and* you if he thinks he can get away with it." He bent his knees, facing her at her level, matching her defiant stance. "He's not the kind of man who's satisfied with one woman. It doesn't have to be you. It's a game. He wants to score whenever and however he can. I just told him you weren't available to play."

The fire bled from her eyes. He didn't need any damn gift to see the color draining from her face. Something he'd said had triggered a hurt, a painful memory or fear that knocked the fight right out of his feisty she-bear.

"What did I say?" he asked, more concerned by her 180-degree turn in self-assurance than by de Vega's lecherous threat.

"Stop doing that!" Tension fluttered across her expression and landed in the grim set of her beautiful mouth. He'd seen that look before, dozens of times. It was the disgust of someone realizing the full scope of his bizarre talents. The denial of the man because the powers wouldn't go away. "It's an invasion of privacy. I feel like I'm being violated."

Hawk jerked back as though she'd slapped him. He'd dropped his guard with Sarah, and this was payback time. He'd been steering toward this kind of censure right from the start. He shouldn't expect her to be any different from the rest of the world. In her mind, he rated no better than de

Vega or that preppy boyfriend of hers back home.
The distinction wasn't lost on him.

Stoic silence had been his ally for many years.
He straightened to his full height and watched
Sarah back off as the difference in size and demeanor between them registered. He didn't care,
he told himself. He didn't care what Sarah
thought of him. He was here to do a job, not to
play bodyguard-slash-whipping boy to a naive,
virginal schoolmarm from Smalltown, U.S.A.,
who was so far out of her element that he might
have laughed if he could allow himself the liberty
of mirth.

"I'll try to remember that," he muttered, turning away from the abhorrence he'd heard in her
voice and the black spot of heartsick pain he saw
in the wavering light surrounding her.

"Miss Mack! Miss Mack!"

Pounding footsteps crashed down the path toward them. Hawk stopped as the two girls approached, but he didn't move any closer. He
recognized Colleen Walks-a-Deer immediately,
and had learned that the older girl's name was
Denise.

"What is it?" Sarah glanced at her watch and
frowned, apparently forgetting or ignoring her
new aversion to him.

"Lyndsay's missing," said Denise. "She said she
was going to the latrine over an hour ago. Then
the rain hit. She hasn't come back. We went to
look for her, but the generator wasn't even turned
on to power up the lights there. We can't find
her."

"Did you check Andrea and Lynnette's tent?"

Denise nodded. "They're out looking for her
now."

Damn foolishness! Hawk barged into the conversation uninvited. "Did they stay on the path?" He stepped up to Sarah's elbow. "The predators come out at night. A novice can get turned around even in the daylight. At night, if your girls stray away from the influence of man, they'll be sitting ducks for one of the big cats."

Sarah looked up at him with barely checked fear clouding her eyes. "I'm more worried about where Martín's been the past hour."

Hawk felt his self-controlled resentment fading. She might not appreciate his chivalric attempts to defend *her*, but she'd sacrifice pride and principle when it came to protecting her charges. "His clothes were dry when he talked to you. He'd have been soaked to the skin if he were up to mischief earlier."

"He could have done something to her and then changed."

"Let's not panic yet." Hawk squeezed her shoulder, then wondered if she hated his physical touch as much as she despised his extrasensory contact. He pulled away and primed himself to do what he used to do best. Take the point. Find the objective, then relay the information back to base.

He'd failed on just such a mission once before, but he didn't see the need to share that information with Sarah. She already had enough doubts about him to dissuade her trust. He pointed to Colleen and Denise. "You two find Andrea and Lynnette, then go back to your tent and stay put. We don't need to lose track of anyone else."

"But we can help," argued Denise. "Wouldn't more eyes make it easier to find her?"

In daylight or on familiar ground, that might

have been a sensible offer. But there was nothing familiar about the night on Tenebrosa. "What I foresee are more footprints wiping out whatever trail the rain hasn't already destroyed."

He was thankful when Sarah backed him up on this. "Hawk's right. Find the others and stay in your tent. Give a loud holler if Lyndsay shows up before we get back."

With a groan that was a mixture of worry and teenage envy at not being treated as adults, the two girls returned to camp. When Sarah stepped toward the fire pit instead of her own tent, Hawk snagged her by the elbow and stopped her midstride.

"We?"

"She's my responsibility."

"You got turned around in the jungle yourself. You have no business searching for Lyndsay."

She pulled away and made a sweeping gesture around the campsite. "I can't just sit here and do nothing!"

"You can follow your own advice." Hawk kept his tone soft and authoritative, the way he often did when advising a patient. "Stay put so I don't worry about you. I need you here to keep everyone else in line. I'll find her as quick as I can and bring her back. I promise."

Her eyes flickered in the glow of the lantern and she hesitated. Maybe she doubted the reliability of those last two words as much as he did.

"I know you will," she whispered, surprising him with her humble faith in him.

Hawk reached out then and cupped her cheek, ignoring her request to keep anything personal out of their relationship. Like a territorial male instead of the enlightened man he sought to be, he cradled the very cheek de Vega had stroked earlier, putting *his* stamp on Sarah and canceling out the other man's touch.

He lingered a moment when she didn't flinch away or flay him with her tongue, and basked in the healing beauty of her timid smile. He didn't have the words to thank her for the simple trust, and he couldn't ask her to believe in him unconditionally, but for now it was enough that she entrusted him with this.

"Stay here," he ordered, closing his fingers into his fist and pulling away, knowing he had to ignore his longings at this moment. "Keep the others safe."

Sarah nodded and Hawk strode across the compound to Lyndsay's tent. The mud immediately outside the flap had been smushed into a pulp of unrecognizable tracks. Undaunted, Hawk circled the tent until he found what he was looking for—a single boot print, intact beneath the sheltering overhang of a tree root. Hawk allowed himself the slightest of smiles. Barring catastrophe, Lyndsay was as good as found.

Sarah watched Hawk stoop and touch something on the ground. Then he pulled a flashlight from that curious vest of his and vanished into the jungle. She marveled at his supreme self-assurance, and understood how, as a soldier, he would inspire confidence in the men who served with him.

His ability to sense her emotions, robbing her of a well-used shield that normally allowed her to distance herself from uncomfortable situations, still unnerved her. But that particular talent didn't worry her so much as his deep-rooted penchant toward gallantry. He was a protector by nature, a man who made restitution when he inflicted a hurt. A man who treated her like a lady of value, a woman of desire.

Despite her bold, commonsense arguments to the contrary, she craved his touch, whether it was the untamed passion that made her forget who she was, or the gentle reassurance of his hand on her shoulder or her face. She could quickly get used to Hawk's protection and kindness, and knew they could become dangerous addictions.

And how foolish was that?

She didn't fear him. She was afraid of herself. Afraid of the woman she could be if a man like Hawk cared about her. A woman she would never be because a man like Hawk was too exotic, too male, too powerful, ever to be a part of her real world.

And she should be thinking about the real world right now, about how she might possibly come up with a plausible speech for Lyndsay's parents to explain their daughter's disappearance, or how she could withstand Walter's condescending *I told you so* every time she met him on the street in Marysville.

She'd botched everything on the trip so far. It was high time she got something right. Andrea and Lynnette reported that Lyndsay hadn't gone down to the lagoon. After repeated reassurances that Martín hadn't spoken to them since lunch, Sarah helped the girls move their sleeping bags and had them all bunk on the floor of her tent. Then, restless to do more than hold down the fort, she borrowed a flashlight from Denise and walked across the compound. If Hawk couldn't find Lyndsay in half an hour, then maybe he needed help.

She approached the door to Luis's tent and cleared her throat loudly, hoping he'd wake on his own before she actually called his name. "Señor Salazar," she finally said. "Luis?"

Dead silence answered her. She patted the damp canvas, creating a thumping noise like that of a bass drum. "Luis, it's Sarah. Are you in there?"

She shined her light through the net opening. Inside, the tent was totally dark. And empty.

Maybe the girls' commotion had alerted him to the trouble, and he had already joined in the search. She walked on to the next tent, a larger one that slept four men. "Antonio? Raul?"

Again, empty silence.

A shuffling sound drew her attention to the mess hall. She'd heard something similar once at her father's fishing cabin, when a raccoon had broken in and chewed its way through several Tupperware containers. She wondered what form of raccoon the jungle produced. So far the native fauna had been bigger, wilder, and more dangerous than anything she knew back home.

Sarah's frown of curiosity quickly reversed into a smile of triumph. Her jungle raccoon might just be the sounds of a hungry teenager scrounging for her own midnight snack.

Metal clanked against metal. Before reaching the entrance, she heard the *thwump* of a solid mass hitting wood, followed by a string of garbled curses. Hardly ladylike, but Sarah had long ago accepted that the curb she put on her own vocabulary was rarely shared by the young women of the next generation.

She opened the door of the small wooden structure and peered inside. "Hello? Lyndsay?"

"Señorita."

Sarah swung her light around until her beam picked up the reclining figure on the floor near the ice chest. Slitted black eyes leered up at her, and Martín de Vega saluted her with an open beer bottle. A wooden bench lay overturned on its side, and she suspected he'd tripped on his way to or from getting his booze.

He drank deeply, then wiped the dribble from his lips with the back of his hand. "You have come to see me after all."

"You're disgusting." She spun around to leave and find some actually useful way to spend her time.

"But I am doing my job well, no?" She stopped at his taunting laugh. "You and Señor Hawk are very busy, no?"

Sarah slowly turned and forced herself to look at the living, breathing slime. "What do you mean, we're busy? Do you know where Lyndsay is?"

Her stomach lurched and sank to her toes as horrible images of gang rape and cult sacrifice blurred across her mind. Martín seemed to smell her fear. With an awkward lack of grace, he lurched to his feet and shuffled toward her with that awful smirk plastered across his face. "Lyndsay is the one with the pretty red hair, no?"

He rolled the word *pretty* around his tongue as if he could taste what he described.

"If you've done anything to hurt her . . ."

"I don't like girls." He stopped as if her threat held some substance for him. Then he pointed to her with his bottle and laughed at his own joke. "As much as I like women."

He swigged another draft and stopped laughing. "I don't know where the girl is. But if you're

113

looking for her, then I don't have to worry about your Indian friend's threats."

"What threats?"

"He is very possessive of you, señorita." He draped his gaze over her body, and she fought back the urge to cover her breasts with her hands. "You are full of secrets. A man can find that irresistible. Perhaps I will discover your answers before he does."

Sarah shivered, feeling her skin crawl beneath the visual assault. What kind of idiot was she, bringing her students down to this spider-infested jungle to work with boozing, lecherous slime like this sorry excuse for a man?

First thing in the morning—no, the second she found Luis tonight, she would insist on returning to El Espanto. Though it galled her no end, she had to admit this whole trip was a mistake, from her pitiful motives for coming in the first place to the frightening danger of what might have happened to Lyndsay.

Sarah pulled her shoulders back and turned up her nose at the crude proposition. "Save your energy, Martín. I'm not that interesting."

She walked out, his laughter trailing behind her.

Sarah slogged across the compound, the mud on her boots weighing her down as heavily as her guilt. She'd been such a fool. Such a stupid, naive fool to think that after thirty-four years of living life as a wallflower she could suddenly break free and experience the adventure of a lifetime.

Adventures were for other people who knew something about the world. Other people who communicated easily; other people who could spot a slimebag at thirty feet and know to keep their distance; other people who could be responsible not only for themselves, but for anyone entrusted to their care.

Adventures happened to people like Hawk.

Hawk *was* an adventure.

And if she needed anything else to point out just how foolish this over-the-rainbow wish of hers had been, then her feelings for Hawk completed the humiliation. Her fascination with such an unattainable man mirrored the futility of her dream to experience life in one grand, glorious finale. She had less in common with Hawk than the tropics had with the dry plains of Kansas. She belonged in this high-temp adventure just about as much as she could ever belong to a man like Hawk.

"Sarah?"

Caught up in her stew of self-pity, she'd failed to notice Hawk walk into the clearing, framed by a teenager on either side of him.

"Lyndsay? Thank God." Forgetting decorum, Sarah ran over and hugged her, pouring her relief into the squeezing force of her arms. "Are you all right? Are you hurt?"

Sarah stepped back and inspected her from head to toe. *Sheepish* might best describe the downturned face and expectant expression in Lyndsay's eyes. She was apparently safe, though drenched to the skin, so Sarah turned her focus to the other teen.

Embarrassment blotched Raul Salazar's cheeks. He scuffed his toe in the mud and concentrated on the ooze spreading across the top of his boot. Without eye contact or forthcoming explanations from either teen, Sarah turned to Hawk. "What happened?"

"I found them about a hundred yards from

here, holed up in a cave. They got caught outside when the rain hit. They were, um . . . together."

He spoke the last word in a low, husky pitch. The sound of it whispered along her nerve endings, gathering strength until the significance of that one word settled at the core beneath her belly. "Together?"

Her lips tingled at the memory of his kiss. Pinpricks of remembered awareness skittered over the surface of her skin. She looked up and saw an answering gleam in the shadowy midnight of his eyes. Had his memory drifted back to that same clearing in the jungle? Could he sense how raw the memory of it made her feel? The unwavering intensity in his eyes made her think he knew exactly what she was thinking. She forced herself to look away so she could deal with the situation at hand.

Together? Sarah hoped Hawk's definition of together was a chaste kiss and a grope or two, rather than that indecent, unstoppable, clutching, clinging embrace they'd shared in the jungle. The first option she could tolerate; infatuation and hormones were an inescapable part of teenage life. But the latter . . .

And to think someone almost twenty years younger would behave in the same abandoned way . . .

Sarah's guilt evolved into anger when it became clear that neither teen had broken anything more than their curfew. "What were you thinking? Making out with him? We laid down rules, and I expected you to follow them. Isn't that what our concensus was all about?"

Lyndsay's head shot up, her green eyes sparking

in protest. "We weren't making out. We went for a walk. We just wanted to talk. And then the storm came, and Raul found the cave. He held me because I was cold. We just kind of lost track of time."

Sarah glared in silence as Lyndsay's final words petered out. Unmoved, she propped her hands on her hips and passed sentence. "Go pack your things. We're leaving in the morning."

"What? We just got here. We haven't even done any digging yet!" Lyndsay protested.

"It's too dangerous. If I can't trust you to do what you're told, then there's no way—"

"Miss Mack! Don't punish everyone because of me. We have to stay."

Sarah kept her voice steady and stifled the childish urge to argue with the teen. "Go pack your things."

Lyndsay's groan covered three different pitches. She stalked off, and her waiting friends engulfed her in a rush of hugs. She gave them the news of their early departure, but Sarah's stern look told the girls that now was not a good time to lodge their complaints.

Raul stepped forward, beseeching Sarah. "It is my fault, Señorita Mack. I invited Lyndsay to walk with me. Do not punish her for the rain or my intentions."

"Your intentions?" Sarah turned on him. "I have a responsibility to keep these girls safe. If that means confining them to their tents or taking them home to keep them safe from the likes of you, then so be it."

"Sarah," Hawk's quiet voice interrupted. "They did the smart thing to find shelter instead of making their way back during the storm. Why don't you wait until you've cooled off a little to make any decisions?"

She swiveled her chin and met the blank wall of those impossibly dark eyes. With him around, her own safety and sound judgment were as much at stake as the girls'. "We aren't your concern," she bit out, forgetting even to thank him for returning Lyndsay safely or to apologize for her insulting accusations about his psychic abilities. "No one invited you along in the first place. You should be glad to see us go."

"Not like this."

She ignored the seductive softness of his whisper and turned on Raul, who watched the interchange with cautious curiosity. "As for you, wait until I tell your uncle."

"You've seen Luis?" Raul shifted uncomfortably, dragging his fingers through his damp, dark hair. "Tonight?"

Sarah didn't miss the catch in his voice, but couldn't take time to analyze it right then. "No. But as soon as I find him, I'm making arrangements to leave. And I'll advise him to screen his staff more carefully before he takes another group on any expedition." She relented a fraction when she observed the mature straightening of the young man's shoulders as he accepted his responsibility. "You'd better get to bed, too. In *your* tent."

Half of Raul's mouth curved into a smile. "Sí, señorita. Good night."

She waited for the flap of his tent to close behind him before she risked another glance at Hawk. "You were right. I had no business bringing those girls to Tenebrosa. Isn't that what you wanted to hear? You were right."

She was halfway to her tent when she felt his touch on her arm. She hadn't even heard him following her. Startled, she jerked against him, but the quiet complexity in his gaze snared her. His hand felt gentle as a cat's paw on her arm, yet the steel beneath his grip reminded her of a jaguar's strength.

"This isn't a victory for me, Sarah. I won't lie and say I've changed my mind about the wisdom of your being here, but don't be so hard on the kids. Or yourself. You haven't failed."

Failed.

That was exactly what she'd done. Exactly what always happened when she stepped beyond the limits of her meager talents. Her dream had been so simple, really. Just to spend one week out of her life living more fully, more completely than her ordinary existence. Just one week to live her life the way other people lived theirs, with a richness and fulfillment and purpose that filled their empty hearts and restored hope to their empty souls.

Just one week.

And she couldn't even get that right.

With those eerie eyes evaluating her like a big cat's prey, she slipped from his grip and crossed her arms in front of her, sheltering herself as much as pulling away from him. "Is that the psychologist or the shaman assessment of my performance?"

He braced his feet apart and splayed his fingers across his hips in a loose-limbed stance that hinted at relaxed ease, yet the piercing darkness of his eyes left no doubt in her mind that he could pounce in an instant. "I'd like to think it's the observation of a friend."

"I don't have friends like you, Hawk." She turned and matched his stance. "I know the names of my friends. I understand their behavior. Dealing with them doesn't turn my life upside down."

He stood there silently, the stillest part of this interminable night, unable to find an argument to back up his claim to friendship.

Sarah nodded, expecting as much. Or as little. "I need to get back to those friends. I need to get back to that life. I thought you wanted me to."

The unanswering silence stretched on, punctuated by the caw of a wild bird and the screech of an animal in the distance. Sarah stood her ground, matching his obsession with the quiet. Then, with swift, businesslike efficiency, he broke the standoff. "I'll go find Salazar and alert him to your change in plans."

Without comment, without a wink or a nod or a smile, he turned and strode away. She didn't need any outside observer—friend or otherwise—to point out how foolish she'd been to leave her predictable, secure, maiden aunt–infested home in Marysville.

She'd checked her thesaurus, the hand-tooled leather edition that Walter had given her for their six-month anniversary. In it, she'd found forty-three words that meant *fool*.

And she knew the list by heart.

"Luis, you work for me, not the other way around. I demand that we go now."

The morning had dawned bright and humid, and in the clearing surrounding Las Lagumas the sun beat down with a merciless hand. Despite a brimmed hat, long sleeves and a coating of sunscreen, Sarah could almost feel the freckles popping out on her sweaty skin, one by one. Her normal abundance of patience had gone by the wayside, needing the replenishment of a good night's sleep and the cooperation of her preoccupied host.

Luis turned on the step above and scowled down at her with impatience. Her charming host had been replaced by this bleary-eyed, sharp-tongued stranger. "I am sorry that Raul forgot his place with your girl. But we worked late into the night preparing the site for you. It will take us at least another day to cover and restore it."

The girls accompanied Sarah, hoping for one last look at the tomb before being packed up and sent home. Andrea stepped up beside Sarah, her worn book in hand. "You don't need to cover up anything you've dug. The walls of the pyramid were designed to shelter the interior chambers from any direct contact with the elements. Besides, won't that just make more work for you to uncover it again when you bring the next tour?"

Luis shifted his peevish glare to the young blonde, and Sarah curled her arm around Andrea's shoulders, shielding her from the wordless attack. "She makes sense. I've never heard of archaeologists digging up something and then burying it again. Not for any legitimate reason."

He slid his tongue around his lips, licking the layer of dust that turned his black mustache a grayish white. By the time he turned his head and spat, Sarah realized he was reacting to her subconscious choice of words. *Legitimate.*

A shiver of awareness quaked through her. Either Luis was a greater devotee of archaeology than she had imagined, or he was up to something. She quickly glanced around to make sure all the girls were accounted for. One, two, three, four, five.

And, darn it all, where was Hawk this morning? Why wasn't he here to back her up? He must be angry with her. She could just imagine him hidden in the trees nearby, watching her attempts to persuade Luis flounder. He was probably so frustrated with her ineptitude as an expedition leader—and as a woman—that he was laughing at her now, thinking she deserved this uphill battle for respect.

Luis intruded on her condemning thoughts, and Sarah now recognized his old-world charm as a facade that hid a very driven man beneath the sham of manners and culture. "Let me show you what you are asking me to give up by leaving early."

The girls swarmed past her, eagerly following Luis into the passageway that led to Meczaquatl's chamber. Sarah hesitated at the opening, remembering the poisonous atmosphere that had altered Hawk's personality and nearly suffocated her.

This morning the tomb was a hive of activity, with men going in and out, pushing wheelbarrows, carting boxes and heavy packs, as well as shovels, picks and torches. She hadn't imagined the miasmic atmosphere inside the antechamber last night. Her fingers fluttered to the sore muscles at her throat. Nor had she imagined Hawk's savage reaction to it.

Yet no one else seemed to notice any potential danger. No one else seem affected by the air. And now her girls were in there. Her responsibility. Swallowing her fear, Sarah walked inside.

Unlike last night, the passage was well lit. She easily followed the stirrings of dust and noise and quickly found the antechamber.

And froze in her tracks.

Luis and his men must have worked around the clock. Last night a dusty, painted wall had separated her from the burial chamber of King Meczaquatl. Today, a hole had been gouged out of that wall. Stacks of numbered stones were piled to one side of an opening supported by long metal poles. Beyond that, a blinding light reflected off gold and jewels and polished bronze.

Sarah stared in wide-eyed wonderment at the preserved perfection of a gold-encrusted teakwood sarcophagus, with emeralds and whorls of color defining the image of the dead ruler on its lid.

"It seems disrespectful to disturb the dead," whispered Colleen beside her.

The others joined in the mute awe of the once-in-a-lifetime discovery: a centuries-old king and the priceless treasures buried with him, revealed for the first time in eons. Sarah and her girls were witnesses to that history.

Satisfaction, honor, and adventure sparked in Sarah's heart for an instant. And then she realized what was happening around her, making her schoolgirl fantasy seem like pure folly. One of Luis's men walked out of the burial chamber carrying a sealed wooden crate. Another man walked in with a torch, followed closely by Antonio with an open crate.

"I thought it was illegal to disturb Meczaquatl's chamber." Sarah raised her voice so that it car-

ried to Luis and penetrated the lustful fog surrounding him as he watched another box of artifacts being crated out. "Raul said your country
doesn't allow—"

"Raul is a boy!" Luis whipped around, silenc-
ing her.

"You're raiding the tomb," she accused. "You're
violating a man's resting place and stealing national treasures and . . . " She marched up to him,
more angry than she'd been since Walter had humiliated her so. "We won't be a part of this. Why
did you have to involve us?"

Luis shoved her back. She would have fallen if
her momentum hadn't carried her straight into
Denise and Lyndsay. "Get back! You have been a
nuisance from the start. The other groups were
much easier to control."

"You've done this before?" She gasped. "Used
innocent people—children—as a cover?"

Luis ignored her protests. From the corner of
her eye, she noticed some of his men circling
around. Sarah pulled the girls in close and faced
Luis. "I want to leave. Now."

"Miss Mack?" Lynnette's breathy voice turned
Sarah's attention to the side. Antonio stood in the
man-made archway, leveling an automatic
weapon straight at the teenager.

Sarah ducked in front of Lynnette, placing herself between the girl and the gun. "Damn you,
Luis! These are innocent children."

Then she realized how futile her protective
show of bravery had been. Four other men, including Luis, now held guns, each pointed at one
of her girls. Sarah's breath seeped out of her
lungs. This nightmare didn't make any sense.
"What are you going to do with us?"

Luis's thin lips curled into a smile that did not reach his eyes. "I didn't plan to hurt any of you. But I'm afraid I can't allow you to leave now. It's so hard to sell these goods from a jail cell. Martín!"

Answering like the snap of a military command, the greasy man appeared in the opening of the tomb wall. His leering gaze swept across the women, then landed with disdain on Luis. "*Sí?*"

"Put them with Señor Hawk." Martín nodded, then wrapped his dirty fingers around Sarah's upper arm, dragging her forward. She cringed at his touch, but followed along meekly when she saw the other men pushing the girls behind them with their guns.

"And Martín?" Luis's suave voice echoed through the antechamber. All the men had gone silent, awaiting his instructions. "The Indian. If he is awake . . . hit him again."

Chapter Six

The field trip from hell.

The subtitle for this ill-fated trip clanged in Sarah's head like a death knell.

Antonio and another man dragged Hawk's unconscious body out to the fire pit and dropped him at Sarah's feet. She fell to her knees, and the girls crowded around while she checked his neck for a pulse.

"Thank God," she said in relief, feeling a strong, steady beat beneath his smooth skin.

Then she inspected the extent of his injuries. She'd learned CPR and basic first aid to better care for her parents and aunts. She quickly identified the contusions and abrasions around his knuckles and mouth. Whatever had happened to him, he'd put up a good fight.

She was more concerned by the dried blood

caked around the bruised swelling at his temple. "How long has he been unconscious?"

She looked directly at Antonio and he frowned, taken aback by the sharp query. "He came to us last night. He was not a welcome visitor."

"That's an understatement," she muttered beneath her breath, noting the knotted ropes that bound his ankles and wrists together. "How long?" she asked again.

Martín sidled in beside Antonio, his rifle lazily tucked in the crook of his elbow. But Sarah didn't doubt he or any of the other men would hesitate to shoot if pushed too far. "We subdued him last night. Apparently he was not welcome in your bed and sought out other men with whom to commiserate."

"He was looking for Luis. We were ready to leave last night." Martín laughed at her explanation. "Hawk had a bad feeling about this trip even before we knew what you were up to."

"Yes, he is a very observant man." Martín's smile faded. He patted the butt of his rifle. "He tried to escape at about three this morning, and that is when I hit him. He has been in and out of consciousness since then."

"Five hours," she said softly, wishing a properly staffed emergency room were closer than the mainland. "He needs water."

She raised her voice as a plea. Dehydration and infection were two symptoms she could treat. She could only pray his head wound wasn't as bad as it looked.

"Stop where you are!" She heard a series of clicks that she imagined must be safeties being thrown or triggers locked into place. Sarah spun around.

127

"Denise!"

Her eldest charge stood ramrod straight several feet from the group, defying the business end of one of the men's rifles. In a firm voice, much calmer than Sarah's had been, Denise looked the man in the eye and said, "He needs water."

Stunned by her defiant show of resistance, the man glanced over at Antonio and Martín, clearly unsure how he should respond. Antonio, too, seemed unprepared for this civil disobedience. But Martín took it all in stride. "Get them the water," he said.

The man scurried off to the mess tent and returned with a red plastic jug of water. Denise took it from him and knelt by Sarah's side. The rush of air in her sigh told Sarah just what that show of bravado had cost her. She quickly caught Denise's gaze and winked. "Thank you."

Then she reached across and squeezed Denise's hand before turning her attention back to Hawk. Color returned to Denise's cheeks, and she helped pour the water into Sarah's handkerchief. Sarah dabbed at Hawk's wounds. The cut at his temple was small, but ideally could use a couple of stitches for it to heal neatly. Colleen scrounged a bandage from her pocket, and together the three of them tended to Hawk.

They worked for several minutes, putting aside the threat that surrounded them. But when Sarah touched the binding at Hawk's wrists, her captors spoke again.

"Enough!" shouted Martín. "Move away from him."

"Wake up, Hawk," she whispered close to his ear. And then, reluctantly, she obeyed. Sarah stood and pulled the girls with her to the opposite side of the pit, keeping Hawk's prone body in view.

A truck pulled into the compound and the driver shouted something at Antonio in Spanish. The men surrounding them, except for Martín, lowered their weapons and ran to the truck. They climbed into the back and sped away.

Lyndsay leaned over to Sarah and whispered, "He said something about getting the last one loaded so they can leave."

"Are they going to leave us here?" asked Lynnette, voicing the panic that thrummed through Sarah's veins.

She put her arm around Lynnette's shoulders and hugged her. "I don't know. Let's just do what they say for now."

Hawk moaned and rolled over onto his side. Even at this distance, Sarah could see that his eyes didn't open. Martín moved toward him, spinning his gun around to use it as a club.

"Don't!" Sarah jumped forward, pushing Lynnette behind her. "He's no threat to you in his condition."

Martín rolled his gaze up to her, a curious expression clouding his eyes. "I do not trust this one, señorita. He is not like other men."

He blinked and a familiar lecherous gleam replaced his faraway look. "Even you sense it. Perhaps that is why you refused him. But you would not refuse a normal man, no?"

"You never give up, do you?"

"Not with a challenging woman like you, so ripe for the picking."

This man's obsession with sex conjured up familiar memories in Sarah. Ingrained defenses raised their voices in a cruel litany inside her

129

head. She brushed errant wisps of hair behind her ears and advanced on him, heedless of the self-reproach in her voice or the effect she had on Martín.

"There's no challenge here." She spread her arms wide, giving him a good look at her plain khaki blouse and shorts, and the equally plain figure hidden underneath. "I'm not a 'Baywatch' babe. I'm no knockout. And experience? None. I'm not woman enough for you, believe me. So zip your mouth. And everything else."

"You tell him, Miss Mack." A young voice cheered her on.

He stroked his dirty fingers across his mustache, apparently considering her excuse for refusing him. "Then perhaps you will learn by watching."

To Sarah's horror, Martín reached for Lyndsay. "The one with the pretty red hair will help me."

"No!" Sarah smashed her fist down on his wrist, knocking his hand out of Lyndsay's hair. Lyndsay sank back into the circle of her friends, and Sarah positioned herself squarely between Martín and the girls. "Keep your hands off them!"

"De Vega, you bastard . . . " The deep-pitched croak sounded from the ground behind her.

Not daring to take her eyes off their captor, Sarah could only hope the shuffling in the dirt behind her meant Hawk was conscious and climbing to his feet. Even in his injured state, Hawk had the most beautiful voice in the world. The rich, soft sound vibrated along her taut nerve endings, calming her, allowing her to discover her own untapped strength.

A groan punctuated by the thud of something solid hitting the ground behind her cut short her upsurge of renewed determination. Sinister laughter rolled from Martín's lips. "Your threats are not so tough now, Indian."

Sarah glanced over her shoulder and saw Hawk struggle onto his elbows and then push himself up on his knees. But he met the resistance of the rope at his ankles, lost his balance, and fell. His long hair shielded his face like a curtain until he recovered his breath and strength enough to lift his face. Though not directed at her, the absolute blackness in his eyes absorbed the morning light and left Sarah chilled.

"Luis said I should find a way to keep you occupied, Indian. I think I will save myself the trouble." He raised his gun and aimed it. Sarah saw the movement from the corner of her eye and spun around, sticking her hands up in surrender.

"Don't shoot!" She swallowed past the knot of fear lodged in her throat. "I'll go with you."

"Sarah, no!"

She ignored Hawk's plea and stepped toward Martín. He tested her sudden acquiescence by taking one hand from his rifle and cupping her breast. She jerked at the disgusting contact and swatted his hand away.

His curious smile vanished, and Sarah stared into brown eyes darkened with the menace of displeasure. She gritted her teeth and forced herself not to wrench free of his touch again. He unfastened the barrette at her nape and dropped it to the ground. With one hand holding the tip of the rifle at the base of her throat, he dug his fingers into her hair and combed his way through it all the way to the ends, pulling it over her shoulder and draping it across her chest.

He pressed his lips to the exposed side of her

neck and nipped her. Sarah turned her face away and squeezed her stomach muscles to avoid retching at the stench of his hot breath. She had to keep him busy, she told herself. He didn't seem to care what she looked like, so long as she was female. If she could distract him long enough, the girls could untie Hawk, and even injured as he was, he could overpower their lone captor and they could escape this nightmare.

The girls would be safe. Hawk would be alive.

And suddenly she realized that her need to protect Hawk stemmed from something more than fear of surviving this alone, or even a healthy conscience that inspired her to help others. She needed time to learn more about him. She needed to understand why he behaved so mysteriously, and why her foolish attraction to him wouldn't go away, despite her track record with men.

If she could distract Martín long enough, she could buy them the time they needed.

If only she had understood the flaw in her plan.

Martín grabbed her blouse by the front placket. His grimy fingers rubbed against her. She jerked away from the offensive touch and the top three buttons popped off her shirt.

"Miss Mack!" Concern and unmasked fear echoed in the chorus of young voices.

Grinning wickedly, Martín snatched the material in his fist and pulled. "If any one of you moves to follow me, I will kill her."

With the order delivered, he backed toward the trees between the staff's tents. Sarah grabbed his wrist for balance and staggered after him, understanding too late that she'd been playing a dangerous game she had no hope of winning.

"Help him." She looked back at Hawk and

prayed the girls would follow her command quickly once she was out of sight. He might be their only chance out of there.

Her only chance.

"Sarah!"

Martín yanked her beyond the tree line. She stumbled over a tree root and fell, landing with a painful jab on her side. Before she could regain her footing, Martín was on top of her, ripping open the front of her blouse. He dropped his rifle on the ground within arm's reach beside him and tugged at her belt.

Hawk's hoarse, desperate shout was the last thing she heard before blackness swam through her head.

The last thing Hawk saw was Sarah's golden-brown hair fanning through the air as she fell. When the dizziness cleared and he could focus again, neither Sarah nor the bastard were in sight.

His head felt like a lead pendulum swinging off-kilter atop his neck. Still, he had to get to Sarah. Lying with his face in the dirt wasn't the way to do it.

Ignoring the ache in his ribs where he'd been kicked, he concentrated on sitting up and leaned his back against the brick perimeter of the fire pit. The earth spun madly, rising up toward him, then falling away. He squeezed his eyes shut and turned his focus to the calm center within him, that peaceful place of balance and beauty where he turned for wisdom. In this case, he sought to clear his head of the pain and vertigo that rendered him useless.

"Sarah!" he called again, blindly seeking her out.

He heard her scream. The fearful sound pierced his soul before being silenced into a muffled cry. The bastard had his hands on her! He had her mouth! That sweet, beautiful, sexy mouth. Martín's touch violated her mouth. He would soon violate her in other ways too unforgivable for Hawk to allow himself to imagine.

Rage boiled within him, overwhelming his attempt to regroup, bubbling up alongside a shame and doubt that drove him up to his hands and knees. If only he could stand!

"Hawk!"

Faces swarmed around him, joining the whirlpool of images spinning in and out of his line of sight. He felt hands on his shoulders and a tugging at his wrists. The girls.

"I can't get them. We need something to cut it."

They balanced him on either side and tried to free him. Hawk shook them away, needing to get to Sarah before it was too late. He tried to stand, but the bindings on his feet kept him in place. The girls tried to break his fall, but he took two of them with him when he crashed to the ground again.

"Knife." He spat out a mouthful of dirt. "In my vest. Salazar's tent."

"I'll get it."

One of them ran off and Hawk pulled himself in the opposite direction, toward the scuffling noise at the foot of the trees.

He'd fail her.

Damn it! He couldn't get there in time. He couldn't help. He'd fail her.

"Sarah!" He cried out her name desperately. Frustration and helplessness weighed him down. He crawled farther, pulling himself with his hands, pushing with his feet. His sluggish movements propelled him forward in laughable slow motion. But the bear was a talisman of power. If he could get closer to Sarah, his strength would return.

Hawk was a master of cunning and gifted with second sight. But those powers would do him little good if he couldn't reach Sarah in time.

He hadn't reached Jonathan in time. His commanding officer had died.

On Tenebrosa.

The nightmare of his failure played itself out a second time.

"Help me up." The four girls struggled to drag him to his feet, then held him steady when Colleen returned with his weapon. "My feet first," he commanded.

He chomped on the inside of his lip, waiting a lifetime for the milliseconds to pass before he could move his legs again. He moved out when the pressure eased around his ankles. Colleen trotted alongside him, sticking the knife between his hands and trying to cut while he reeled toward the flattened break of ferns and leaves amid the trees.

"Sarah, hold on!" he shouted again, feeling the pull of her powerful spirit, praying to the Ancient Ones to watch over her until he could get to her.

The crack of a gunshot reverberated in the air, stopping Hawk in his tracks.

"Sarah?" Fear knifed through him, taking the steadying rush of blood from his head. He reached inside his shirt and clutched the sicun that hung around his neck. The smooth spirit stone felt cold and lifeless, robbing him of hope.

His shock spread through the girls, freezing

them in a chain reaction behind him. But he'd been a soldier once. He'd served as spiritual leader to his tribe, a community elder to others. This wasn't the time for him to feel pain. It wasn't the place to mourn the loss of something that had never been his. It was a time for action.

Pressing a finger to his lips, he silenced their questions. He took the knife from Colleen and inched forward, swearing to wring the bastard's neck with his bare hands before ramming the knife up under his gullet.

Sarah's death was his fault. He'd add her innocent life to his guilt. But first he'd take de Vega's life as a small token of retribution. Then he'd track down the others one by one and punish them for bringing Sarah to this island of evil in the first place. He'd punish them all for destroying her.

"He's dead."

A break in the undergrowth parted and Sarah stepped out. She clutched the bloody front of her blouse together in her left fist. Martín's gun dangled from her right.

"Anybody have a safety pin?" Her gaze swung around the stunned semicircle waiting for her.

Hawk tucked his knife in a cargo pocket and rushed forward. "What happened?"

He grabbed her shoulders, slid his palms across her chest and stomach, looking for her wound. He pressed his hand to the reassuring strength of her powerful heart. She closed her fingers over his wrist and pulled him away.

"I asked you not to touch me."

Her request was understandable, in light of what she had just endured. But they weren't the words of an injured woman repelled by the touch of a man. They belonged to the sharp-tongued schoolmarm putting him in his place.

"Are you hurt?" Perplexed by her reaction, but honoring the shield she had erected around herself, he let go of her and stepped back.

"Nothing serious."

Hawk studied her from the slight distance. A flat dullness had snuffed the gleam from her golden eyes. He tried to read her aura, but the halo of light proved dim, grayish, like fog. He saw no fear in her. No relief. Nothing.

She had removed herself from the horror, shut down that part of herself that would reveal fear or disgust or anger or any other emotion. She was probably in the preliminary stages of shock. She was certainly in denial.

"It's not a safety pin, but it might help." Hawk looked down at the girl beside him. The sensitive one, Lynnette, held out a button that had been pinned to her shirt.

"Thanks." Sarah took it, handed Hawk the rifle, then proceeded to double up the front of her blouse and pin it into place. Incognizant of the dark dampness of the material clinging to her skin, she worked diligently, covering herself modestly if not completely. "There."

The slogan on the button mocked the duty the pin behind it served. I GIVE UP. WHAT PLANET ARE YOU FROM?

"Okay." She reached for the gun, but Hawk tightened his grip.

"I don't think that's a good idea."

She tilted her chin, and for an instant their eyes locked. The blankness in her gaze wavered a fraction. His mind glimpsed the image of that powerful Kodiak with its heart ripped out. But just as

137

quickly as the impression hit him, her eyes shuttered and she let go.

She circled behind him to the girls, snapping orders with soft-voiced precision. "Grab your packs and whatever water you can carry. We'll hide out in the jungle until they leave. Denise, get the radio out of the mess tent. We'll call El Espanto and have someone pick us up."

"Yes, ma'am." Despite the hesitancy of confusion in Denise's voice, she and the others scattered like bees from the hive to do Sarah's bidding.

Sarah herself wasted no time. She recapped the water jug and set it next to his vest. Then she fell to her hands and knees and scavenged through the dirt and mud surrounding the fire pit. Her hair cascaded over her shoulders. With manic twists of her wrist, she knotted the toffee strands into a rope and tossed it behind her back. Uttering a breathy, frantic grunt, she dug her fingers into the soil again.

"What are you doing?" Hawk asked.

"I have to find my barrette. I have to keep this hair out of my face."

He patted the air, placating her from a cautious distance. "Sarah, honey, calm down. You'll scare the girls, acting like this."

"I don't have time for that *honey* stuff right now." In one jerky motion, she stood and spun around, advancing on him. "I have to get them out of here. Are you going to help me, or are you just going to stand there?"

A wild streak flared in her eyes, then vanished beneath a flat hazel squint. "Are you hurt?" With renewed worry, she held up her hand. "How many fingers do you see?"

Hawk gently wrapped his fingers around hers and pulled down her hand. "I've got a killer headache, but I'm going to be fine."

"You probably shouldn't sleep. Or if you do, we'll wake you every few hours to be sure you're not unconscious."

"Sarah." Concerned by the coolness of her clammy skin and the rapid-fire delivery of her words, he added a touch of steel to his soothing counselor's voice. "Your adrenaline is wearing off and shock is setting in. You need to sit down and relax before you collapse."

"Relax!" She jerked her hand away and rubbed at her palm as though wiping away his touch. "We're surrounded by thieves and perverts with guns, and you want me to relax?"

"Here's the radio." Denise lugged the leather-shrouded box onto the brick wall of the grill.

Sarah pulled out the headphones and trailed her fingers across the face of switches and dials. "Do you know how to work this?"

Hawk identified the markings as old Soviet issue, a relic discarded from Cuba or traded on the illegal market. Definitely not state-of-the-art, current technology. If that thing reached fifty miles into El Espanto, he'd wear a crew cut and deny his Pawnee heritage.

"Do you?" she repeated, distress raising her voice to a higher pitch.

He closed his fingers around Sarah's slender shoulder. "We'd have to hike that radio twenty, thirty miles closer before we'd be in range."

"Fine. Let's do it." Jerking away from his touch, she turned and slipped her arms through the radio's webbed straps and slid it on like a backpack.

139

Denise raised her pale gray gaze from Sarah up to Hawk. The girl's mounting fear shimmered around her face. Hawk nodded to her, conveying calm and reassurance. "Get your pack like the others."

"We've got it." Colleen handed an extra pack to Denise while the other girls gathered around them. Hawk smelled their wariness in the air. He didn't need to turn to see the worry etched on their faces or ringed in their auras.

He reached behind Sarah and lifted the radio with his free hand. "Enough. We'll find another way out of this. Let it go."

She clawed at empty air, trying to retrieve the radio he set beyond her reach. The roar of heavy machinery in the jungle diverted his efforts to calm her.

"We need that!" she yelled. "Give it back!"

The unmistakable sound of diesel engines grinding through their gears too quickly shifted even Sarah's focus to the three trucks that skidded to a halt at the edge of the clearing, their motors still running. Luis Salazar jumped from the cab of the first truck, his fingers caressing the butt-end of a SIG 9mm as he strode toward them.

He motioned with the government-class weapon and Antonio leaped off the third truck. "Take Señor Hawk's gun."

With the business end of Antonio's pistol pointed at Sarah, Hawk set his rifle on the ground and made no protest when Antonio picked it up and tossed it to Raul in the back of the truck. Without moving his gaze from Luis, Hawk sensed the boy's reluctance to comply. He only hoped the teen wouldn't do anything foolish.

The timing for heroics couldn't be worse with Sarah and the girls lined up in the sights of various guns from each of the trucks.

"What are you going to do with us?" Sarah's voice cracked as she worked to control the shock that taxed her mental and emotional strength.

"Not a thing, señorita." She visibly flinched when Luis tried to charm her with a false smile. Hawk swayed a step toward her, but Salazar stopped him short. "Do not move, señor, or I will kill her. You have been an unanticipated thorn in my side since the beginning of our journey."

Without moving his gun, he faced Hawk. "I asked Martín to keep you occupied so you would not discover our plan. His attentions to your woman kept you very distracted, no?"

His woman. The phrase spread with a possessive rightness through Hawk. But the staggering depth of the connection he felt to Sarah held a bittersweet aftertaste.

All this was his fault. The gun pointed at her now, the attempted rape, both were his fault. She could have blissfully completed her field trip without being traumatized by these goons. But his appearance had altered Salazar's plans. Instead of the expedition serving as an unknowing front while he and his men pillaged Las Lagumas, Hawk's presence turned Sarah and her girls into expendable pawns. Made them vulnerable to one greedy man's deception.

Guilt warred with hatred in Hawk's gut, but he was powerless to act on either emotion. Salazar smiled, and the supreme satisfaction on his face indicated that he understood and enjoyed Hawk's helplessness. "The gunshot we heard," Luis taunted, "I suppose you took care of Martín?"

"I shot him."

Salazar cocked an eyebrow at Sarah's weak protest. He glanced at her chest, as though noticing the bloodstain there for the first time. He bowed in a mocking display of respect. "Impressive. I did not think you were strong enough to do such a thing."

Could no one else see her limitless courage?

"He tried to rape her." Sarah didn't need to justify her actions, especially to this bastard. But Hawk defended her anyway. He grabbed the tip of Antonio's gun and shoved it away from his ribs. Surprised, the smaller man made no protest. "She killed him in self-defense."

At Salazar's command, Antonio backed off, then turned and scurried back onto the truck. "Most unfortunate," said Luis. He bowed to Sarah. "*Gracias*. Now I have only four men to pay.

"By the way"—he shifted his aim to the radio— "you won't be needing that."

Hawk alone braced for the thundering report. Glass shattered and the radio sailed across the fire pit, landing with a crash at Lynnette's feet. The girl screamed and jumped back. Sarah and the others rushed to her side, seeking and giving comfort to fight their universal terror.

Clearly outgunned, Hawk stayed his ground and watched Salazar wave the drivers into motion and scramble into the back of the last truck. Luis's reasoning made cold-blooded sense. He didn't have to do anything to ensure their silence. Abandonment this far into the jungle was as good as a death sentence.

Unless one had been trained in military logistics and survival skills. He might be rusty, but he had a damn sight more experience than his sheltered schoolmarm and her bevy of bookish girls.

This was his third chance to make things right in Tenebrosa. If he didn't get Sarah and the others safely home, then he didn't deserve any more chances.

"But Uncle, they will die if you leave them like this! I cannot live with that!"

Hawk swerved his attention to the back of the truck, loaded with crates from the tomb. Raul Salazar obviously hadn't counted on murder being a part of his uncle's scheme.

"Fine! You join them." Luis's family loyalty proved nonexistent. He snatched the rifle from the boy's grasp, flattened his boot in Raul's midsection and kicked him off. The boy landed hard and rolled away as the trucks picked up speed. Before he could climb to his feet, his uncle waved a fist. "Now I pay only three."

Lyndsay ran to Raul and helped him up, ignoring the young man's string of foreign obscenities, shouted loudly enough to drown out his uncle's laughter. Lynnette's screams faded into sobs, but her cries were joined by others. Hawk heard the repetitive chant of someone reciting prayers. Above the frenzied din, he heard Sarah pleading with them to stay calm.

When the trucks disappeared around the bend in the road, Hawk pulled his knife and dashed toward the tree line. Three men plus Salazar. Two on the last truck and only the driver on each of the others. If he worked quickly, he could pick them off one by one. Maybe he needed to take out only Salazar. Antonio, at least, possessed a weak stomach for violence and could easily be persuaded to surrender his weapon.

He'd hacked his way to an undetected spot past the next curve before he shivered with the awareness of being followed. He flattened himself on the ground and hid from the unseen stalker. He breathed against his hand to dispel his breath and prevent the canopy of greenery from moving and giving away his location.

Where had the fifth man come from? Maybe Martín had only been wounded. Or was Raul recklessly trying to help?

The thunder of the engines approached. Hawk could not be seen from the road, and the first truck passed him by. The prickle on his neck froze into an outright chill as the sensation behind him moved closer. He turned his knife in his grip, prepared to kill.

The second truck hit a rut and tossed mud across his shoulders and back before bouncing on by. The unnatural awareness shimmied down his spine and he stopped breathing.

Rolling over, he looked up in grim horror and saw a glimmering chimera of gold and black and prismatic colors hovering in the air above him. Sweat popped out on his top lip despite the arctic cold front seeping from the swirling miasma.

No. He mouthed the word and closed his fist around his burning sicun. A combative heat radiated from the smooth obsidian pendant.

The third truck wheezed around the bend, its engine grinding in an earsplitting roar as the driver shifted into a higher gear. The distorted air above Hawk flashed and jerked as though startled by the sound.

The spinning whirpool stopped, and the two-dimensional being elongated itself, listening.

Hawk gave the specter human characteristics even though he knew the thing was not human. It hadn't been for centuries.

But it was alive.

It was angry.

It was full of hate.

And it sped after the retreating truck, disappearing inside beneath a slim flap of canvas.

Chapter Seven

Hawk's footsteps resounded like hoofbeats on the densely packed jungle floor. He retraced his path without the silent finesse he'd used to follow the convoy. If that *thing*—if *he* was loose, then he would have passed right through the camp on his way to Salazar.

Luis Salazar didn't believe in the spirit world. He clearly didn't respect it or he would never have violated Meczaquatl's burial chamber. Hawk not only believed in the immortal existence of spirits, but he believed in the sentience of such beings. His own tribal history and the Christian tenets of his faith taught him of an everlasting afterlife.

But Meczaquatl's spirit had yet to find peace with this world, had yet to pass over into the next. Something had disturbed the Aztec king's immortal slumber long before Salazar and his men opened up the walls of the tomb with plastic explosives and pry bars. Hawk had felt it when he'd entered the antechamber the night before.

The king's restless spirit had touched Hawk's mind then, exploited his clairvoyance into the spirit realm. Channeling through Hawk, he'd seen Sarah as an intruder. A threat to all he held dear. Using Hawk's own hands, he'd tried to kill her.

Would he still see her as a threat? Would Meczaquatl equate Sarah's presence with Salazar's crime? Would he turn someone else against her? Someone who wouldn't know that they were killing her until it was too late?

"Sarah!" he hollered, panic pushing him to ignore the painful pressure of his lungs expanding against his bruised ribs. The beating he'd taken was nothing compared to the pain squeezing his heart.

Sarah had pulled him from that spell. Her gentle touch, her sensual innocence, her selfless concern had reached the man in him. She had broken through Meczaquatl's control and found his spirit. She'd touched his soul and his heart and his body, and made him human again.

Not a mystic. Not a soldier. Not a freak.

But a man.

He'd be damned if he'd allow that vengeful entity to hurt her again.

"Sarah!" The heavy, humid air swallowed up his cry like a sponge soaking up water. "Colleen! Lyndsay!"

He hadn't found Jonathan. Alive or dead.

He prayed he'd find Sarah and the girls unharmed.

"This never should have happened!"

"I'm supposed to be taking pictures for my scrapbook."

"If Andrea can't fix the radio, we're history. And it's all your fault!"

Hawk heard agitated young voices and burst into the clearing, counting four healthy teenagers in a circle around the broken radio. "Is everyone all right?" he asked. "Where's Colleen?"

Lynnette spun around and launched herself at his chest. Wincing at the tight hug around his middle, Hawk lowered a comforting arm around her trembling shoulders. "I want to go home," she said, sobbing against his shirt.

"I'll get you there," he promised, unsure he believed those words yet.

"This looks so different from the pictures." Andrea spoke her thoughts aloud.

Hawk released Lynnette and knelt beside Andrea. "Do you know what you're doing?"

The young blonde frowned at the open back of the radio. She chewed on the stub of a fingernail before glancing up to answer Hawk's question. "I read one of my brother's books on electronics. I think if we switch the circuits around, we can still transmit. But we won't be able to tell if anybody answers us."

Hawk squeezed her shoulder. "Do what you can."

His mind flashed briefly on his old buddy, Rafe Del Rio, and his former comrade's uncanny ability to fix anything. If Del Rio were here now, he could turn that archaic piece of junk into a broad-based scanner.

Better still, Rafe would have sabotaged those trucks' engines in the first place, and helped Hawk take out the enemy. Then, like a mechanical miracle, he'd have the trucks up and running again, and their transportation to safety would still be on hand.

But Rafe wasn't here. These barely grown children had only him. Hawk hoped he could rise to the challenge this time. He cupped the back of Andrea's head and reassured her. "I know you'll do your best."

When Hawk stood, Raul stepped forward, his hand clenched tightly around Lyndsay's. The boy wore a man's brave face, but Hawk could see the doubt clouding around him. "Did you catch my uncle?"

"No. But I don't think they'll get very far." Hawk worried about the spirit finding its way into the truck and wondered at its evil intent.

"I am sorry," said Raul, looking at his feet.

"Your apology doesn't do Miss Mack much good." Hawk shifted his focus at the sharp accusation in Denise's voice.

"This isn't Raul's fault." Lyndsay jumped to his defense. "He didn't know what Señor Salazar was up to."

Denise moved closer, and Lyndsay stepped out. "If he wasn't so greedy, he wouldn't have been on this trip in the first place."

The two friends advanced to argue further. Hawk grabbed Denise, and Raul tugged on Lyndsay. "Where are Sarah and Colleen?" asked Hawk, defusing the situation before it got out of hand.

In answer, all four turned toward the mess tent. Undisguised fear flooded their auras with coppery hues. A reborn sense of urgency propelled him across the compound in just a few long strides.

He found Colleen in the doorway. A strident

plea distorted her calm, sweet voice. "Miss Mack, please. Just come outside with the others and I'll find the scissors for you."

"Colleen?" He whispered her name so he wouldn't startle her with his touch. He gripped her strong shoulders in his hands and held her until some of the tension eased out.

She reached up and covered his hand, offering an almost adult reassurance to him. "I'm fine," she said, "but I don't know what's wrong with her."

Hawk followed her gaze to the tall metal storage cabinet at the far end of the mess hall. The doors had been flung open. Pans and plates were strewn across the floor and nearby tables. Sarah hovered in front of the cabinet.

She slammed shut the top drawer and whisked open the second. She reached in and pulled out cooking utensils. She glanced at the ladle in her fist, then slung it over her shoulder. Two other large spoons sailed through the air before Hawk spoke again.

He whispered firm instructions into Colleen's ear. "Tell the others to lighten their packs. They won't need extra clothes or sleeping bags. Load up any food you brought and blankets only. Tell Raul we're trekking through the jungle on foot. He should be able to help."

Colleen nodded. "Do you think she'll hurt herself?"

Hawk knew the girl's immediate concern was Sarah. Hawk brushed his fingers across her cheek and smiled, as proud of this girl's strength as if she were his own daughter. "I'll take care of Sarah. I'll keep her safe."

Colleen smiled gamely and hurried off to the

others. Hawk sucked in a fortifying breath and expelled it slowly, observing and analyzing Sarah before taking any action. Her hair haloed around her head and shoulders in wild disarray, blocking him from seeing her face. But he could interpret the invisible signals she sent out. Fear and confusion and determination warred for dominance. Cause for concern, yes, but to his trained counselor's eye, this was a much healthier reaction to what had happened and what she needed to face than denial and shutting down had been.

"Sarah." He called her name across the room. She halted her manic search for an instant, then resumed digging through and tossing aside utensils, hot pads, and storage containers.

"Scissors," she said in a hiss between her teeth. "I have to find scissors."

A long strand of hair fell over her shoulder and she jerked as though a live snake had fallen there instead. "Get away!"

She clutched the strand in a tight fist and tucked it back behind her ear. She released it abruptly, as though the snake had sunk its fangs into her hand. "Get off me!"

Hesitating no longer, Hawk crossed the room. He dodged a flying fork and called her name again. "I'm going to touch you," he explained, struggling to remain the counselor in control of the situation and not the man frightened by her shaking form.

She allowed him to take her by the arms, pull her away from the mess she had created, and turn her slowly to face him. His resolve to stay impersonal nose-dived at the sight of her blanched skin and huge, tear-swollen eyes.

She focused on the shredded placket of her

blouse. "I can't get it off." Her teeth nearly chattered with the strain of emotions overtaking her. She ripped the material in her hands, tearing off a patch and flinging it to the floor. Then she tore at it again. That long strand of hair fell over her shoulder one more time and she jerked.

"Get it off me!"

She captured the lock in one fist and pulled ruthlessly at the ends of it with the other. Then she flipped it behind her back, scoured her palms together and went back to work at the front of her blouse. "I can't get it off me."

Hawk finally understood.

Blood had caked in the tips of her hair, and the front of her blouse was soaked in de Vega's blood. He must have been right on top of her, close enough for her to see his eyes when she shot him. With an eerie similarity to the madness of Lady Macbeth, she worked feverishly to rid herself of the damning reminders of taking a man's life and surviving an attempted rape.

He wanted to shelter her in his arms and pledge his sorrow and apology to her. But she didn't need his guilt. And he wasn't sure what more he had to offer her. Instead, he squeezed his eyes shut and looked inside himself, not to that peaceful center of strength, but to that cold, unconnected place that allowed him to be a soldier. He tapped into the ancient brotherhood of warriors that he'd laid to rest so long ago and allowed their clarity and cunning to flow through him.

Tightening his hands around her shoulders, he steeled himself against her pain. "Come with me."

"I can't get it off." Her hoarse voice reached his heart, but he didn't allow his sensitivities to sway him from his purpose.

He pulled her out the door, sweeping her up in his arms when her stumbling feet threw her off balance. She curled into a ball, concentrating on rubbing her stained fingers. Devoted to her task, she seemed unaware that her feet had even left the ground.

But Hawk was keenly aware of every hill and hollow of her slim figure pressed against him. His skin tingled with a surging heat where her hip and shoulder brushed his stomach and chest, and his lips throbbed with the desire to taste her beautiful mouth again.

He half hoped that she would come to her senses, slap his face and chastise him for his improper thoughts. But the feisty schoolmarm who had come to his tent last night and warned him not to touch her was absent. In her place was this tortured waif of delicate beauty.

The spirit of the warrior, driven to protect his own, swelled in his heart. He pulled her closer and pressed a kiss to her temple. He held her there, tasting the salty tang of her heated skin and inhaling the fresh, unperfumed scent that was Sarah.

He rocked her close a moment longer, calming her and his own need. He stilled when his nostrils picked up a different scent. The spoiled odor of sweat tainted her hair. De Vega's smell.

And suddenly the same madness that consumed Sarah swept through him. Her subconscious desires became a very conscious need for Hawk.

He carried her toward the path to the lagoon, snapping orders to the others. "Colleen, bring me soap and a towel. Andrea, pack up the radio. Raul, find a way to carry any fresh water you can find."

153

"But we do not have that much. . . . "

"Do it!"

He took Sarah to the water's edge, setting her on her feet in a clearing blocked from view of the others by an outcropping of ferns and hyacinths. Putting aside a half-formed fantasy, he stripped off her clothes with doctorlike precision. He pushed aside her hindering hands and peeled away the material to reveal her pale beauty.

Hawk's breath lodged in his throat when he saw her naked figure. Unadorned perfection. In his eyes, Sarah McCormick represented the essence of woman the way nature intended her to be. Proud, slender shoulders; elegant, eloquent hands; small breasts, seductively tipped in pale peach; full, flaring hips that could welcome a man or nurture an unborn child.

He savored a rush of heat, the answering cry of his body to hers. But that base reaction of his manhood reminded him why he had brought her here in the first place. He wanted to cleanse her. To wash away her fears, her shock, and another man's touch.

Her conscious mind might not welcome his attention, but she had not welcomed de Vega, either. She had offered to sacrifice her body to protect her girls, then sacrificed her peaceful existence by destroying the threat to them all.

He owed her this duty. As a counselor, as a protector, and as a man.

Shoving aside possessive motives, he quickly pulled off his boots, socks and shirt, and scooped her into his arms. In his native Pawnee language, he whispered to her, pledging fealty and offering soothing reassurances as he walked into the water with her. He went in to his waist and bent his knees, pulling her down with him.

Startled by the wet, sluicing warmth on her chilled body, Sarah screeched and scrambled up his chest. She clutched him around the neck and clung to him like a lifeline.

"Shh." He hushed her and stroked her back beneath her hair, dipping his hand into the water and letting it dribble along her skin until she got used to the sensation. He turned his head and chanted more native words in her ear, a song of strength and power. He called to her spirit bear, thanking it for saving her life, asking it to save her again.

Prayers of his own ran through his mind and buried themselves in his soul. When she gentled her death grip, he lowered her into the water again, more slowly this time. Her hair fanned out across the surface, encircling them both, cloaking her fine alabaster skin beneath the green-tinted water.

He held her close and rocked her like a baby, beating down his own internal need and fighting to remain detached. He felt her mouth move against the hollow between his neck and shoulder and sensed rather than heard her cries of distress settle into sobs of grief.

The warmth of her tears trickled down his chest and merged with the cooler temperature of the water. Though warm as a bath, the water's heat couldn't compare with the tortured anguish he imagined in each teardrop.

Ignoring the wisdom of his own counsel, Hawk altered his clinical grip and folded Sarah into a more loving embrace. "Let me bathe you. I'll be gentle," he promised, pressing a kiss to the crown of her hair. "I'll try to make you whole again."

A shy voice intruded from the bank. "I brought the soap." Shielding Sarah from curious eyes, Hawk turned only his head to look at Colleen.

"Thank you." The girl's quiet strength impressed Hawk. The girl deserved comfort, too, but right now Sarah needed him more. "You're going to be fine. So will she."

"I know. My father said you're a man we can trust."

Her unwavering faith reminded Hawk of the times he had failed. The hurt in his heart made his reply unintentionally harsh. "Take Sarah's clothes and burn them."

Seemingly nonplussed, Colleen collected Sarah's things and left. Before he could distance his emotions again, Sarah spoke. Her lips grazed his heated skin with an innocent caress.

"I scared them terribly, didn't I?"

Hawk continued to stroke her back. "I expected something like this. You've been through a lot. There was no way you could keep it all bottled up inside. It's a natural reaction."

"Still, I should—"

"Enough." He pressed a finger to her lips and silenced her. "They're a great group of kids. They believe in you and they'll be fine. Right now it's time to take care of you."

"But—"

"For once in your life, can't you put yourself first?"

Her head snapped back and she impaled him with a mixture of fear and surprise shimmering in her golden eyes. He immediately regretted the frustration that had seeped into his voice. Despite her amazing inner strength, this woman was a fragile thing. Her shy outward appearance was matched by the delicacy of her ego. He wanted to show her her beauty, help her believe in the loveliness he perceived.

He traced the elegant curve of her jaw and spoke gently. His anger receded as he realized it was focused on others who had hurt her and not on Sarah herself. "I don't think anyone has ever really taken care of you, Sarah. Just for a few minutes, let me."

"But I have to be strong."

Hawk shook his head at her rhetorical protest. "Not right now. Can you stand?" he asked.

She nodded in meek compliance. She crossed her arms and covered herself when he moved away. In seconds he returned with the soap and a shaky resolve to help her in any way she needed without acknowledging the growing interest of his own body and the burgeoning need within his own heart.

"Turn around." Respecting her rediscovered modesty, he gathered up her Godiva-like hair and rubbed the strands with the soap between his hands. He concentrated on working the lather through her hair, washing it from the roots to the ends, averting his gaze from the determined angle of her chin and the slight trembling in her shoulders. She said nothing more, and from the intermittent catch of her breath, he guessed she was crying silent tears.

He ignored the urge to gather her back into his arms, and tipped her head back to rinse the soap from her hair. His lips quivered at the creamy temptation of her arched neck, then pursed into a grim line when he glimpsed the purplish discoloration of the bruises around her throat, bruises that he had put there.

To carry him beyond his anger, he reminded himself that he was here for Sarah, not to assuage his own guilt. Trying to shut down that whole distracting line of thought, he moved the bar of soap to her shoulders and back and started talking. "The winds of fate have scattered your strength before them. But I have seen a vision of your strength, and I know that the most powerful spirit guide has joined with you."

He smoothed his sudsy hands down her arms and along her spine. He reached around and soaped her stomach. He skimmed his hands across her breasts and around her hips. Her acceptance of his touch humbled him, made his hands tender worshipers of the treasure of trust she gave him. "The she-bear may be wounded, but she will not fail her cubs."

He slipped his hands lower, sliding the soap across her bottom and the supple length of her legs. He dunked his head to reach her ankles and feet, bringing him to eye level with all that was most feminine about her. The pulsing surge of heat in his body made him wish for cold water. He swallowed hard, gulping in enough water to lower his carnal thoughts to a simmer. Sputtering with embarrassment, he surfaced, bringing his palm up along the inside of her leg, carrying the bar of soap higher.

Sarah's lithe fingers closed over his hand midthigh. Jolted by the unexpected contact, already flooded with maddening thoughts, he unclenched his hand. The soap slipped from his grip and shot to the surface. Hawk backed away with the same abrupt motion.

"Am I the she-bear?"

Short of breath and good sense, he could only stare when she turned and faced him. She clutched the soap between her supplicant hands, then crossed her arms over her breasts. But as much as her tempting Venus body mesmerized him, he found he couldn't look away from the hopeful curiosity in her golden-green eyes.

"Yes," he answered simply. "I saw you on a vision quest. Last December. Seeing Brodie Maxwell again, when his wife was in trouble, reminded me of some things I needed to deal with. I went home to Nebraska to visit my mentor, Otis Peace Hands. He helped me with the ceremonies and led me to the vision."

"Of me?"

Many in the Anglo world didn't have patience or interest in learning the details of his native traditions. But he sensed—he hoped—that Sarah might be different. She possessed the curious mind of a true scholar. And right now she was a frightened vessel, set adrift in the world, needing answers to questions to regain security and a sense of balance.

He rarely shared this side of himself. He'd been rejected before for being strange, unnatural, even heathen. But he'd been able to resist little where Sarah McCormick was concerned. And here in this sheltered glade, feeling warm and wet and tired, humbled by Sarah's trust, he found he could no more resist her pleading, needy request than a starving man could say no to a morsel of food.

"I didn't know it was you at the time," he explained. "But certain signs tell me that you are the mother Kodiak I saw."

159

"What signs?" She swayed closer. Automatically, Hawk clasped his fingers over her hips to steady her at arm's length.

"Your hair, for one." He pulled a strand of its silky length from the water and draped it over her milky white shoulder like a modest cloak. "It's the same caramel-brown color of Kodiak fur.

"And your eyes . . . " He swept his gaze back to the irresistible golden light there. "Tawny. Like the bear's."

Though her lids were pink and puffy, her gaze was clear and bright. "You have the most beautiful eyes." It pained him to do anything that might douse the light there. But she had asked for the truth.

"The bear in my vision had her heart ripped out. She had a red, bloody wound on her chest."

Sarah squeezed her hands tightly against her heart. Her voice was little more than a mournful wheeze. "Like the blood on my shirt today."

"Not exactly." Hawk breathed in deeply, turning his face to the sound of a pair of wild macaws, calling in the treetops above them. How could he explain the aura of heartsickness he'd read in her that first night at the town meeting? How could he tell her that he'd envisioned her as his salvation? And knowing that, how could he justify having failed to keep her safe time and again?

"This is difficult for you to talk about, isn't it?"

In a move as miraculous as it was gentle, Sarah touched his brow. She trailed her fingertips along the lines of tension that spanned from his forehead to his temple. Then she laid her hand to rest against his cheek.

He basked in the healing power of her attentions, unable and unwilling to pull away. He

Thrill to the most sensual, adventure-filled Romances on the market today...

FROM  LOVE SPELL BOOKS

As a home subscriber to the Love Spell Romance Book Club, you'll enjoy the best in today's BRAND-NEW Time Travel, Futuristic, Legendary Lovers, Perfect Heroes and other genre romance fiction. For five years, Love Spell has brought you the award-winning, high-quality authors you know and love to read. Each Love Spell romance will sweep you away to a world of high adventure...and intimate romance. Discover for yourself all the passion and excitement millions of readers thrill to each and every month.

Save $5.00 Each Time You Buy!

Every other month, the Love Spell Romance Book Club brings you four brand-new titles from Love Spell Books. EACH PACKAGE WILL SAVE YOU AT LEAST $5.00 FROM THE BOOK-STORE PRICE! And you'll never miss a new title with our convenient home delivery service.

Here's how we do it: Each package will carry a FREE 10-DAY EXAMINATION privilege. At the end of that time, if you decide to keep your books, simply pay the low invoice price of $17.96, no shipping or handling charges added. HOME DELIVERY IS ALWAYS FREE. With today's top romance novels selling for $5.99 and higher, our price SAVES YOU AT LEAST $5.00 with each shipment.

AND YOUR FIRST TWO-BOOK SHIP-MENT IS TOTALLY FREE!

IT'S A BARGAIN YOU CAN'T BEAT! A SUPER $11.48 Value!

Love Spell ✦ A Division of Dorchester Publishing Co., Inc.

GET YOUR 2 FREE BOOKS NOW—AN $11.48 VALUE!

Mail the Free Book Certificate Today!

TWO FREE BOOKS

Free Books Certificate

YES! I want to subscribe to the Love Spell Romance Book Club. Please send me my 2 FREE BOOKS. Then every other month I'll receive the four newest Love Spell selections to Preview FREE for 10 days. If I decide to keep them, I will pay the Special Member's Only discounted price of just $4.49 each, a total of $17.96. This is a SAVINGS of at least $5.00 off the bookstore price. There are no shipping, handling, or other charges. There is no minimum number of books I must buy and I may cancel the program at any time. In any case, the 2 FREE BOOKS are mine to keep—A BIG $11.48 Value!

Offer valid only in the U.S.A.

Name _____

Address _____

City _____

State _____ *Zip* _____

Telephone _____

Signature _____

If under 18, Parent or Guardian must sign. Terms, prices and conditions subject to change. Subscription subject to acceptance. Leisure Books reserves the right to reject any order or cancel any subscription.

A $11.48 VALUE

Get Two Books Totally
FREE —
An $11.48 Value!

▼ Tear Here and Mail Your FREE Book Card Today! ▼

PLEASE RUSH
MY TWO FREE
BOOKS TO ME
RIGHT AWAY!

Love Spell Romance Book Club
P.O. Box 6613
Edison, NJ 08818-6613

AFFIX
STAMP
HERE

looked down at her and mimicked the same actions with his own fingers on her face.

"You always help when you're needed, don't you? It's not in your heart to let anyone else suffer. The bear spirit is so strong in you. Let it heal you, too. Don't give away what you need for yourself."

He felt the timid pressure of her fingertips in his hairline. "Does your bear die?"

He felt a tremble shimmy through her body, or maybe it was his own trembling response to the piteous plea in her voice. "I don't know."

He tightened his grip and tilted her face up to his. "I do know she was fierce and valiant, and she saved her cubs."

He cradled her face in both hands now, possessively, tenderly, beseechingly. "We have to write our own endings to what we envision in life. And I swear to you, despite my failures, that I will keep you safe. I will get you home."

"The girls are my cubs?"

"I think so."

"Thank you." That merest of whispers caressed his ears and settled like a balm over his own doubtful heart. "Thank you for sharing that with me."

"You're welcome." Her words healed his vulnerability. And the aura surrounding her head and shoulders lightened with a silvery glow. Her bath, his words—somehow, he had finally done the right thing and helped her. He'd led her back to her own strength, and in doing so, had rediscovered his own.

"You're welcome, schoolmarm."

And then it seemed like the most natural thing in the world to dip his head and capture her mouth in a gentle kiss. In one intake of breath he remembered her request the night before, the impropriety she worried about, something deeper she feared in his touch.

But in the next breath his worry had disappeared. She didn't pull away. She didn't murmur a protest. She slid her fingers into his hair and parted her lips and welcomed him.

Hawk explored her mouth with a reverence and gratitude befitting the esteemed status of her spirit guide. He tasted the sweet, tender skin along the inside of her mouth and sipped at the corner with his tongue. Then he felt a delicate suckle along the harder rim of his mouth, the unmistakable tug of her soft lips shyly demanding something more from him.

Barely aware of his own chest-deep groan, he gathered her in, flattening his hands over the smooth lines of her back and pulling her close. She wound her arms around his neck and stretched herself tightly against him like a cat settling into her lair. She angled her mouth to offer him greater access, and Hawk plunged in, claiming her with a natural rightness reserved for normal men.

An equal partner in this embrace, Sarah made gentle demands of his lips, and Hawk willingly complied. She was eager to learn and he was eager to teach the teacher the simple, ecstatic joys of a nip on her earlobe, or the tracing of a damp pattern of kisses down the column of her neck. And the teacher turned the tables, teaching herself, and him, the delights of little nibbles along his jaw, or the press of a kiss to the soft underside of his chin.

Never had any loving felt so pure, so perfect.

Never had a kiss made Hawk feel so powerful, so human. Never had a woman felt so right.

Hawk reclaimed her mouth and Sarah squirmed against him, the tips of her breasts beading like tiny brands piercing his chest. An unbidden, welcome rush of heat pelted his body below his waist. He slipped his hands lower, captured her hips, and rubbed himself against her. The heart-stopping friction eased his ache, yet intensified his desire.

And scared Sarah to death.

At least, the sudden whimper in her throat and the startled push of her hands against his chest and the quick ducking of her face made him think he had scared her. He sensed she was new to all this, she'd just been traumatized, and still, like an insensitive brute, he'd overwhelmed her with his own needs.

"I'm sorry," he whispered as she pulled away. He moved his hands to the neutral location of her shoulders, needing her to balance him as much as he intended to balance her.

Water swept in between them, along with concern and regret for Hawk. "Sarah, that was unforgivable. I didn't mean to—"

"Don't." She touched his chest and he fell silent.

Water lapped at the tops of her breasts, creating a hushed drumbeat of sound as she tried to even out her breathing. Hawk inhaled deeply, lifting his gaze from the tempting sight. He drank in the air, filled with the sickeningly sweet perfume of flowers, and found the steamy atmosphere couldn't quite provide his lungs the revivifying air they needed.

Maybe his lungs weren't working properly, because Sarah began to pet him. She brushed her fingertips along his chest, his face, his neck and shoulders. They were gentle, apologetic strokes, as though she wanted to soothe a restless beast.

Did she see him that way? A primitive man-beast who couldn't control his wants or temper? Hadn't he behaved in exactly that way?

"Honey . . ."

The endearment slipped out, but he quickly snatched it back with silence when the caressing stopped and she clenched her hand into a fist between them.

"You must think I'm a terrible, mixed-up, teasing, prudish spinster."

She spoke the apology to his chest, and a flash of anger aimed at the men who had made her believe such garbage mingled with his own regret. "I think you're an incredibly courageous, first-class lady who's been through hell today."

She tipped her chin up and met his gaze, looking surprised by the vehemence in his voice.

"I apologize for taking advantage of that. But I don't for one minute believe that you're a tease or a prude." He shook his head, not sure how to make her understand. "A man doesn't get turned on like that by an unresponsive woman. You make me crazy with the way you touch me. Being shy doesn't make you a tease, and being unmarried sure as hell doesn't mean you're a prude."

He tightened his fingers around her shoulders to emphasize his sincerity. "I'm only sorry I pushed you into this today. I wanted you, and I didn't take into account how you might be feeling."

"I wanted you to kiss me." Her quiet voice stunned him into silence. "You weren't taking advantage. I needed to be held like that. I needed you. You brought me back to reality. I'm sure I'm not through this yet. But I have to be strong for the girls right now, and you helped me. You made me feel almost . . . "

Her eyes rounded, big as saucers, then shuttered again.

"Almost what?" Hawk prodded.

She smiled, but the sweet curve of her mouth didn't reach her eyes. "I'm glad you're with us. I'll try to be a little less crazy from now on, okay?"

"Sarah?"

But she had already left him, slogging her way through the water toward the shore. She covered herself as the water got shallow. Exposed to her hips, she stopped. "I don't have any clothes."

She kept her back to him, and Hawk bit down on the urge to tell her that her reticence came too late. He'd already seen and felt most of her. But he didn't think of her as a lady without good cause.

With a gut-deep sigh that revealed the remnants of frustration, anger, caring and desire, Hawk quickly waded to shore and picked up the black T-shirt he had discarded earlier. "Here. You can wear this until you get back to your tent and change."

She stared at the material dangling from his hand and then looked up at him expectantly. Then she did the damnedest thing and twirled her finger in the air, asking him to turn around. His initial reaction to her belated modesty cooled into something bordering on possessiveness and protection. If she wanted to cover herself, then he wanted her to be covered.

With his back to her, he heard the water dripping from her skin as she climbed out, and the slippery thud of her footsteps on the muddy beach. She snatched the shirt from his grasp, and he imagined he could hear the whisper of soft cotton settling over her softer skin.

"Thank you," she whispered, then darted around him down the path, carrying her boots.

Hawk stood where he was, transfixed, breathing deeply, or maybe not even breathing at all. She'd wound her hair into a cord and pulled it over her shoulder, giving him a clear view of her backside scurrying down the path. His shirt engulfed her slender figure, hanging to her thighs. But it clung to her wet skin, hinting at the graceful length of her back, the slim nip of her waist, and the seductive flare of her hips.

Hawk dove back into the water and prayed for a self-discipline his body couldn't seem to remember around Sarah. A cold shower would have been a greater blessing than this warm bath. But he reckoned that a man who couldn't do his job right and couldn't remember his place got what he deserved.

Chapter Eight

I am He who commands the sun.

All others of this earth are but petty ants that swarm at My feet. I provide all that is needed. I take all that is due Me.

I am He. . . .

The royal litany, first spoken by the gods for Him, obeyed by peasants and soldiers alike, rang through His consciousness like a war cry.

But why was He at war? Had He not brought peace to the land, and ruled with Prini at His side for long, fruitful years? Long enough to build a great city from the black rock from the far side of the island. Long enough to secure the tribute of the native tribes. Long enough to see His people know him for a god and make His will their own.

What had disturbed Him? Who had dared to invade His kingdom? Why had He been summoned from the land of the gods?

He focused His mind and tried to make sense of His surroundings. He traveled quickly, like a canoe manned by eight powerful slaves. But He did not hear the silent rhythm of their matched strokes. These noises were uncommonly loud, not the natural sounds of the jungle. The whining cacophany was a cruel attack on His ears, and difficult to ignore.

He wished for the blessed peace He had once known. But the sounds were not new. They had first come to Him like the distant rumble of thunder, the faint, incoherent stirrings of a gathering enemy. Now His enemies were close at hand, close enough to touch, close enough to make out words of a language He did not understand.

He'd been fast asleep when the first disturbance had jarred Him into a level of dreamlike slumber. In a dimly remembered passage of minutes, or perhaps eons, He heard the sounds again. Over and over. It had taken Him a long time to awaken. A long time to acknowledge the presence of an enemy.

And an even longer time to understand that He was alone.

They'd left Him alone for all eternity.

Fools!

The petty fools had defied His wishes. They had taken it in their small mortal minds to disobey His final request.

Rage boiled within Him. Glimpses of dreams became clear-minded purpose. He sped along under a power not His own, carried in a land canoe with thunder captured in its prow. Inspecting the cargo beneath him, He realized these thieves carried booty that was rightfully His. He moved into a container, felt the familiar warmth of things cherished. He hovered there, absorbing the bold-spirited heat of a gold icon. It was set atop a staff of carved, polished teak. Men had cowered before that symbol of power.

Marriages had been bestowed. Harvests blessed. Men killed by the one who had wielded that staff.

He surfaced, feeling stronger now. The abhorrent sounds receded, and He could sense the presence of another. This one was weak, not like the warrior's mind He had first touched, then trailed from the tomb.

He passed through walls, following the peculiar stench as much as the simple mind. A peasant, He could tell at once, hovering in the small confines beside the man. His clothing might look different, but the sun-weathered skin and small-minded expression were the same.

This peasant held a circlet of gold in his right hand while he steered the land canoe by a round, black rudder in his left. He recognized the golden gift and watched how this rank peasant defiled the gold by touching it and fondling the garnets and emeralds once worn by His beloved.

He gathered Himself, focused on His rage. The peasant glanced around nervously, like a small animal sensing the presence of something much larger about to spring upon it for dinner. He watched the telltale beads of sweat break out on the peasant's upper lip. And like the victorious hunter, He knew the prey was His.

He reached out.

Pitiful little man.

The peasant saw Him with his mind and screamed.

He gave a little nudge, laughing inside at the small man whose screams jarred the air in the tiny land canoe. The man jerked and He pulled away, freeing Himself from the acrid smell of imminent death.

The canoe careened into the trees like hunted prey cornering itself. It smashed through the trunks and leaves and sailed into the air, soaring for a moment like the great harpy eagle. Then it plummeted to earth and burst into flame.

A common peasant was hardly a worthy sacrifice, but the burning pyre at the foot of the cliff soothed the obsessive quest for vindication.

He gathered Himself after the exertion of the hunt, savoring the victory, enjoying the semblance of silence.

But He turned when He sensed others coming. Others who had violated His sanctuary and denied Him the one thing He wanted most.

He would find them.

He would find them all and punish them for what they had done.

I am He who commands the sun. Bow down before Me.

Or know My wrath.

Sarah stared at the toffee-colored plait of hair she held in her fist and remembered her father's sad words when she'd cut it short back in college. *You don't look like my little girl anymore.* He'd meant it as a compliment, a signal that he knew she was growing up. But shortly after that, her mother had been diagnosed with cancer. And other than a regular trim to keep it looking neat, she hadn't cut it since. Her father had found great comfort in familiar things.

She'd found comfort in them, too.

But little in Tenebrosa felt familiar. And nothing about today left her feeling like a little girl.

She flung the braid behind her back, knowing what she must do. But it wasn't easy. Dear Lord, it wasn't easy.

Hawk had bathed her and calmed her and comforted her with his gentle hands and voice. He had washed away the touch of another man, but he couldn't reach inside and cleanse her of what she herself had done.

She'd selfishly taken five innocent children away from their homes and families just so she could experience the adventure of a lifetime.

Some adventure.

She'd killed a man. She'd involved the girls in covering up a crime against Tenebrosa. And now, because of her, they'd been left to die.

Sarah studied the pile of drab, shapeless clothes she'd been told to leave behind. The tans, whites, and browns represented a lot more than her safe, boring taste in clothing. They symbolized the woman she'd always been. Reserved, predictable, responsible. She'd always done what was expected of her.

Until this trip.

Until running up against the enigmatic wall of Hawk Echohawk and his strange, beautiful ways.

She didn't know herself anymore. Had she hit some sort of midlife crisis? Her experience with Walter had left her feeling embarrassingly ancient and past the point of being of any use to anybody. Looking back on the miserable end to that relationship, she could blame her desperate need to make this journey on him. She'd wanted a final fling to prove to herself that her lonely life hadn't been wasted.

But could her needs justify what she had done to those five girls? Hawk had said this was a mistake from the very beginning, and she hadn't listened.

She was listening now.

Sarah sighed, the frustrated sound echoing deeply in her chest. Picking up her lightened backpack and canteen, she slung them over her shoulder and gave one final look at everything she was leaving behind. She couldn't afford to be the old Sarah any longer.

She needed to be more like that mother bear in Hawk's vision. His odd words had given her strength. They had touched a part of her imagination, and struck her with a rightness that was almost like a memory. As he spoke, it had felt like a dream coming back to her.

Sarah shook her head, displeased with herself for allowing such wistful imaginings. When had her dreams ever come true? Those fanciful urges of her quiet heart had only brought her trouble, time and again.

She needed to be more like Hawk. Focused. Alert. Wise about people.

She needed to leave the old Sarah behind and be strong enough and smart enough to help get those girls home. Comfort and familiarity had no place on their daunting hike back to El Espanto.

Girding herself in a show of strength, she shut down the rising flood of doubt inside her and turned to join the others.

Hawk paced restlessly, anxious for Sarah to join them at the fire pit. The others were packed and ready to go, a young but indomitable brigade. What they lacked in experience, they made up for in trust and cooperation.

His first trip to Tenebrosa had been in the company of savvy, highly trained Marine Corps intelligence operatives, each bringing their individual talents to the elite group. He supposed Sarah's girls had their own unique talents, too.

Denise, their leader. Andrea, a storehouse of knowledge. Lyndsay, the risk-taker, the emotional one unafraid to take action. Lynnette formed the heart of the group, providing that nameless cohesion that bonded them into a single unit. Colleen was most like him, intuitive about the needs of others, quietly doing what needed to be done. Even Raul, with his altered loyalties and newfound idealism, fit in as the rebel joining their fight.

And Sarah . . . she was the commanding officer every soldier wished he had, the teacher who taught more than facts. She helped them understand themselves and their world. She molded them into confident, caring human beings with a respect for themselves and others. Then she quietly stepped back and allowed her students to shine for themselves.

Like the mother bear, who nurtured her cubs and defended them with a vengeance until they could take care of themselves.

Only *he* remained the outcast, without a niche to fit into the group—except when Sarah dropped her ladylike reserve and reached out to him. Then he felt connected. For those few brief moments, first in the jungle, and then in the lagoon, he felt that he had a purpose here. That he belonged.

But belonging was just an illusion, wasn't it? To some extent, he belonged to many different worlds. Soldier. Friend. Counselor. Pawnee. A man of the earth. A man of the spirit world.

But there was not one place where all the elements that made him who he was were accepted as a whole. Not one place where some element of him wasn't resented, or questioned, or loathed.

Not one place.

Except with Sarah.

Sweet, brave, gentle Sarah, full of surprises, and frightened of all he wanted from her. Of all she wanted for herself. Gritty courage aside, she was a lady through and through. She was a woman who needed courtship, who should be led gently to the discoveries of loving. She deserved a storybook marriage with a successful, three-piece-suit kind of guy; not a brief, coarse, passionate affair in the tropics with a used-up shadow man like himself.

Still, it felt so good to belong. Like a parched man in the desert of loneliness, he basked in her rare, glorious smiles, and found soul-nurturing sustenance in the gift of her kisses. The ultimate acceptance he would find buried deep inside her was a tribute too far out of reach for a man so alien to her world.

Besides, he had come to Tenebrosa for a different kind of healing. He wanted closure for the unexplained mistakes of his past. The one time when it had counted most, his abilities had failed him. That truth would have to stay hidden for now. He had a larger responsibility on his hands, because not seeing Sarah and the others safely home would be a failure he couldn't live with.

Wasting time wishing for things that could never be would only distract him from what needed to be done. He buried his feelings, hardened his resolve, and gave up his pacing.

He strode straight to Sarah's tent. "Damn it, schoolmarm, what's taking you so long?"

The flap opened and Sarah materialized right in front of him, looking so small and fragile and delicate that he had to clench his hands into fists to keep from pulling her into his arms. Her chin was bowed below its normal regal tilt, but she lifted her beseeching golden gaze to his and whispered quietly, "I need to ask you a favor."

The tremor in her voice and the pull of her eyes threatened to undermine his resolve to stay emotionally unattached. Fighting off the desire to stop and give the lady whatever she asked, when he knew damn well they should have been on the road an hour ago, he made his own voice tighten to a clipped growl. "We'll never get ten yards, much less ten miles, down the road at this rate. What do you want?"

She tipped up her chin and leaned back as if his harshness surprised her. The glimmer of fear surrounding her ebbed in a swirl of amber confusion. Then, in the space of a heartbeat, her familiar blue aura asserted itself as she summoned her courage.

Reaching behind her, she pulled out her braid and held it up to him like an offering. "I want you to cut my hair."

Hawk glanced from the determination in her eyes to the beautiful twist of Kodiak brown in her hand. "Not your hair."

Her focus followed his own and she looked at the braid as though she held a poisonous snake in her hand. "It won't dry like this, and it will be hot and heavy to wear while we're hiking. Just as you said before we left the airport in Kansas City." Her breath caught in a tiny little gasp. "And he . . . he . . . "

Suddenly Hawk remembered de Vega's hands

on Sarah, and the way he'd combed his grubby fingers through her hair. With a matching catch of his own breath, Hawk lifted the braid from her hand. He'd counseled women who had been abused by their spouses, but never a woman who'd been victimized by a crime the way Sarah had. Dealing with her emotional wounds required a different kind of strategy than he could give her, especially since his reaction to her request was male and territorial, and not at all detached, the way he'd promised himself earlier.

But he supposed the nearest therapist or crisis center lay across the Bay of Yucatán in mainland Mexico. And since he had no books or colleagues to consult, he had to rely on his instincts. Those instincts said to give Sarah what she wanted. Despite how the color of her hair had drawn him like the symbol in his vision. Despite the old-fashioned ladylike quality its length gave her. Despite its sensuous beauty when it had floated around them both in the water and he had caressed its silky texture between his hands.

"I don't know if I can," he murmured aloud, torn between the impulse to wipe de Vega's touch from her and his desire to preserve a thing of beauty.

"I'm not *asking* you."

She wrapped her fingers around his wrist and forced his gaze to meet hers. He recognized the schoolmarm determination in the gold-green depths and realized that no matter how he argued, he would bow to her will in this.

He nodded slowly and unsnapped the sheath on his vest. "Turn around."

Her rallying spirit eased his doubts only momentarily. With her back to him, she tucked her chin to her chest, exposing the creamy length of her neck. Hawk swallowed hard, feeling like an executioner about to slaughter an innocent. He twisted her hair twice around his left hand and pulled it taut. He laid the knife against the braid and stopped, entranced by the shiny glints reflected in the smooth steel blade.

She must have sensed his hesitation. "Do it."

He balked at her command, knowing he could hack it like a vine in one or two sure strokes. But that would be too cruel, too much like cutting into Sarah herself.

"Hawk, please."

The breathy plea reached all the way to his soul. Hawk was a master of self-control, but something about this shy woman's bravery shamed him. Her resilient strength in the face of unending obstacles made him wonder why he, too, refused to take more chances.

He should be in charge here, and yet he found himself once again unable to deny her need. Clenching his jaw, he began sawing back and forth through her hair. With each stroke, damp strands popped loose, and, freed from the weight of the heavy braid, they kinked into tiny loose curls that sprang away from his hands.

When he finished, Sarah patted the back of her neck as if checking the tenderness of a wound. Hawk muttered an apology and stepped back, mourning the loss he held in his hand.

"I have some manicure scissors in my pack." Hawk barely heard her as she turned and spoke. "I'll have one of the girls trim it up a little more evenly.

"Thank you. For . . . everything."

The shyness of her voice pulled his attention

back to her. Before he could refute her misplaced gratitude, she flattened her palm against his chest for balance and leaned in on tiptoe to press a chaste kiss to the square jut of his jaw.

Then she ducked her head and scooted past him to the others.

Hawk stood mute, absorbing the tantalizing sensation of her soft lips against his sun-roughened skin. He could still feel the whispery pressure of her hand and hear the demure awkwardness in her voice.

"Ten minutes, schoolmarm!" he yelled over his shoulder. "And then we hit the road."

Hawk barked the order in an automatic attempt to distance himself from the inexplicable warmth that suffused him. That quick kiss probably had cost her more than any other physical contact they'd shared, because she had initiated it. That tiny risk of kindness eased a hurtful place inside him. It soothed his guilt and reminded him of his strength.

And it made him realize how vulnerable he was. How deeply that quiet, bossy stick of a woman had insinuated herself into his life in just a few short days.

And how utterly impossible it would be for them to become anything more than friends or lovers. And how a deeply buried part of him wanted all that and more from Sarah. But back in Marysville, Kansas, when she was surrounded by familiar people and familiar things, she wouldn't want him for anything. She wouldn't need him.

She would be polite. Hawk could picture Sarah treating him with the same gracious patience that she had used with Kensit after the town meeting. Her family background wouldn't allow her to be anything less than courteous. But a cool, polite brush-off was still a brush-off.

She wouldn't need him at all in the real world.

And caring about the woman, one way or the other, admiring her courage, liking—no, going out of his mind with—her touch, and memorizing endearing little traits, like a shy stammer or a twist of her fingers or a dazzling smile, would only lead to trouble. Hell, it already had.

She clouded his judgment, altered his priorities. Made him care about things he had no right caring about.

Hawk looked down at the braid in his hand and remembered the symbols in his vision. With every moment that passed, he had no doubt that Sarah was the Kodiak, and the girls her cubs. The world freezing and turning to gray could loosely be interpreted in her momentary and understandable breakdown after de Vega's attack. Something in her past made her heartsick, yet Sarah continued to fight as valiantly as the mother bear.

What he couldn't yet understand was the oblivion when the world in his vision had shattered and collapsed all around them. Were Sarah and the girls doomed to that unacceptable fate? Hawk would die himself before allowing that to happen.

Or was that shattered world his own destiny? The price he had to pay for caring?

He couldn't escape Otis Peace Hands's dire warning that Hawk must save the bear in order to save his own life. He wondered how Sarah could possibly save him. She knew little about survival skills, next to nothing about the jungle, and nil about criminals. Otis must have misinterpreted the dream. Surely he meant that Sarah would die without *him*.

But then he thought of his silly, softening reaction to that innocent kiss, and how her gentle touch and selfless concern in the jungle had totally freed him from Meczaquatl's control. The hair in his hand seemed to glow with heat.

There was something more at work here. Something still beyond his understanding, something not yet under his control.

Hawk wasn't a man to take chances. Purposefully pushing aside any inklings of sentimentality, he pulled two strands of Sarah's hair from the braid, wound them into a tiny knot and snapped them inside a pocket on his vest. He'd add them to his medicine pouch when he sought his next vision.

He'd keep them as a reminder of what they might have shared.

He tossed the braid on the cot inside her tent, then patted the pocket of his vest.

He might not understand it, but he couldn't ignore an omen.

On the other hand, he'd do his damnedest to ignore his feelings for pretty Sarah McCormick.

It was a matter of survival.

His.

Four hundred fifty-two, four hundred fifty-three . . .

"Hold up."

Sarah halted, as ordered. Four hundred fifty-four steps since Hawk's last words, and that had been a terse *Eyes right* to warn them to give wide berth to the snake wrapped around a tree limb that hung out over the road.

What was wrong with him? Was this his jungle mode? The soldier in him taking charge of their survival? Didn't he realize these were children, not troops he was commanding? Taciturn, mysterious exterior aside, he had shown her he was a deeply spiritual, compassionate man. What had happened?

What had she done to make him withdraw into caustic silence like this? Maybe her going wacko had turned him off to any kind feelings he had toward her. But his kiss had come after that, hadn't it? When he was talking about his vision.

Maybe that explained his mood. He had shared something intensely personal with her, and now he regretted it. She'd listened to his story as if hearing the soothing words of a prayer. But maybe Hawk hadn't intended them that way; perhaps he was only doing what needed to be done to comfort her.

Perhaps her misinterpretation of his help had embarrassed him. He was trying to be a good friend, and she . . .

She felt the temperature of her already hot skin rise, nearly suffocating her. Sarah opened her mouth and sucked in a deep breath.

You're nothing remarkable. Not terribly pretty. And sexy?

Walter had said she was lucky he'd shown an interest in her. Lucky that he'd found other qualities to like about her. Like her bank account and her family lineage.

She'd been *lucky* to have his attentions. It had taken her far too long to realize just how insincere they had been. Why should Hawk be any different from any other man?

She'd be a fool to interpret Hawk's actions as anything other than friendship. Or anything more than what an experienced man like him was willing to do to ensure their survival.

She might be slow to learn about men, but she was no fool.

Hiking the road had actually proved to be an easier trip than riding over it in the back of a truck had been. The ruts that had jarred Sarah's bones into putty en route to Las Lagumas now served as a clear path back to El Espanto.

But nothing else was easy about this hike. With the break, she eased out of her pack, twisting to avoid brushing the sore skin at the back of her neck, which hadn't seen direct sunlight in nearly fifteen years. She rubbed at the front of her right shoulder and rotated her arm, working out the stiffness there. She might be used to walking for exercise, but she wasn't used to carrying a pack.

And with the excess humidity, she'd discovered that one of the drawbacks to having short hair was its tendency to frizz and fly around her face. The wispy ends tickled her chin and stuck to the perspiration on her forehead. She pushed the annoying curls away from her temples and tried to figure out what Hawk was studying in the mud at the side of the road.

"What is it?" questioned Lynnette.

The youngest member of their group had stayed on Hawk's heels for the past three miles. The others trailed along in single file while Sarah brought up the rear. Hawk had commanded her to holler if anyone straggled too far behind, but it was Sarah's intention to adjust her pace so that none of the girls would feel they were holding the group back.

Raul shrugged out of the radio pack and opened the jug of water he carried. "Is it all right if we have a drink?" he asked Hawk.

For a moment, Sarah didn't think he'd heard

the boy. Hawk stood and stared down the embankment through the trees. The girls crowded in behind Raul, panting in deep breaths of hot air, waiting for Hawk's answer.

Sarah herself was about to repeat the question when Hawk whipped his head around. "Three swallows apiece. Drop your packs and rest for fifteen minutes. I want to check something out."

The thumps of packs, teens and supplies hitting the ground sounded like a drumbeat. Only Lynnette seemed inclined to follow Hawk into the trees. Sarah hurried and caught Lynnette's arm, pulling her back.

"Do what he says. You need to keep up your strength."

The girl looked at Sarah, then reluctantly nodded. Andrea held out her canteen to share, and Lynnette took it and sat down beside her friend.

When Sarah turned around, Hawk had already dropped out of sight down the steep incline. But she saw a clear trail where the undergrowth had been crushed and trail markers had been gouged into the sides of some of the tree trunks.

Swelling with pride, Sarah noted that the girls hadn't complained once about the heat or the pace. But glancing over at them, she couldn't help but notice their slumped shoulders, some of them heaving to catch their breath. Denise and Colleen had already stretched out with their heads resting on their packs.

Whatever Hawk's grievance with her might be, he didn't need to take it out on the girls by pushing them so hard.

"You guys stay together," she said, hoping to buy them some more rest time. "I'll find out what's going on."

Tucking a bothersome curl behind her ear, Sarah stepped across a decaying fallen tree and started down the hill. At first she used the trunks and branches for handholds on her way down. But then the slope became rocky and dropped off sharply, and recent rains had turned the mud and crumpled greenery into a slick mock-up of an amusement park ride. She planted her boot against an exposed root, but slipped on the wet surface and plopped down hard on her bottom.

Sarah lost her grip and went flying down Mother Nature's slide. She grabbed at handfuls of ferns and roots, but her momentum ripped them out of the earth and tilted her sideways.

"Hawk!" She hollered his name, crashed into a tree root, tumbled head over heels and watched her world spin out of control. In one last effort to right herself, she stuck out her feet, planted her heels and straightened. She would have flipped over face-first into the mud, but she slammed into warm, solid man first.

"Damn it, schoolmarm, what are you doing now?"

For a few wonderful, sane seconds, Hawk held her as tightly as she latched on to him. He was the one thing in the jungle that wasn't spinning.

Then he abruptly pushed her away, leaving Sarah to sway back and forth on her own two feet.

"Are you all right?" His clipped tone revealed standard politeness rather than genuine concern.

Sarah silently accounted the extent of her injuries. Other than the throbbing pain in her hip where she'd smacked into the tree, her ego seemed to be the only part of her that had suffered serious bruising. "I'll be fine."

She rubbed at her hip and blinked to focus. She pushed her hair back from her face and saw Hawk circle back to a large, blocky shape hidden in the trees. Sarah followed. "Why did you leave? Wouldn't it be better if we stayed on the road? Or is this a shortcut?"

"I thought I told you to wait up there."

His harsh voice cleared her dizziness faster than finding herself on relatively flat terrain again. "What is wrong with you? You're pushing the girls like you don't have a heart in you anymore. If you're mad at me, take it out on me! Not them."

"This has nothing to do with you."

He looked at her coldly, then pointed toward a clearing. Sarah followed the angle of his arm and gasped in shock at the twisted wreckage of one of Luis Salazar's trucks wrapped around a tree.

"Oh, my God . . . " Her hand flew to her heart as her voice trailed away, her indignation forgotten.

"I saw tracks running off the road up there. There were no signs of him hitting the brakes. It looks like he sped up and leaped the curve on purpose."

Sarah stumbled over to the truck, touching the open tailgate as though needing tactile proof that the crash had really occurred. "Was Luis inside?"

"No. Just the driver. Hernandez."

"Is he . . . ?" She stared into the shadowy void beneath the twisted frame and torn canvas at the back of the truck. She knew before Hawk nodded that Hernandez had died in the crash.

Her moment of compassion was brief, her feeling of justice served short-lived. Suspicion set in, and she altered her stance by splaying both hands around her waist.

"Where's the treasure that was inside?" she asked.

"I spotted an extra set of tire tracks up top, and drag marks through the trees. I imagine they came back and unloaded whatever they could carry."

This refresher course in the depravity of the criminal mind propelled her to the driver's side of the truck cab. She jerked the door open a moment before she heard Hawk swear and overtake her from behind.

But in the split second before he jerked on her arm and smothered her against his chest, she caught a glimpse of the grisly corpse behind the wheel. Hawk's nylon canvas vest abraded her cheeks, but she clutched handfuls of it and buried her face in the warmth radiating from Hawk's body, willing his sheltering arms to drive the bloody image of the dead man from her mind.

"They took time to unload their precious artifacts, but not to save their own man?"

"I would have spared you that." Hawk whispered the words beside her ear. "The engine caught fire. He never had a chance. Sometimes you're too pigheaded for your own good."

The critical words sounded oddly like a compliment. The strength they inspired allowed Sarah the freedom to vent her temper.

"Those bastards!" She thumped her fists against him.

"Sarah!" Hawk pushed her away, gripping her by the shoulders and zeroing his gaze in on hers. "I don't think I like hearing you curse."

"What would you call them?"

"That and worse. But you're a lady. I don't expect that kind of language from you."

"A lady?" A derisive laugh bubbled up in her throat at the misnomer. "If I hadn't been living my life out of my aunts' etiquette books, and had paid more attention to how the real world works, I'd never have gotten us into this mess in the first place."

He seized her chin between his thumb and forefinger and tipped it up. His anger vibrated along with hers. "This isn't your fault."

"Isn't it? If I'd listened to you and half of Marysville a month ago, we wouldn't be here!"

"Schoolmarm . . . " His voice dropped to a dangerous purr, and the darkness in his eyes flickered. "Guilt is a terrible load to bear. And yours is misplaced. You can only do what you think is best at any given time, and let your conscience guide you."

"What do you know about guilt?" She jerked her chin away from his touch, heedless of the growing storm in his eyes. "You'd be out of here by now if it weren't for us. You'd never have come in the first place. . . . "

"I let a man die, Sarah."

She shook her head, confused. The cool stoicism in his voice mocked his words. "What, Hernandez? He was alive? I thought you said the fire—"

"No. My best friend. Five years ago, right here on Tenebrosa. I let him die."

187

Chapter Nine

"You let your best friend die?"

Sarah pulled away and rubbed her hands up and down her arms. An uneasy chill permeated the humid air around her. Hawk was a rescuer, a soldier who defended his country, a leader who guided his community. He couldn't be capable of such a violation of trust.

And yet the absolute blackness shadowing his eyes warned her to believe that he was.

She hugged herself and stared at him, waiting for him to contradict the expression on his rugged features. He didn't.

"I know all about guilt," he said. "I should have found the colonel and saved him. But I didn't."

"But if his death was in the line of duty?" She wanted to find an acceptable explanation for his guilt.

"My duty was to get him off this island. I didn't.

I had to go back to Kansas City and tell his wife and baby girl he wouldn't be home for Christmas. *That's* guilt."

Beneath the hushed anger in his voice, Sarah heard something else. A mournful plea. A heart breaking beneath the weight of so much condemnation. The soul of a man living in torment.

Her own soul responded to that plea, and she reached out to him. "I'm sorry."

Hawk's gaze burned holes in her peace offering. She curled her fingers into her palm and tucked her hand beneath her crossed arms.

"Your girls are still alive. Salazar's the villain here, not you. Put your guilt aside and concentrate on how much your students look up to you. If you want something to worry about, you worry about me. About whether or not I can get you home."

She lifted her gaze from the muddy tips of his black boots. "Is that why you're acting so strangely? I'm not worried about your abilities. I trust you."

"Do you?" Something darker than the night flashed in his eyes. "I tried to strangle you in Meczaquatl's tomb, didn't I? Haven't you ended up pushing me away every time I kiss you? Is that a sign of trust?"

"But that's not your fault. I—"

"Go back to the others." He silenced her by refusing to listen. Angling sideways to avoid touching her, he slid up to the cab of the truck. "Tell Raul we'll set up camp in the road. Get a fire going. I'll be up as soon as I do what I can here."

Stung by his dismissal, Sarah watched him pull the charred body from the cab and gently carry the smaller man to the bed of the truck, where he laid him down and unfolded a blanket. Was it guilt that made Hawk give such tender care to a man who had left him for dead? He tucked the blanket securely around the body, then went back to the cab to retrieve whatever was left of Hernandez's personal belongings.

Was it guilt that made Hawk say such magical things to her, that he'd seen her in a vision, and credited her with a strength she didn't feel? Was it guilt that made him kiss her? Hold her? That made her feel desirable and powerful and cherished?

Was it guilt that brought him into her life in the first place?

Walter had been kind to her, had said pretty things. She'd been naive and slow to learn, but eventually she figured out that Walter's interest had been based purely on financial opportunity. Her naivete then had resulted in the humiliating destruction of her heart and ego.

Her fragile sense of self had been slow to heal. But with Hawk—his spirit, his touch, his words—she found herself making a miraculous, if hard-fought, recovery. Had she foolishly fallen for another man who saw her only as a means to an end? A man who was using her to make retribution for the perceived sins of his past?

Was she a poor student who never learned from her mistakes? She'd either chosen the wrong man a second time, or she was letting a last chance at love slip through her fingers because she was too much of a coward to fight for it.

No matter what, she'd lose.

"Damn it, schoolmarm, quit looking at me like that and get the hell out of here."

Snared in the endless night of his eyes, Sarah realized she'd been staring. Her eyes burned with the need to blink, as if she'd been afraid that looking away would make something she wanted disappear.

But Hawk could never really be hers.

She forced her eyes to close and turned away. She could hear the quiet, efficient sounds of him returning to his work behind her. She'd walked away from her heart before.

Walter's patronizing voice intruded on her thoughts. She trampled through the underbrush, blazing her own path up the hill, trying to drown out the painful scene unfolding in her memory.

"I'm warning you, Sarah. Nobody's lined up at your door waiting for you. You throw this away and you'll have nothing. I'm as good for you as you are for me."

"But what about love, Walter?"

"I love you, sweetie, you know that."

"Do you love Wendy, too?"

He smiled at her with that boyish little tilt of the mouth that usually turned her knees to mush and made her forget the common sense drilled into her since childhood. "Wendy's not the woman I plan to marry."

"But she's the woman you sleep with." Sarah went to the sink and plunged her hands into the sudsy water. If she didn't keep them busy, she'd be wringing Walter's neck.

"I told you, you misunderstood. We work for the same company. It's inevitable that we'll have meetings together when I'm out on the road." He moved behind her and wrapped his dish towel around her waist, pulling her back against him in a cutesy maneuver that made her feel imprisoned instead of embraced. "Don't worry, sweetie. I have the utmost respect for you. I want to have kids. I

promise to show you all about making love after we're married."

Sarah shifted out of his grasp and moved away, dripping water over the counter as she reached for the skillet on the stove. "I don't think it's respect that keeps you from making love to me before the wedding."

"It's true you have a lot to learn, but you'll do fine once you learn to relax and enjoy letting a man touch you."

"Maybe I would if it was a man I trusted."

Sarah stopped in her tracks so suddenly that she had to grab a nearby tree to keep her balance. "A man I trust . . . " she murmured out loud.

Hawk had kindled a fire in her by simply touching his thumb to her lips. Walter's lengthy courtship hadn't made her feel any more desirable than just a brief, direct glance from Hawk did. Walter's kisses made her feel clumsy and naive. Hawk's kisses made her feel womanly and whole.

He didn't need to believe in her trust.

She did.

"Hawk?" The heavy weight of the air absorbed the breathy substance of her plea.

She'd stumbled down this hill with the petty goal of finding out what made him so moody. And now she was slinking away, knowing she had contributed to his justified silence, even if she wasn't the direct cause, knowing she could help him if she cared enough to stay.

Walter might have robbed her of her confidence. But he hadn't taken away her ability to care.

Sarah had no idea what to say to Hawk, but she

knew that running away wouldn't help her find the words.

She slid down the slope on her feet, praying for divine inspiration to tell her what to say or do. But then she hit the clearing, and saw that she'd been saying the wrong prayers.

Hawk stood at the rear of the truck, holding a shiny gold object in his hands. The late-afternoon sunlight glinted halolike off the burnished artifact. He stared down at it, transfixed by its lustrous beauty.

Sarah stared too, caught by the mesmerizing glow that soaked the atmosphere around it. The air above Hawk's hands quivered, as though distorted by rising heat. His glassy eyes seemed to absorb the unnatural distortion, hypnotizing him.

Just like . . .

"Hawk!"

Sarah screamed his name. Startled by the sound, a flock of brightly colored birds screeched and took wing. He never so much as blinked. She moved a step closer and called to him again.

Another storm was building high in the sky. The churning pocket of low pressure dropped the temperature below ninety degrees. But the chill that shivered down Sarah's spine wasn't forged by Mother Nature. It emanated from the circle in Hawk's hands, luring his shaman powers and the essence of the man who owned them down into its frozen depths.

"Hawk?" She reached up and touched his cheek. The chiseled angles felt as cold as the copper granite they resembled. She molded her palm against the beloved planes. "Can you hear me?"

A tremor vibrated along his jaw.

"How can I help you?" she asked.

A sickening familiarity was reflected in the shadowy hollows of his eyes. "Get away from here," he said in a raspy voice.

The chill where she touched him ran along her fingertips and down her arm. Sensing the helplessness of his paralyzing stupor, Sarah shook her head. "I'm not leaving without you."

"He's so angry." His voice broke on a desperate plea. "He doesn't want us here."

"Who?"

Guided by an instinct beyond her conscious thought, Sarah wrapped her fingers around the gold artifact and gently pried it from his grasp.

"Mecza . . . "

Still holding his cheek in her right hand, she slowly set the the small tiaralike object on the bumper of the truck. "Meczaquatl?"

The void in his eyes brightened and he forced his gaze up to hers. "Gave it to her . . . "

Sarah nodded, pretending she understood. She backed away, pulling Hawk along with her. "Come with me."

"So angry . . . " His first step jerked.

"That's it." She clutched his hand and stroked his cheek. "Just another step."

"Didn't honor death . . . " He worked his mouth and swallowed, as though battling a parched throat. "He . . . killed . . . sacrifice."

"Hawk, please. Don't talk now." Sarah begged him to listen. She coaxed him along to the foot of the hill, and he followed her like a wary panther on a leash made of sweet words and tender touches.

Partway up the hill, Hawk's resistance weakened. His stealthy grace returned, and she quickened their pace. She remembered the wild run they'd had escaping from the tomb and figured the more distance they put between Hawk and the wreck, the safer they'd be.

"Just a bit farther." She wished she knew his given name or had the right to use an endearment, some special word that would have more significance than any other. A word that would wake him from this trance and bring him back to her.

With her back to the slope behind her, Sarah stepped on a moss-covered rock face of smooth black basalt. Her boot slipped. Her feet flew out from under her, and she and Hawk went down in a tangle of arms and legs. Their combined weight acted like an anchor, but they slid only a few feet until friction stopped them on a damp bed of ferns and fronds.

In a swift spasm of reaction, Hawk levered himself onto his elbows above her. He squeezed his eyes shut and shook his head. Trapped flat on the ground beneath him, Sarah had no choice but to watch the tortured constriction of muscles across his face as man battled demon. His eyes snapped open, dark and compelling as ever, but without the shadowy dullness that had polluted them down by the truck. The man had won.

Exhaling an aching sigh of relief, Sarah brushed the midnight waterfall of hair behind his ear and trailed her fingertips along his stubborn jaw. "Welcome back."

"Did he hurt you? Did I hurt you?" Propelled by a sudden impulse, Hawk shifted onto his side and ran his hands up and down her body. With rough, tender, protective touches, he checked her face, arms, legs, stomach and neck.

Each brush of his fingers, every probing pressure woke a part of her body. As if her senses had been asleep, her blood rushed to each pulse point, overriding her fear for his safety. With Hawk's body pressed to her side, his strong hand at her hip, he felt as solid and vital as the earth itself. Sarah melted into him, like the rain that sinks into the dust. She caught her breath and drank in the green smell of the damp trees and Hawk's own earthy scent. A whirlwind of sensations built up inside her, as natural as the elements, and as powerful as the gathering storm.

But before the clouds burst open and she embarrassed herself with an inappropriate response, she folded his hand between both of hers and pressed it close to her heart. "We fell. I lost my footing, and with you off balance, too, I couldn't recover. I'll have a few bumps and bruises. But that's from my own klutziness, not you."

His inky gaze traveled down the length of his arm to the juncture of their hands above her left breast. She wondered if he could feel the hammering of her heart in her chest. She glanced down, too, and trembled at the intensity of her reaction to this intimate touch. But before she could decide whether to protest or welcome him, he rolled onto his back, carrying her on top of him. He swallowed her up in a crushing hug, breathing raggedly in a sporadic rhythm that sounded almost like crying.

Draped like a rag doll over him, from his chest to his ankles, Sarah wondered if she had the backbone to allow him this comfort without giving in to her own simmering needs.

"Hawk?" She tried to scoot away, but he squeezed her tighter, locking her in his desperate embrace.

"No." He buried his nose in the crown of her

hair and breathed in deeply. "Just let me hold you for a minute. Please. I was cold. So damn cold. I need your light and warmth. I need to hold on to you."

The husky plea in his voice couldn't have spoken more eloquently to her heart. Allowing herself the rare privilege, Sarah laid aside her doubts. She refused to think about the past or worry about the future. Right now, for these few moments, she let her love for Hawk shine through. She freed her arms and wound them around his neck, clinging to him with the same fierce possessiveness with which his arms held her.

"As long as you need me," she promised, her voice shaky with the emotion behind that vow. "I'm here as long as you need me."

Three hours later, with the predictably heavy thunderstorm caking the dust on his boots into mud, Hawk roamed the perimeter of their makeshift camp. The solid wall of rain that blocked out the light from the stars and moon would also keep the predators at bay.

If they were man or beast.

An uneasy apprehension propelled his footsteps through the darkness. Something was pursuing them. Something far more dangerous than smugglers. Far more unpredictable than the hazards of the jungle.

Alive with hatred and grief and confusion, yet not alive.

Attuned to Hawk and his accursed intuitive powers.

Afraid of Sarah.

He pulled the black band from his forehead and laughed, a deep, hollow sound, devoid of real humor. Sweet Sarah, that little slip of a thing, dainty and delicate and delectable, from the soft new curls that framed her face down to the demure pedicure on her toes, shouldn't be able to frighten an annoying fly.

Yet she had stood up to seasoned criminals. She had risked her life to protect her children. She had cleansed the vengeful spirit from Hawk's sensitive aura.

She had turned his solitary life upside down and made him fall in love.

Hawk stopped beneath a canopy of milk vine and slowly exhaled. Did she have any idea what kind of impact she had on the world? On him?

As long as you need me.

She'd been talking about Meczaquatl's influence over him. She'd stay at his side and fight the demon she couldn't possibly understand because it was necessary for his survival, and therefore for hers. She saw him as a protector, said she believed in him. And maybe, on that level, she did. She depended on him to be an anchor in her time of crisis, a rudder to steer her safely back to civilization.

But he was more than that. He was a man.

A man who terrified her. Even before de Vega had assaulted her, she'd been afraid. Despite a physical attraction, or maybe it was naive curiosity on her part, she'd been afraid. It radiated with the bitter tang of copper from her aura.

For a moment he considered that he'd been too rough with his kisses, too frank in his admiration for her. Too unsettling with his strange abilities. But he suspected there was more to her reticence in accepting him than old-fashioned, ladylike shyness.

As long as you need me.

The man in him wanted her forever. But he sensed she wouldn't be willing to give him that. Did he even have the right to ask? Maybe he could give her the time and space she needed to work through whatever troubled her. Court her slowly and keep a respectful distance until she was ready to trust him.

But concessions had never worked in the past. His job with the corps or his shaman spirituality or his guilt over losing Jonathan had always gotten in the way of lasting relationships. Would he be content to share a few brief encounters of genuine passion with Sarah and then move on?

Would he be disappointed in her if his sweet, shy lady said yes to such a decadent proposition?

Hawk squeezed the excess water from his headband and tied it back in place to help shield his eyes from the rain. Avoiding her hadn't changed the truth any. He loved her. He wanted her. And like the prophecy in his vision, he understood that he needed her.

Forever had never been a real possibility for him. He couldn't give it himself; he couldn't expect it from others. But for the first time since he was a child, having forever with someone mattered.

With Sarah, it mattered.

He smelled her rain-soft scent moments before he heard her speak. "Hungry?" she asked, pointing a misshapen, foil-wrapped bar of chocolate in his direction. "You didn't eat anything at dinner."

She stood beside him beneath the overhang, close enough to be shielded from most of the rain, far enough away so he couldn't touch her without moving. Despite the friendly overture, he felt her cautious distance like a verbal reprimand.

She'd withdrawn into her shell again, protecting herself as best she could. But from what? If he said he needed her, would she drop those defensive walls again?

"I'll save the trail mix for you and the girls. I grabbed a snack when I was out on patrol."

"What did you eat?" she asked, tightening her wool blanket around her shoulders. "Bugs?"

Hawk did know of several varieties of edible grubs and arthropods, but he'd opted for a vegetarian meal over their obvious source of protein. Sarah's dubious scowl gave him the boyish urge to kiss the crinkled tip of her nose. "Not this time," he answered.

"Will we have to eat bugs?"

The look of absolute ick on her face was priceless. And irresistible. He reached out, and with a single finger tucked a toffee-rich curl behind her ear. "It won't come to that for several days," he reassured her. "And we'll be home by then."

Her shoulders lifted and sank with a sigh of relief. And though she hadn't resisted, he pulled his hand away.

She had no reason to stay, now that he'd rejected her offer of food. But he wasn't ready for her to leave just yet. "The main thing is that we don't dehydrate. A person can survive several days longer without food than they can without water."

"I wish we had a better way to collect some of this rain," she said. "I told the girls to set out their cups, but it's coming down so hard, the water splashes back out. I just want to turn my face up to the sky and let it wash down my throat."

She imitated her words, and the graceful arch of her neck drew his awareness like a winged raptor spotting its prey. Hawk clamped down on the talons of desire that stabbed through him and forced his gaze away, not wanting to scare her off. "Water isn't the only liquid source out there. But I don't want any of you sampling anything natural unless I check it out first. There's a lot of poison out there. But there's also a lot of good."

Seeing that he had her attention, Hawk took out his knife and pulled down one of the overhanging vines. He hacked it twice, cutting a deep gash down to the core. He sheathed his knife and broke the vine in two. A milky white substance dripped out. Hawk tipped his head and shook several swallows of the bitter, sticky liquid into his mouth.

"Its nickname is milk vine. It's a good way to quench your thirst. Here."

Hawk pulled the vine down to Sarah, and squeezed and shook it until a steady stream of sap trickled out. The first drop hit her chin, but then she stepped closer and caught the drink in her mouth.

"It tastes like a tree."

"It'll taste like manna if you're truly thirsty." Hawk helped himself to another sip of the reviving fluid before tipping the ends up and tucking the vine out of the way.

"You're sure you don't want any of this?" Again Sarah held out the candy bar, an innocent gesture that bordered on temptation for Hawk.

"Only if you'll share it with me," he countered.

His agreement earned him a smile. "Good. I want to get rid of the taste of that milk vine. Besides, what goes better with milk than chocolate?"

Sarah sat down on an outcropping of rock and divided the candy in half. Hawk settled on the ground beside her. He took a bite and watched as she quickly devoured three sections of chocolate.

"Mmm. Much better aftertaste," she critiqued between chews, politely covering her mouth with her fingers. She must have felt the milk vine's residue then. Stretching her cheek, she tried to wipe it clean. But Hawk had a better view of the mess than she did. He reached up and touched her jaw, then rubbed his thumb across her chin and bottom lip.

He froze when she did, his thumb on the sensuous curve of her smile, his fingers on the delicate arch of her throat. Her breathless gasp provided the only sound beneath the steady drumbeat of rain around them. The storm cocooned them on three sides. With their backs to an unbending wall of rock, Hawk felt detached from the rest of the world, secluded from the Salazars and spirits and ghosts from their pasts that threatened to rip Sarah right out of his world.

"Are the kids asleep?" He eventually found his voice, but the rest of his body couldn't seem to put any distance between them.

Sarah nodded. "They were out almost as soon as we put up the tarp."

"You should be with them," he cautioned her. "You've got a hell of a long walk tomorrow."

"And you don't?"

He locked onto her hazel eyes and glimpsed a stubborn determination glowing in their depths. "I'm used to the rigors of survival, Sarah. You're not."

With an arrogant tip of her chin, she broke the connection between them. But the way she huddled inside her blanket spoke of a vulnerability her bold words couldn't hide.

"I couldn't sleep if I wanted to," she said, staring into the dark. "This has been the longest day of my life. I don't think I could ever go back to . . . to . . . "

Her words faltered. She glanced down at him, her eyes and aura beseeching him in a way that no man could resist.

Instinctively protecting her, loving her, Hawk stood up and pulled the poncho he'd been wearing off his shoulders. He spread it on the ground and then reached for her. She walked into his embrace without a protest, without a single word of doubt or a flicker of mistrust in her eyes. He palmed the side of her head and pressed her cheek against his heart.

Her folded arms between them kept him from pulling her as close as he would like. But he crooned soothing words to her and stroked her back, treating her with the same tender patience he'd use to calm a skittish wild animal. Gradually he felt the stiffness drain out of her. She shifted, and he felt her fingers clutching at his vest and shirt, searching for a grip that suited her. The blanket fell from her shoulders and she shrugged, trying to catch it in the crook of her arms. She grew fidgety, restless. She couldn't be comforted.

Hawk stepped back and clasped her shoulders, stilling her struggles. She looked up at him, her aura alight with a spectrum of color. But he could read the turbulent emotions in her hazel eyes, flashing green and gold at the same time. Her gaze sought something from him, something he could read and understand more easily than she even knew how to ask.

He dropped his hands, but maintained unblinking contact with her eyes. He unzipped his vest and dropped it to the ground. He untangled the blanket from her arms and then knelt at her feet. She angled her gaze to his uplifted hand, and after several silent moments, folded her own hands around it and knelt on the poncho beside him.

Such shaky trust. But a courageous gesture all the same. Hawk shook the blanket, then wrapped them both inside it, pulling Sarah into his arms as he sat back against the rock. She nestled against him, tucking her head beneath his chin. She splayed her fingers across his chest, digging the tips in slightly to anchor herself, finding peace.

"A little body heat won't hurt us tonight," he whispered. "I can't risk your going into delayed shock or exhaustion."

She burrowed a little closer, as if his words upset her or made her think when she didn't want to. He waited in silence for several minutes, treasuring the opportunity to hold her this way. Though they were relatively dry in their makeshift shelter, the dampness in the air around them brought out the dank smell of wool and the uniquely feminine scent of soap and freshness in Sarah's hair. Something deep inside Hawk unclenched and dropped its guard. If he could dream himself to a contented place, this would be it. The soldier and the schoolmarm. Man and woman. Hawk and Sarah.

"Can I ask you something?" she murmured. Her lips whispered like a caress against his neck.

That unguarded place shivered with awareness. "I don't know if I can be as objective as a counselor needs to be with you. But if you need to talk, I'll listen."

Her lips moved again, and he imagined he could feel her smiling. "I don't think it's the counselor I need to talk to."

Hawk closed his eyes to block out her aura. He wanted to be able to listen to what was in her heart, and not judge her by any subtext she might not wish to reveal. "I'll still listen," he offered.

"What happened this afternoon at the truck?"

Even without his powers, he sensed she was avoiding something. Or maybe this was her roundabout way of getting to what she needed to discuss. "To Hernandez or me?"

Truth be told, he didn't think the causes were all that dissimilar.

"You're the one I worried about."

"Me?"

Her right hand moved on his chest, tracing random circles. Nerves, he told himself. "When you held that crown in your hands, it was like you were . . . possessed. Your eyes looked so dull and lifeless. I didn't think you were with me anymore."

He covered her hand and stilled it. He didn't want to answer these questions. Didn't want her to know these things about him. But how could he be anything less than honest when she was so bravely opening herself up to him?

"One of my powers . . . as a shaman . . . " He tilted his face up to the heavens and willed his spirit guide and creator to strengthen him on this difficult journey. "I'm attuned to the spirit world. Through many of my visions I have visited there. It makes me one with them sometimes. They can channel through me to this world. I can feel their presence, even when they don't wish to communicate. Much like I can read the energy fields that surround people."

When he dared to open his eyes and read the skepticism on her face, he found Sarah propped up on one elbow, looking at him, her eyes shimmering an iridescent green beneath a veil of unshed tears.

"They use you?" she asked.

"Oh, honey . . . " He brushed her cheek and caught a teardrop where it began to fall. He had expected censure or denial or more curious questions. He had never expected compassion. He never realized how much he needed it.

He tunneled his fingers into her hair and brought her closer. He kissed away the salty moisture from her eyelids, then lowered his head to her mouth. The kiss was gentle, healing, reverent. And the shy pressure of her response catapulted him from the role of healer to patient. He held her close and gratefully accepted her restorative touch on his mouth.

Humbled by her generous gift, Hawk ended the kiss and brought her to rest on top of him, hugging her slender form in his big arms until he thought she might snap. He didn't have the words to thank her for believing in him.

The tremulous flutter in her whisper told him that the kiss had been as soul-shattering for her. "At the tomb, the king's spirit was using you to see into this world?"

"He felt violated." Hawk feathered her hair through his fingers and begged apology for his actions there. "He thought you were the intruder who had disturbed his rest. That's why I tried to kill you."

"*He* tried to kill me. *You* saved my life by getting me out of there." The distinction in her words thawed a hurtful place around his heart. He almost missed the hesitancy in her next question. "So why didn't he try to hurt me at the truck?"

"He's awake now. Fully aware. He knows that Salazar and his men are responsible for stealing his treasures and disturbing his eternal rest." Despite the melding of their bodies beneath the blanket, Hawk felt the blood run colder in his veins. "I believe he killed Hernandez somehow, and he's pursuing the others. I felt the resonance of his presence in that crown. It's something important to him. Something that, if he were a physical entity, he wouldn't leave behind."

"So when I took it away from you, that broke the connection?"

"You touched the crown?"

She nodded. "I pried it from your fingers so I could lead you out of there. It seemed to hypnotize you as long as you held it."

He'd been cold before, but now his soul bottomed out like Arctic ice. Sarah must have sensed the change in him. She stiffened as if his chill touched her, too. "Didn't I do the right thing?"

Hawk captured her head between his hands, roughly framing her face and forcing her to look at him. "You didn't feel it? His hatred? The pain? That need for retribution?"

Her eyes widened in fear. "No. I just set it down. I wanted to help you."

"And you did. I couldn't break free. But . . . "

"But what?"

"I don't know." Hawk sighed deeply and loosened his hold. Sarah trembled above him. Only a real bastard would scare Sarah the way he just had, and he never wanted anything or anyone, especially himself, ever to cause her to doubt herself or be afraid. He relaxed and rolled over, laying Sarah on the ground cover. He lay on his side next to her and tucked the blanket securely around her.

"There's an answer there somewhere," he tried to explain in calmer tones. "Something with you or that crown makes a difference to Meczaquatl. He may never rest until we figure it out."

He brushed a curl off her forehead and kissed the spot, trying to atone for his behavior. "I know you must have some power over him. You've reached me each time he . . . took over. I don't understand it yet, but I'm grateful."

Sarah's hands fluttered to the edge of the blanket, pulling it up to her chin. "Is that why you held me like that? After the tomb, and on the hillside? Because I keep the evil spirits away? Is that why you like to hold me?"

Chapter Ten

"You're joking, right?"

Hawk hovered in silence above her, waiting for her answer. He hoped she'd smile and bat her eyes, let him know this subtle turn in the conversation was a display of feminine wile, staged for his benefit to elicit a compliment or put him off until she grew more comfortable having him so physically close to her.

But Sarah had never been a teaser. Finding the words to express herself might prove challenging at times, but she'd yet to speak words that weren't true to her heart. His radar tapped into the underlying question she had asked. Not why did holding her help him resist Meczaquatl's influence. But why *her*. The fact that she'd mentioned it at all put him on alert. It made him wary, and absolutely positive that the issue needed to be resolved now, or it would fester and grow, paralyzing the fragile trust blossoming between them.

But he'd stopped to analyze his observations a fraction too long. Something about his utter stillness must have alarmed her. Her fingers clenched and unclenched on the blanket, creasing it with wrinkles similar to the lines of apology marring her face. "Don't get me wrong. I'm glad I can help you. I will, no matter what. It's just that . . . I was curious."

"Curious?"

Hazel eyes met midnight and she flinched. Suddenly she was pushing at the blanket and rolling away. "I can't have this conversation."

Hawk caught her by the shoulder and pulled her back down. He threw his leg across her thighs and pinned her beside him. His Sarah had proven herself time and again to be a woman of courage. He wouldn't let her back away from this challenge.

"I think we'd better."

"I'm sorry. I shouldn't have asked."

She squirmed beneath him and pushed at his chest. He would have released her at once if he hadn't sensed the halfhearted effort behind her struggles. Something inside her was killing her, like the mother Kodiak with her heart ripped out. She wanted to share this. She needed to. But acknowledging that need humiliated her.

She waged an inner battle as savagely soul-stealing as his war with Meczaquatl, though he suspected her demon came from a source much closer to earth. If Hawk didn't force her to deal with it now, she might bury the hurt so deeply that it could never get out, and his beautiful, brave she-bear would slowly die from the inside.

"Sarah." The fists that had pushed against him now clutched handfuls of his shirtfront. She lay still beneath him, staring up at her own hands. "Why would I hold you for any other reason than that I wanted to? I needed to?"

"People need each other for a lot of reasons."

"They do," he agreed. "Sex, for one."

Color stained her cheeks immediately, and he heartened at the speed of her healthy response.

"What about warmth? And comfort? Human compassion?" He released her shoulder and covered one of her hands with his own. "What about a need so strong in here to connect with another person, or else you'll waste away and die? To have somebody see you and accept you for what you are?"

She blinked twice, long, languid brushes of caramel lashes on her creamy, smooth cheeks. And then she lifted her gaze to his. Awash in green and gold and sparked with a tremulous hope, her eyes met his. She looked into him. She wanted to listen. She wanted to understand.

Hawk swallowed hard, awed by her willingness to trust, humbled by the responsibility she gave him. He chose his next words very carefully. "When I hold you I forget about my demons. I'm so turned on and lucky and grateful, I think like a man. I react like a man. Not something weird or outcast."

"Do . . . do you think I'm attractive?"

She held his gaze as if it were the riskiest thing she had ever done. Hawk stared back in disbelief. A tiny kernel of resentment took root inside him, licked slowly through his veins. Someone had done something awful to this woman. His woman.

She'd been hurt. Purposefully or carelessly, she'd had a wound inflicted in the most vulnerable part of her—her shy sense of self. He gritted his teeth and concentrated on keeping his face smooth and expressionless while rage spiraled through him. He knew an uncharacteristically violent urge to ram his fist down the nameless destroyer's throat. He turned his focus to his hands, willing them to remain gentle where they touched her.

"If I didn't know you better," he said, his voice barely more than a whisper, "I'd think you were fishing for compliments. But you're not that type."

She nodded and dropped her gaze. Her brave light faded and she began to slip back into her protective shell. "I'm not like other women."

"No, you're not." Giving in to a flare of temper, he grabbed her chin and made her look at him. "You're special."

"That's not true!"

"You're calling me a liar?"

She snatched at his wrist to pull his hand away, but he clearly outmatched her strength. He held on gently, without fear of losing his grip. She stopped tugging at him, but tightened her fingers around his arm. "No, it's . . . you're being kind. You're a nice man. You would be."

She wanted to reason away his compliment? He'd been as patient as a counselor could be and had gotten nowhere. She'd claimed she needed to talk to the man in him earlier. That man in him surged forth, giving vent to temper and need.

"Who did this to you?" He heard the edge in his own voice, saw it reflected in the widening of her eyes. "Who made you think you were anything less than beautiful and desirable and perfect?"

"I'm not—"

"Stop saying that!" He brushed her hair off her forehead, atoning for the harshness in his voice. Then he opened up his heart and let all the emotion stored there speak for him.

"You want to know what I think?" He dropped his gaze to the unadorned lushness of her lips. She caught her breath and they parted. Hawk stroked her bottom lip with his thumb, loving the soft suppleness beneath his callused touch. "I think you have the sexiest mouth I've ever seen on a woman."

And then, because she needed him to, because he needed to, he moved his thumb and covered the spot with his mouth. He apologized for his temper, praised her, beseeched her. He tasted and stroked, wooing her gently, urgently, begging for a response.

He felt the telltale pressure of her fingers clutching at him. She angled her face slightly, and then she lifted her mouth to his. The combustion was instantaneous. A gratifying rush of triumph flowed through him. He pushed her mouth open and deepened the kiss. She tasted of chocolate, a womanly confection whose essence was sweeter than any he had ever known. He savored her a moment longer, then drew his mouth away to sample the smooth, creamy skin along the delicate curve of her jaw.

Her hands fluttered over his chest, up across his neck and face, and then in a bold move that delighted him, she buried her fingers in his hair and pulled his mouth back to hers. Hawk dutifully obeyed, gave her all she asked for and more.

While they explored each other's mouths, teaching and learning about pleasure, Hawk ran his hand down the graceful column of her throat. His fingers slipped lower, discovering the soft neckline of a black cotton T-shirt. His shirt on her. His scent on her. Something powerful and primitive exploded in his veins.

He tipped her head back and ran his tongue along the path his fingers had traced. He kissed the warm pulse point at the base of her neck, and moved his hand lower to cover her breast. Through cotton and lace and ladylike inhibition, she swelled beneath the warmth of his palm. He squeezed her once, learning her size and shape, marveling at the perfection of nature that made them the right proportion for the slender contours of her body.

"I love how you respond to me," he praised her. "Such a lady with the rest of the world, but like fire when I kiss you." He slipped his mouth lower and drew the sensitized peak into his mouth.

"You shouldn't—" She gasped aloud, as startled by her body's immediate reaction as he. Eager to know more of her, he tugged at the hem of the shirt, pulling it free. He spread his hand across her middle, his splayed fingers nearly spanning her rib cage. She was so delicate, so feminine, and the soft skin beneath his hard palm felt hot to the touch.

His body throbbed in anticipation. He skimmed his hand upward beneath the shirt and found the treasure he sought encased in satin and lace. She whimpered with the first stroke of his tongue there. Hawk pushed the material aside and laved the protruding bead, filling his mouth with her. Filling his mind and his heart with nothing but Sarah.

Her hands flailed at his shoulders. "They're too small," he heard with the tap of one weak fist. She gasped when he moved his attentions to the other breast. "You'll be disappoint—"

"They're perfect." Anger warred with the desire humming through his body, making his voice a ragged breath of air. "Any bigger would mar their natural beauty, in such perfect harmony with the rest of your body."

"But Walter said—"

"He's an idiot. A fool." Hawk lifted his mouth to hers, taking in the dazed wonder of her hooded eyes before claiming her mouth in a searing stake of possession.

His blood thundered into a roar inside his ears. His senses filled with the fresh woman scent of her. His mouth gloried in her sweet, passion-drugged taste. He drowned out the sound of another man's name on her lips and filled himself with the heady knowledge of her clutching, demanding fingers paying no heed to the caution in her words.

He ran his hand down her side, roughly skimming her exposed breast and searching lower, finding the feminine indentation of her waist and sliding down to cup the flaring earth-mother cradle of her hip. He pulled her into the vee of his legs, pinning her most feminine center beneath his most masculine response to her.

Hawk groaned at the sheer, nearly painful delight of the friction between them. Unable to help himself, he rubbed against her. Sarah caught her breath and pressed her face into his neck, riding

215

the same physical tidal wave that threatened to carry him away.

"Don't you know what a turn-on you are?" He rasped the question into her ear, kissed her temple, clasped her in his embrace. "I know what it costs you because you're shy, but you respond as if you can't help yourself, as if you're so turned on by me you can't resist. As if I'm the only man you've ever kissed this way."

"You are."

She whispered the admission, soft as the abating rain, against his sun-roughened skin. She pulled her fingers from his hair and curled them into the collar of his shirt. Hawk recognized the symptoms of withdrawal. Though stretched out beneath him, he imagined her curling into a ball deep within herself.

Hawk lifted his head to study her face. Her lips were pink and swollen, branded with the imprint of his kisses. Her hair fell in a wildly sexy disarray around her face. But her eyes were unreadable. Downcast, they were looking at her own hands again.

"What's wrong?" He touched his forehead to hers, inhaling deeply, knowing his body would have a difficult time recovering from this passion, this unbridled need for her. But he suspected his heart would have an even more difficult time, judging by the quivering hesitancy of her bottom lip.

"I . . . you want something more, don't you?"

"Yes," he answered simply and honestly. "But not until you're ready."

A horrible eternity passed in silence, only a moment of real time, but long enough for Hawk to finally fully understand the damage done to this woman.

"I may never be ready. When I was engaged, there were certain things . . . certain aspects of our relationship that took me a while to warm up to."

"You mean sex?" He wished he could retract the bluntness of his question. He wished he had Walter Kensit's neck between his hands.

Her cheeks colored with a rosy blush. "We never . . . I never . . . "

"I suspected you were a virgin."

The heightened color drained from her cheeks. "It's that obvious?"

"Because of your morals, your outlook. Not because there's a stamp on your forehead. That doesn't make you undesirable. If anything, it adds to your appeal. You're waiting for the right man. It makes me hope that *I'm* the right man. I can scarcely hide how badly I want you." Hawk shifted slightly, easing the pressure on their lower bodies.

She might be inexperienced, but she was no prude. She clearly understood the evidence between them. "But Walter said . . . "

"What the hell did Walter say to make you believe there's something wrong with you?"

Her gaze flashed up and met his; she seemed startled by his anger, but not yet persuaded by it. "He didn't. I . . . he wanted . . . " She smoothed the collar of his shirt absentmindedly. "I couldn't . . . "

A hard and painful knot of compassion cooled the unfulfilled needs of his body. "Did you like the way he touched you?"

He waited patiently while she chose her words. "I thought it was kind of fun at first. It was all so new. But then, sometimes, I wanted something . . . "

"He didn't listen to your wants?"

"I didn't have any experience. What did I know?"

"You know what feels good to you and what doesn't." He mimicked her soothing motion, stroking the hair at her temple behind her ear.

"Sometimes I felt trapped. It wasn't . . . and he wouldn't stop."

His hand froze and his blood boiled with thoughts of vengeance. "Did he force you?"

She reached up and wrapped her long fingers around his, protecting him from his own vile thoughts. "No. Never. He just . . . lost interest. He found someone who could give a man what he needed."

Hawk couldn't speak for several minutes. But when Sarah began to squirm, he knew he had to get past his anger so she wouldn't misinterpret his silence as acknowledgment of her perceived deficiencies. "He found someone who gave a self-ish egomaniac what *he* wanted. Making love is a two-way street, Sarah. If both partners don't enjoy it, then that's not making love. That's taking. Using. Making love between a man and a woman should be all about giving."

He turned his hand and squeezed her fingers. "Have I done anything that scares you? Or makes you uncomfortable?"

"No. That's just it . . . " She cupped his jaw in the feminine strength of her hands, reassuring him with her touch as much as her words. "I like when you touch me. I love the way you kiss me, too."

Her moment of bravado faded into a whisper.

"I just don't want to disappoint you."

"You couldn't, schoolmarm."

He was relieved to know he hadn't hurt her, hadn't reminded her of Kensit or her encounter with de Vega. But the tension that goaded him refused to drain away.

"Sarah, how long were you engaged to your fiancé?"

"A year and a half. Whirlwind courtship, huh?" She tried to laugh at her own irony, but the weak sound found no answer in him.

"In all that time, didn't he once tell you that you were beautiful?"

She stiffened in his arms, and he had his answer before she spoke. "There was no reason for him to."

He rolled over and sat up, bringing her with him. He made himself as comfortable as he could with the rock at his back, pledging silently to be there the whole night through for Sarah. Wishing he could pledge something more.

He tucked her head beneath his chin, pulled down her shirt and covered her with the blanket. He held her as tightly as he dared without breaking her. But he knew he couldn't hold her securely enough to erase all her doubts. That would take time. Rebuilding the ego that Kensit had attacked with criticism and indifference, then left to slowly wither and die would take a lot of time. It would require a little nourishment each day to nurse her spirit back to health.

But time was a luxury he might not have with Sarah. Here in the jungle, alone in the middle of the night, she was his. With patience, he could teach her to believe what he believed, teach her to believe in herself again.

But back in the civilized world, where he lived on the fringes of Sarah's venerable Anglo society, he wouldn't have the freedom or the opportunity to pull her close and help her through this. A man who had failed as he had had little right to try to prove that she *hadn't* failed. Those doubts could sink their talons into her again, and tear her fragile self-esteem into unmendable shreds.

He was more patient than most men. If he had the time, he'd pay her a tiny compliment every day. He could think of a million ways to praise her. But he didn't have a million days to do it.

With Sarah, he might not have even one.

"Hawk?" Once he had settled, she spoke into the front of his chest. "Is it all right if I stay here for a while?"

Her whispered request touched him. He pressed a kiss into the crown of her hair. "I didn't intend to let you go."

Once she accepted his welcome, she relaxed and burrowed into him, seeking a more comfortable position. She kept her fingers curled into the front of his shirt. The timorous connection warmed him with an illusion of hope. For now, he told himself, he wanted nothing more than this night with her in his arms.

"Sarah?"

"Hmm?" She murmured the response without seeming to move a muscle.

"Thank you for sharing your fears with me. I can only imagine what it must have cost you."

Her silence stretched on for so long, he thought she had fallen asleep. She'd gone through more in this one day than most people did in a lifetime. She'd earned her rest.

But she hadn't been sleeping. "It's like an old family secret that no one talks about. But I felt safe sharing it with you."

She deserved the same kind of openness from him. "Speaking of old family secrets . . . I'm Virgil."

He could count on one finger the number of people who called him by his given name. Somehow he didn't think his mother would mind sharing that privilege with Sarah.

"Sarah?"

She yawned and snuggled closer. Hawk risked a smile. He curled his body around hers and closed his eyes, planning to rest and indulge himself in this simple gift of shared trust.

"Your secret is safe with me, Virgil."

He wished his heart could be, too.

Worthless peasants.

He who walked with the gods hovered at the fringes of their encampment. The two thieving servants who had betrayed their rightful master scurried around the dead body like the tiny worker ants that they were.

"Luis!" the younger one shouted, turning the body over to face the sky. A burnished hilt glistened in the early morning light, warming to the rays of the sun the way He warmed to the task of retribution. Their words, spoken in a foreign tongue, made little sense to him, but He understood their frantic terror and suspicion of each other. "Ramon was stealing from us! But look, he fell on the knife."

Satisfied laughter echoed in the dim recesses of his consciousness.

I am Meczaquatl. King of the great waters and

the strong rock and the fertile earth. I walk with the gods. These weak, puny mortals who cover their bodies in strange, white garments are no match for Me. They have no power against My wrath.

He watched the two peasants inspect the sacrifice. In his memory, He could feel the knife's weight in his hand, remember the power He had once felt in the lives He had claimed with it. He swelled with the renewing power He'd felt when the peasant had used the knife at His bidding. The memories made Him stronger.

"This was no accident. I heard Ramon cry out. He was speaking to someone. If he was stealing, we never would have heard him." The man with the silver in his hair tapped the lifeless body with his foot, then lifted his shrewd gaze and scanned the trees at the edge of the clearing.

This silver one might prove a worthy opponent. He recognized the voice of command, the expectation of authority. This one was the leader. This mortal considered himself clever enough and powerful enough to defy His wishes.

But clever or not, He would conquer him. He could show no mercy on those who had defiled Him. Forgotten Him. Betrayed His love for Prini.

The silver one would die. Just as the others would. Just as they all must.

"Antonio." The silver one was speaking again. "Load everything onto one truck and hide it."

"But Luis," the weaker one pleaded, "that will take two men. We have already lost Manuel Hernandez and Martín. Should we not bury Ramon and get out of here as quickly as we can? There is something unholy about this expedition. Too many have died!"

"*Silencio!*" The silver one pointed his weapon at the young peasant, who cowered beside the dead body. "We have made this trip three times without incident. Each time making you a wealthier man than you deserve to be."

"But that was Prini's tomb. This time we have disturbed the great Meczaquatl!"

"You are a superstitious fool." Meczaquatl waited for the silver one's explanation with discerning interest, His thoughts of vengeance gathering like a storm. "Look around you. There has been a struggle. Someone else has been here. We do not know that Martín is dead."

"But the gunshot? And he did not meet us at the rendezvous."

"I told him to kill that Indian. The others will not survive without him."

The weak one rose unsteadily to his feet. "You mean Martín is tracking us? Killing us one by one to take the treasure for himself?"

He hovered beyond the edges of their perception and let His consciousness slip back to the other mortals he had encountered since awakening. He had sensed four men and a boy in His tomb. The boy had deserted these others. He could detect no other men except these two . . . and the warrior.

The warrior had been different. More like Him. The warrior was powerful in ways the weak one could not understand and the silver one could not tolerate.

The two peasants scuttled back and forth, moving His things, touching His tribute. "The empty truck will travel faster," the silver one said. "We will go back and find him before he finds us."

"And if it is not Martín?"

"Then that Indian has survived. And we will kill him."

The silver one slammed his weapon with his fist.

223

A cumbersome weapon, it seemed. Less wieldy than a spear or knife. But He sensed it could be infinitely more powerful. The daring mortal jerked a handle on it so that it made a terrible, deadly, metallic noise.

A worthy opponent, indeed.

The one who walked with the gods shrank down into a tiny, watchful presence. The silver one was a warrior as well. But a warrior without honor, a warrior who would be destroyed for his arrogance.

They would all be destroyed for what they had done to His beloved.

Static crackled from the radio, as heavy and ominous as the humidity that hung in the midday air and sucked the oxygen from her lungs.

Sarah watched Andrea and Raul tinker with the pieced-together communication device. Then Hawk picked up the transmitter and sent another SOS message, giving their approximate location. With the sun high in the sky above them, she couldn't even tell which direction was north, but she had no doubt that the latitude and expected mileage from El Espanto he gave were accurate. Hawk possessed a preternatural ability that went beyond reading auras. She likened him to a mercenary Doctor Dolittle. He seemed to communicate directly with the plants and animals, even the very air surrounding them.

That special gift made him less like a gentle country doctor, though, and more like the wild jungle around them. He seemed so at ease here, so full of purpose. His extraordinary competence filled her with hope for their survival—and made her feel useless.

They'd dumped the last empty water jug that

morning. And with the humidity sapping their strength as they hiked, Sarah wondered just how long the eight of them could go before passing out from heatstroke. But then Hawk had told them to stop and rest for fifteen minutes. While they collapsed, he disappeared into the trees, and came back minutes later with an armload of large, flat leaves. He called them traveler's palms, and showed them how to pierce the base of the leaf stalk and suck out its watery sap to ease their thirsts.

"Shadow Man here. Sending out SOS re this location. Expect to reach El Espanto next A.M. Will need medical attention." *Shadow Man?* Sarah felt Hawk's gaze slide over to her. She lifted her chin and met the question in his look. She wiped the sweat from her forehead with the back of her hand, and pushed aside the sticky curls that clung to her face. She tried to give him a reassuring smile, but wasn't sure her aching muscles had obeyed her wishes. Just as quickly, he turned away. "Repeat. Shadow Man here. Will need medical attention upon arrival."

She must look a sight. No makeup, no bath, no brush for her hair. They hadn't yet spoken about last night. She wasn't sure she could. She'd opened up her deepest scars to him, shown him all her inadequacies. She'd awakened at dawn, when the heat of the rising sun began to burn off the clinging mist of the night. He had still held her in his arms. But he had removed the cherished protection as soon as he knew she was awake. He had tucked the blanket around her and excused himself to wake Raul and gather some breakfast.

He'd made no mention of their conversation

the night before. He hadn't touched her in any way more personal than a chaste kiss on the forehead. His hasty departure left her wondering how big a fool she'd made of herself. Had she imagined the intensity of his reaction to their kissing and talking and holding? Or had she seen what she wanted to see, leaving a kindhearted Hawk with no option but to go along with her wishful thinking?

By the time Hawk and Raul returned with an assortment of edible fruits for breakfast, she had the girls ready to go, and her emotional armor as firmly in place as her tattered defenses would allow.

They'd exchanged several curious, meaningful looks throughout the morning. But Hawk limited his conversation to the business of getting them out of the jungle, and Sarah retreated into cowardly silence.

While the trio worked with the radio, Sarah opened her pack and took out some of the chocolate tree fruit Hawk had brought them. She popped one of the black berries into her mouth and chewed thoughtfully. Hawk had explained that the plant was related to the persimmon tree of North America. Unfortunately, the chocolate-colored flesh beneath the skin tasted more like the tart persimmon than like its sweeter namesake.

The memory of Hawk's chocolate-flavored kisses stirred, unbidden in her mind. Despite the gnawing emptiness in her stomach, her hunger vanished. The natives and conquerors who had settled this island and much of the tropical Americas called chocolate "the food of the gods." But the sweet tenderness and gentle urging of Hawk's mouth and hands had been a far more addictive pleasure.

Walter's erudite kisses had been a perfunctory formality. He would drop a tantalizing tidbit here and there to pique her curiosity, and once he had her full attention, he tried to teach her what she needed to know about the differences between men and women. She had once imagined that by pleasing him, she would find pleasure for herself. But her repeated failures left her wanting as much as Walter did. He took care of his needs elsewhere, while Sarah broke the engagement and embraced her impending spinsterhood with forced relish.

But Hawk's touch had been a gift, one she dared not ask for again, unless she wanted to risk his refusal. He asked for nothing from her, out of consideration, perhaps. But maybe from compassion. Maybe he had tried to spare her the embarrassment of not being able to give him all he needed.

Sarah tried to reason away Hawk's kindnesses, to convince herself he might really want *her*. When Hawk spoke of her hips and breasts, he made her pear-shaped figure sound like a sensuous, irresistible temptation.

But memories of Walter intruded, drowning out the beautiful compliments Hawk had given her. *Let me take you shopping sometime. My treat. There are certain clothes that can camouflage those little imperfections.*

"Can't you do anything to make that static go away?" The shrill question pierced Sarah's downward spiral into self-pity. She glanced up to see Lynnette pacing in tight circles around her pack.

The young girl rubbed at the back of her neck in a nervous motion as tight and deliberate as her footsteps. Sarah rolled onto her feet and stood, tossing aside the berries left in her hand. "Lynnette, you need to calm down so you don't overheat." Sarah nodded toward the radio, and noticed Hawk and the others focused on Lynnette, as well. "The static means the radio is working."

"We don't know that." The girl stopped in her tracks, stared wild-eyed daggers at Sarah, then resumed her pacing. "We can't hear anybody else on that thing. Maybe it's not broadcasting at all. Maybe we walked all this way, and the only ones who can hear us are Señor Salazar and all those other men who went off and"—she sobbed a gasp of air—"left us.

"I have a cat at home," she continued on the next sob. "And if I don't get home at the end of the week, Peanut Butter might run away."

Sarah reached out and wrapped her fingers around Lynnette's wrist. "Calm down. You're not making any sense. Peanut Butter will be at home when you get there, Lynnette. We'll all be home very soon." Though she was taller in stature, the younger girl stopped at the light touch and glared down at her teacher's hand as though she'd been trapped.

"No, we won't," she argued, her reasoning skewed by heat and stress and fear. "We keep stopping every half hour."

Hawk stepped forward, then halted in his tracks when Lynnette jerked her hand away from Sarah. In a low, soothing voice tinged with the cool affirmation of authority, he explained their slow, erratic pace. "With this temperature, we need to take frequent breaks to keep up our strength. If one of us passes out, the others will have to carry him or her. And then, yes, we will be delayed. But we'll all get home, I promise you."

"No, we won't. At this rate we'll never get home. Never!" In a swirl of dark brown hair and high-topped sneakers, Lynnette dashed into the trees, running as hard and fast as her long, coltish legs could carry her.

Sarah waved Hawk back down to the radio. "You stay here. I'll go get her."

She cursed herself as she jumped the ravine and ran into the trees after Lynnette. What was she thinking? She should have seen this coming. If she'd been paying more attention to someone besides herself, she would have recognized that Lynnette was about to snap from all the stress. She'd lost sight of her responsibility to these girls, her charges, all because of a man.

All right, so he might be heroic and handsome. He might be gentle and caring . . . and strange. She might love him. . . .

Sarah would have stopped at the admission if she had the time to think about it and talk herself out of it. She loved Hawk. But she couldn't have him. And if he would somehow give her a chance, she knew she'd never be able to keep him. She wasn't the kind of woman a man pledged eternal devotion to. The kind of woman a man made passionate love to, and shared silly little secrets with, and grew old with. She wasn't that kind of woman.

She was a teacher, a woman who nurtured the minds and spirits of children beyond a parent's love. Right now, she wasn't even doing a very good job of that.

"Lynnette!" She yelled out loud, losing track of the girl when she veered back toward the road. The heavy air and sudden exertion were evident in the painful wheezing of her lungs. Her steps slowed, and Sarah had flashes of telling Lynnette's mother how she'd lost her daughter in the jungle down on Isla Tenebrosa.

An unexpected scream curdled the blood in Sarah's veins. She stumbled over her own feet in her hurry to stop, pausing to get her bearings over her own loud breathing. Lynnette screamed again. "Miss Mack!"

Changing course, Sarah ran out across the road and stopped, almost knocking Lynnette to the ground when she crashed into her. The girl had stopped at the far ditch, glaring down at something hidden there. Sarah hugged her tightly to calm her and then looked down.

A dead body lay facedown in several inches of standing water. Recognizing the white cotton uniform of Salazar's men, Sarah knelt down and turned him over. Lynnette's gasp echoed her own at the man's blue-lipped, bloated features. Sarah could see no other obvious marks on the body. He'd drowned! In six inches of water, the man had drowned!

"Oh, my God." Sarah murmured her prayer, then stood to turn Lynnette away from the gruesome sight. The girl's overt calm worried Sarah more than her hysterical screaming had. "It'll be okay, hon. Let's go find Hawk. He'll take us home."

"That is right, señorita." A falsely charming, accented voice stopped her. Sarah bristled, suddenly on guard, and turned to see Luis Salazar walk out of the trees. "Let us find that Indian friend of yours who has killed all my men."

"Hawk hasn't killed anyone." Her protest was

230

automatic. She had no trouble imagining Hawk capable of killing a man to protect himself or someone else. He'd been a marine, after all. But he wasn't the type of man to kill another in cold blood. To track a man down and drown him at the side of the road for no better reason than revenge. Was he?

Besides, he'd stayed with her all through the night. And she'd followed the broad, steady rhythm of his back all morning. Hawk had never left them long enough to find Antonio and kill him.

"So what happened to my men, then?" He asked the question in jest, sounding as though there could be no other explanation. "Someone is tracking them down, one by one. Tailing us through the jungle. Is this something you or your little girls can do, señorita?"

"Hernandez died in an accident."

Luis laughed out loud. "Señorita, you have quite the imagination." His laughter stopped with the abrupt foreboding of a rattlesnake's silence before it struck. "Now go. I want to take care of your friend before he eliminates me as well."

Ignoring the shock of the dead body and Luis's ridiculous accusation, Sarah resigned herself to his unwelcome company. She needed to think of some way to warn Hawk, some way to alert him to protect himself and get the others to safety. But what could she do that wouldn't get her or Lynnette killed? She thought long and hard, coming up with possibilities, then quickly discarding them. In the end, she simply prayed, and hoped that Hawk's uncanny intuition would pick up on the terror coursing through her.

She wrapped a sheltering arm around Lynnette's shoulders and walked slowly along the mud-packed road, silently obeying the rifle pointed at their backs.

Chapter Eleven

"I don't know where they are," Sarah repeated.

The radio still sat on a rock, crackling with the static of unanswered petitions. Packs and scattered palm fronds littered the flat rise between the rutted ditches. The temporary camp lay ready, like the set and props of a stage, waiting for the actors to walk on and assume their roles.

Only there were no players in sight.

"I am in no mood for games, señorita." Salazar's accent sounded thicker, less refined, couched in that menacing whisper. "Call to him."

Sarah glanced over her shoulder at Luis, using the opportunity to check the perimeter of trees to see if, by some miracle, Hawk had sneaked in behind them, poised to attack. But the jungle closed around them like an isolating green curtain, and there were no allies to be found. At least he had gotten the others securely hidden away. Now she had to see to Lynnette's safety. She hugged the frightened girl around the waist, pulling her close to her side and angling her own body between Lynnette and Luis. "Let her go first."

Luis shook his head. "You are in no position to bargain. Call him."

She knew little about the design of Luis's semi-automatic, but she understood the universal function of the trigger and was keenly aware of how his right index finger caressed the black metal loop framing it. With her gaze pinned to that finger, she raised her voice and spoke. "Hawk? If you're out there, we need you."

Luis turned away, on alert, scanning their surroundings for any sign of movement. Sarah seized the sudden opportunity. She spun around and shoved Lynnette ahead of her, forcing her to run for the trees.

But Luis reacted quickly. "Enough!"

A deafening blow of thunder exploded in the air behind her. Falling to her knees, Sarah pushed Lynnette across a ditch into the protective underbrush. But before she herself could scramble to her feet or crawl to safety, the hard bite of metal tapped the base of her skull. She froze.

"Get up on your feet."

"You're not a killer, Luis." Playing for time, full of blind hope, she tried to reason with him. Appeasing his desperation, she slowly stood and turned around to face the sleek black tip of the rifle pointed at her forehead. It was mere inches from her face, the hot odor of gunpowder stinging her nose, sickening her as much as the senseless, unending threat of this man's greed did.

He shook his head, but the gun remained steady. "It was all so simple. We open the tomb and take the treasure while you sleep. In the morning, you and your students dig up the artifacts we have uncovered."

"The few you leave behind for us, you mean." If Luis wanted to talk, she'd encourage the distraction. Anything to give Lynnette time to reach the others and be safe. "How many expeditions have you used as a cover to raid Las Lagumas? The authorities in El Espanto think you're some kind of savior, rescuing the national treasures of King Meczaquatl and Queen Prini."

"They were easy to fool. Eager to be 'a part of history.' " He quoted the very brochure that had lured Sarah here in the first place. Her stomach flipped over in her self-loathing for how gullible she'd been to fall into his plan so easily and so completely. "And the government believes what I tell them."

"How can you endanger children like this? How do you justify using them?"

"The children were never in any danger. No one ever got hurt until this expedition. Until your Indian friend decided to come along. He is no teacher. No student. He is like no human I have ever seen. He is unnatural." Sarah bristled at the derogatory description, feeling the slur in Luis's voice as painfully as if his words had insulted her instead of Hawk. "He's been a danger to me from the beginning. But I will put a stop to him. Now."

Luis's finger slipped to the trigger. Sarah's breath lodged in her chest. She braced for the impact of the bullet, prayed for forgiveness when she reached the hoped-for peace on the other side.

"Put down the gun."

In the blinding light of midday, Hawk emerged

235

from the trees like a shadow from the darkness. Darkness from darkness, she'd once thought with fear. But no more. Her breath seeped from her lungs with blessed relief. Hawk's reassuring presence fortified her like the cooling relief of evening settling in on a hot day.

He moved silently as a wraith into the clearing, holding up both hands high enough for Luis to see them, high enough for him to see the thick, gleaming blade of the knife he held in his hand.

Without moving his rifle from Sarah, Luis spoke. "Drop it."

Hawk swung his midnight gaze over to Sarah. In that briefest of contacts, she saw deadly conviction and something else. Something deeper, fiery, and full of promise. A feeling of cherished protection washed over Sarah. The sensation was as welcome as it was foreign.

He would die for her, she realized. The predatory gleam in his calm expression held no mercy for Luis. Yet she knew he would willingly sacrifice himself to protect her. Something altered deep inside her, an infinitesimal shift in her spirit that changed her perception of the world, that shone new light on her perception of herself.

Hawk could not die. This gentle, soul-healing man whom she loved could not die. She pleaded with her eyes. She pleaded with her heart. "Hawk, no. Don't do anything—"

"Silence!" Luis shook the gun scant millimeters from her face. Sarah gasped and staggered back a step. "The knife, Indian."

"Do what you want with me," Hawk said in a throaty whisper. The words were barely audible, but they vibrated through the air with unmistakable clarity. "But you hurt her, and I'll track you down. There won't be anyplace in this world you can hide from me."

The threat earned Hawk a thin-lipped sneer from Luis. He knew he had the upper hand as long as he controlled Sarah's fate. "Brave words for a man who is about to die. The knife?"

With his fathomless, unblinking gaze locked on Luis, Hawk knelt down and laid his weapon on the ground. When he straightened, he shook out his arms and shoulders with the controlled, calculating, predatory finesse of a big jungle cat.

But the older man refused to be intimidated. "Now kick it away," ordered Luis.

Hawk obeyed. With the weapon now twenty feet away in the underbrush, Luis's expression broadened into a self-satisfied smile. "I cannot allow you to stop me. You might outsmart my men, but you will not get the best of me. I know this jungle as well as the man who tamed it. I know all its secrets, all its treasures. Meczaquatl built an empire out of rock and gold and intellect and ambition. He eliminated those who defied him, carved them up as offerings to the gods. I have studied the master. I have learned his lessons by heart. I will follow his example. The scavengers will not even be able to smell what is left of you."

Hawk dropped his hands to his sides. "You don't know him at all. You have no respect for all he accomplished. No idea of the power he still commands."

Laughter bubbled up from deep in Luis's chest. It moved up his throat and spilled out in a devilish roar. "You are a madman! I told you he was crazy. *Loco,* this one. I am about to do you a favor, señorita." Luis's gaze darted from Hawk to Sarah. "Facedown in the dirt."

Sarah looked at Hawk, not fully understanding Luis's intentions, but certain the results would be fatal. The granite mask of Hawk's expression never changed, but he gave her the slightest of nods.

"No—" She leaned forward, but a reminding tap on the shoulder from Luis's gun stopped her protest.

"Sarah, please. Do as he says." In that softest of voices, like a lover's call, he begged her to do what he asked.

Left with little choice but to comply, Sarah went down on her knees, sharing one last look with both men. She didn't know which frightened her more, the murderous intent in Luis's expression, or the stalwart look of acceptance on Hawk's. Briefly, she hoped the girls were hidden well enough so that they couldn't witness this execution. But her last thoughts centered around her heart and the painful rendering of knowledge that she had learned to love and trust a man, but that she had learned too late. She spread flat on her stomach and turned her cheek into the mud.

The next few seconds played out like eons. "On your knees, Indian," she heard Luis command.

Hawk made no sound, but she could tell by the shifting of Salazar's feet that he had his unresisting target in the sights of his gun.

"The treasure of Meczaquatl is mine."

A grinding roar crashed through the trees, startling into flight a raucous chorus of birds and sending a skittering, slithering army of tiny animals deeper into the safety of the jungle. Sarah lifted her head and saw a grimy white truck clunking over ruts and barreling toward her. The rapid report of gunshots reverberated loudly above the wild cacophony.

She screamed and rolled into the ditch, narrowly dodging the crushing wheels. Ignoring the slimy water that filled her boots and soaked her clothes, she clawed her way to her feet and watched the truck fly past. She glimpsed a flash of red behind the wheel, noticed a second person hanging out the passenger window, and realized that was where the shots had come from. Lyndsay? Raul? They'd stolen Luis's truck!

New hope surged through her. She dug her fingers into the earth as the truck sped past, and she climbed out of the ditch, desperate to see if Hawk had survived. The two men tumbled back and forth in a twisting heap on the ground. She saw Hawk raise up, watched his fist go down.

Luis jerked beneath him. But then the older man's legs kicked, and suddenly Hawk was in the mud and Luis dove at him. Hawk coiled at the last instant, and Luis crashed to the ground.

Sarah looked around for some way to help Hawk. His knife lay on the opposite side of the brawl from her. But Luis's rifle was closer at hand, in the middle of the road. With the instinct to survive guiding her steps, she ran and picked it up. A resounding thud diverted her attention. Luis flew back toward her, hitting her legs and toppling her to the ground.

"Sarah!"

Hawk's bellow reached her the instant Luis realized his advantage. Suddenly she was clinging to the gun and struggling to hold on to it. But Luis ripped it from her grip.

She scrambled backward, crablike, as he rolled onto his haunches at her feet. In the space of a heartbeat, he had the gun leveled at her and his finger pressed to the trigger.

"Sarah!"

Hawk leaped at them the same time the gun went off. Luis's rifle sailed through the air, and Hawk's dark form crumpled in a lurch, crushing her beneath the rangy shield of his body.

"Hawk! No!"

She felt the warm, sticky ooze seeping between her fingertips. In a catch of breath between a gasp for air and a cry for help, she twisted beneath him to free herself and check his injury. With his right arm he propped himself above her, his chiseled bronze features looking ashen around his mouth when he looked down at her.

Sarah sat up. She touched his face, ran her hand down along his arm and flanks, and found the wound in his left side. She lifted her gaze to the powerful midnight promise in his eyes, then looked over his head and beyond.

Luis staggered to his feet, his weapon in hand. His bloodied mouth hung open, gasping in lungfuls of air. Then he closed it in a laughing smile and trained the gun on them both.

"*Adios*, señorita."

From out of nowhere, a swirling chimera of distorted light rushed at Luis. As startled as she, Luis watched the vortex whip around his head. Then it seemed to spread out around him. The temperature dropped. The strange phenomemon glowed. It grew and ebbed around Luis, spinning more slowly, gathering light. Gathering strength.

The light was alive. The light . . .

Luis screamed. The hovering entity closed in

on him, attacking him with a force that knocked the gun from his hands. He clawed at his chest, gurgling for air as the thing seemed to suck itself down his throat.

"Don't look." Hawk wrapped his right arm around her, pulled her down and tucked her beneath him. Sarah buried her face in his shoulder, clutching him tightly and shielding her eyes from the blinding prism of colors that careened around their would-be killer.

She shivered with the cold, and Hawk wound his body more securely around her. He bent his head to her neck and chanted something into her ear. Foreign words. Indian words. Powerful medicine. A powerful prayer to keep that thing at bay.

Seconds later, minutes later, maybe a lifetime later, the shrieks stopped. She became aware of the warmth of Hawk's body surrounding her, and sensed the jungle air adjusting itself to its normal, sunny hues.

The thing was gone.

As suddenly as it had appeared, it had vanished.

Breathing heavily, Hawk loosened his hold on her and they helped each other to a sitting position. She looked past him and saw Luis Salazar's twisted, pale body lying on the road. The fixed terror in his sightless eyes told her he was dead.

Stunned, she lifted her gaze to Hawk. His sad, pitying stare focused on the corpse of their attacker.

"What was that?" she asked.

Several silent moments passed before he answered.

"Retribution."

* * *

Retribution?

Sarah gripped the steering wheel harder and tried to switch her concentration back to the road. But the deep, meditative silence of the man beside her filled her thoughts.

Hawk never explained his answer, and he hadn't spoken another word to her since Luis's death two hours before. But he knew what had happened; she was sure of that. He understood the horrid, unspeakable thing that had killed Luis. It probably had killed Antonio, too. Maybe even Hernandez.

But she had no answers to the puzzle. A freakish phenomenon of nature had choked the life out of a man right before her eyes, an impossibility to her learned mind. She had a million questions.

Only one man had the answer.

And he wasn't talking.

And the potential consequences of that secretive knowledge frightened her.

"Are you in pain?" she asked. Maybe if she could get him to open up about something else first, she could ease into asking about what had happened. "You lost a lot of blood. You're not going to pass out on me, are you?"

At that moment she hit a rut, and the wheel jerked in her hands. She tugged hard in the opposite direction, fighting to keep her seat and keep the truck on the road at the same time. Once she had the vehicle heading straight again, she turned and offered Hawk a sheepish smile. "Sorry. I guess that's how Lyndsay ended up putting their truck in the ditch."

Still nothing. He continued to look out his window and scan the reflection in the side mirror, as though he expected that someone else—maybe *something* else—was following them. His right hand cradled the barrel of the rifle standing up between his knees, and his left hand rested on the hilt of his long-bladed knife, lying between them on the bench seat.

Sarah wanted nothing more than to reach across the gulf between them and touch that hand. What had once terrified her now fascinated her, the warmth of his skin, the hard lines of sinewed strength over his knuckles and down his long fingers. His touch meant reassurance. It meant strength and understanding, an anchor to latch onto to right herself through turbulent times.

She needed that anchor now.

But something about his edgy silence kept her hands locked on the wheel.

"Is the bandage holding?"

"It's fine." *At last, a response!*

"I still think a doctor should look at it. You'll probably need a few stitches." Her brief flare of hope was absorbed by dead silence. The wild beauty of the jungle and its canopy had become an endless green tunnel leading toward civilization. This whole journey had turned into a never-ending nightmare.

Her nightmare. A lonely woman's rosy-eyed dream had ended up a surreal nightmare of danger and terror.

Read my aura, she heard herself wishing. *Look at me. See my confusion and help me understand.* But her silent pleas went unnoticed.

"The girls really did their part, didn't they?" Sarah purposely steered the one-sided conversation toward a lighter topic. She needed some sound, even an inane monologue on her part, to drown out the terrifying imaginings swimming through her mind. "When Colleen said she and Denise had found this truck loaded with all the artifacts from Las Lagumas, I couldn't believe it. I've always known they were talented and smart young women, but I had no idea just how resourceful my students could be. Lyndsay and Raul saved our lives by distracting Luis. Andrea fixed the radio. Lynnette's writing all of our adventures in her journal. She'll probably turn it into a best-seller someday."

Her forced smile faded along with her bravado. She resigned herself to passing the next two miles listening only to the warring voices speculating inside her head.

She felt as uncomfortable and bewildered as she had at the first and only dance she had attended her freshman year of high school. Her date back then had endured an equally torturous evening of awkward silence. She'd had so many ideas to talk about, so much she wanted to ask about him . . . if she could just come up with the right words and get past the idea that any attempt at conversation on her part would be considered an intrusion or get laughed at for being inconsequential.

The man beside her now was a good deal more mature than Brian What's-his-name had been, and her feelings for Hawk ran deeper than she could possibly have imagined caring for a man back then. She, too, had changed, maybe more in the past few days than in the twenty years since that dance. She could speak her mind on the girls' behalf. She'd even risen to Hawk's defense.

But to broach the subject of her own fears, her own confusion, still terrified her. She felt raw and battered from all she had revealed to him the previous night. She needed for those wounds to heal and make her stronger before she could overcome decades of shyness and confront a man as imposing and important to her as Hawk had become.

So she would do what she did best. She'd be patient, tuck away her fears and concerns, and concentrate on getting something useful done. Except she wouldn't be very much good to anyone if she stranded them out here.

Looking down at the dashboard, Sarah watched the gas gauge teeter toward empty. Having no idea how much farther El Espanto lay, she gritted her teeth against the jarring ride and turned to speak to Hawk.

"How much farther do you think it is? There weren't any gas cans in the back, and I doubt if there's a gas station along the way."

Instead of answering, he shifted his gaze from the open side window to the front windshield. Like a bloodhound picking up a scent, he turned his attention to a distant point ahead of them.

"What is it?" she asked, straining to see what had caught his eye.

"Stop the truck."

Hawk pushed a clip of bullets up into the rifle and slapped it with his palm.

"Hawk?" From the corner of her eye, Sarah watched the former marine slip into his battle mode. She stomped on the clutch, ground her way through the gears and killed the engine. Before the truck jerked to a stop, Hawk stepped out onto the running board and jumped down. He circled the vehicle, surveying the area, ending up in front with Raul close behind.

Sarah hurried out after him, closing her door

and holding out her arm to keep the curious throng of teenage girls from joining the men.

"Hawk, what is it?" she asked again, a crawling sense of foreboding chilling her skin. He tipped his nose to the sky, sniffing the air with his preternatural abilities. With her nerves frayed from the tension of the drive, his unexplained alarm triggered a kaleidoscope of imagined dangers—and her temper. She turned to Denise. "Stay back."

The girl nodded, taking charge of the others while Sarah strode up to Hawk.

"Are you ever going to answer me?" she demanded.

The stillness of the late afternoon echoed in ominous silence. He stared down the road, his heightened senses seeing something in the distance she could not.

"Would Luis have any accomplices in El Espanto?" she asked, considering the possibilities that Hawk refused to share. "Someone who might check on him if he didn't show up at a certain time?"

"No," Raul answered, readying his rifle and moving in to stand shoulder-to-shoulder with Hawk. "My uncle trusted very few people. The man to whom he arranged to sell the artifacts is not Tenebrosan. He would not know his way here."

A ripple of unease quickened Sarah's heart. "Should I put the girls back in the truck? Hide them in the trees?"

She exchanged a look with Raul. The young man shrugged his shoulders and frowned, looking as clueless as she. He was simply following Hawk's lead, unwilling to let down his defensive duty.

Sarah clamped down on the urge to strike out

at Hawk for frightening them all this way. Bracing her fists on her hips, she turned on him. "Damn it, Hawk, talk to me! I don't know what's going on, and you're scaring the hell out of me!"

His stony features softened when he looked down at her, his eyes scanning her upturned face. But he didn't smile. "Not very ladylike, schoolmarm. But always courageous, aren't you?" What he might have intended as a compliment sounded more like a whisper of regret. "I'm sorry." He nodded up ahead. "I think we're about to get rescued."

"How do you know?" she asked, her ire diminished by his odd lack of joy at the news.

"I just know."

He offered no further explanation. He walked forward a few steps, braced his legs and stowed his weapon over his shoulder, forming an imposing sentinel to greet the tan Humvee just now coming into Sarah's view.

The squat, sleek vehicle zipped toward them, unmindful of the road conditions. As it came closer, Sarah could make out the silhouettes of two men behind the windshield. When it came within fifty yards, the driver honked the horn several times. Hawk lifted his hand in greeting.

"It's okay." Sarah waved the girls forward.

The Hummer skidded to a halt, and the driver popped up from behind the wheel. The faded blue Kansas City Royals baseball cap perched on his tobacco-brown hair softened the crisp, mercenary formality of the jungle fatigues he wore.

"Shadow Man!" He vaulted over the door to the ground, a trim, six-foot-plus package of coiled energy. A pair of silver aviator-frame sunglasses only partially hid the devilish glint in his eyes. He held his hand outstretched as he bounded over to Hawk, who met him halfway.

"Rafe." Sarah marveled at the subtle easing of tension around Hawk's shoulders when the two men shook hands. "I wondered if anyone got my message."

The man named Rafe pulled off his glasses, revealing a pair of sparkling green eyes. "It was about time you called in. We'd been in El Espanto a whole twenty-four hours, wondering whether to bide our time or hire a reliable guide to come look for you."

"He *is* the only reliable guide."

Along with the others, Sarah shifted her focus to the second man. He climbed more slowly out of the vehicle and walked toward them, swaying from side to side in a stiff-legged limp. Despite his irregular gait, he carried his shoulders with the regal pride of a military man. His close-cropped cinnamon-brown hair reinforced her observation even before Hawk spoke.

"Major."

"Those days are long past, Hawk." He extended his hand, taking the sting out of his clipped correction.

"Kel."

"Good to see you in one piece." Keeping hold of Hawk's hand, Kel pulled his arm to the side and looked at the hanging tatters of Hawk's bloody shirt. Lifting one brow with a cynical twist, he revised his greeting. "Good to see you. Is that the medical attention you mentioned?"

"Nothing a shot of penicillin won't fix." Hawk pulled his fingers back and splayed them across his hips, nodding to either side and, for the first time, including Sarah and the others in their conversation. "We've got minor scrapes and abrasions, probably a few blisters. Not that any of them would complain."

Hawk's compliment garnered tired, proud smiles from the girls and Raul. "I'm more concerned about the preliminary stages of dehydration and exposure. I'd like to get a solid meal into these kids."

"How do cheeseburgers sound?" Rafe walked past Hawk, introducing himself to each of the girls, one by one.

"Cheeseburgers?" echoed Lynnette.

Rafe's smile crooked with boyish enthusiasm. "Complete with high-fat French fries and the paper wrappers to match."

"Yes!"

"Real food."

"Do you have any ketchup?"

The enthusiasm of the girls' responses to his tempting offer would have misled a stranger about the level of their fatigue.

"American cheeseburgers?" questioned Raul. Sarah's heart warmed at the sound of lust in his voice. He'd acted as a man on their trek, but he still had the bottomless stomach of an eighteen-year-old boy. "I have never eaten one."

Rafe turned and clapped him on the shoulder, smiling. "You can eat as many as you want. Only the best for Kel. When we heard Hawk put teenagers on his team, he had the banquet flown in from Florida."

"Quit flirting, Del Rio. They're just kids," warned Kel.

Rafe stepped in front of Sarah, removing his

hat and capturing her hand in one smooth gesture. "Not all of them."

With a flourish of old-world charm, he brushed a kiss across her knuckles. He tilted his head up and winked at her. Suddenly she was keenly aware of the chapped condition of her lips, the sunburn on her nose, and the unkempt wildness of her hair. Sarah's gaze flew up to Hawk, questioning the sincerity of the appreciation reflected in Rafe's eyes. But the heat in her cheeks went unnoticed, as Hawk had taken Kel aside for an urgent, whispered discussion.

Uncomfortable with Rafe's close scrutiny, she licked her dry lips and pulled away, thrown off-kilter at the sudden change of events. She'd been in survival mode for so long, enduring physical stress and emotional upheavals, that it left her struggling now to remember some basic rules of social etiquette—such as answering when spoken to.

But this wasn't a man with a gun threatening her students, and it wasn't a journey across miles of unfamiliar terrain; this was just a man. A man with enough boyish charm to remind her of one of her students. She breathed in deeply and forced herself to look into Rafe's striking green eyes.

"Can I assume you're friends of Hawk's?" she asked, embarrassed by the shaky quality of her voice.

"I'm Rafael Del Rio," he said, easily excusing the lull in the conversation. "We served in the corps together a few years back. My friends call me Rafe. The serious guy's Kelton Murphy."

That name sounded familiar, but in the midst of remembering her manners, keeping a nervous eye on Hawk, worrying about getting the girls a regular meal and a full night's rest, and trying to judge the level of sincerity in Rafe's flirtations, she couldn't place him. She filed the information away to consider later and found herself able to answer Rafe with a genuine smile. "Then I take it you're *not* the serious one."

"Not if I can help it."

She laughed at the severe face he made. The buoyant release tapped into the capped well of repressed emotions buried inside her. Rafe joined her laughter, eliminating any self-consciousness she felt. His gift of humor lightened the burden of shyness she carried on her shoulders.

But her laughter dissipated at the abrupt end to Hawk's conversation with Kel. He swung around to look at her, his heated focus pinning her across the heavy air as clearly as the urgent stroke of his hand on her skin. She saw a flicker of light in his shadowy midnight eyes, read the question crinkling around the corners of his mouth.

She curled her lips into a silent *O*. "What . . . ?"

But he blinked and the light vanished. He turned back to Kel. "Do you think we can do that?"

Kel nodded, his face a grim mask. "I'll make the arrangements. Give me a day to get it done."

Get what done? Now what dreadful secret was Hawk hiding from her? For a brief instant, when she had laughed, it was as if he had awakened from the spell of the seasoned warrior and become the gentle spirit-healer she had fallen in love with. But in the blink of an eye that man had vanished, and the silent mercenary had replaced him.

Kel whispered something else to Hawk, who eyed him for a moment before giving a single nod. Then Kel raised his voice for all to hear and snapped an order to Rafe. "Break out the canteens and let's get some water to these kids."

"You bet."

The girls and Raul eagerly traipsed after Rafe to the back of the Hummer. Kel retrieved a map from beneath the front seat and spread it open across the hood. "Hawk?"

The two men leaned over the map and fell into a deep, intent conversation, pointing out geographic positions and plotting some sort of strategy. Sarah crossed her arms and rubbed at the sudden chill spreading through her. Abandonment. She recognized the symptoms. She was an old hand at dealing with the overwhelming loneliness that could attack a person unaware. She'd lost the important people in her life, or been betrayed by them. And now, with Hawk . . . maybe she'd already lost him two hours ago. If he'd ever been hers to lose.

Before the numbing paralysis of self-pity could overtake her, Sarah moved to the back of the truck and began to rearrange the crates that had been moved to accommodate the kids. She climbed inside, stepping over backpacks to continue her work.

Busy hands, her aunts had often advised her, after losing her parents. *Busy hands will heal your heart.* It was Millie and Doris's own platitude. Sarah didn't know if she believed in the healing part of it, but she knew that staying busy provided a practical distraction from debilitating thoughts. She could wear herself out until she was too tired to think one way or the other about her pain.

She leaned her shoulder into a crate and

pushed it into the center to balance the load of the truck. Weary from her brain to her toes, she sighed as she straightened, then reached for the next crate. An iron hand cinched her around the waist from behind. Startled, she had no chance to protest when Hawk lifted her from the back of the truck.

Still holding her, he pulled her back flush to his chest and circled his other arm around the front of her shoulders. He dipped his lips to the crown of her hair and rocked her back and forth, holding her tight.

"I've never heard you laugh before." His lips brushed against her ear. She felt a trembling in his powerful arms, heard the hesitancy in his soft voice. "You sounded so free, so open. I'm so glad you can be. We haven't beaten you yet, have we?"

"We?" she said in a shaky voice, thanking heaven for his reassuring embrace, yet questioning the underlying message he hadn't put into words.

His arms stiffened. She felt him withdraw inside himself before he pulled away. For a flashing moment, Sarah wished she had Hawk's powers of perception so she could understand what demon was torturing him so. But she had no such magic, only a rusty feminine intuition that advised her to hold her tongue about deeper matters and keep the conversation light and impersonal to give him the space and time he needed to wrestle with that demon.

She turned and faced him, trying to align her mouth into a teasing grin. "Have you two figured out your battle strategy?"

She glimpsed the regret stamped in stone across his features before he, too, forced a slight smile. "Think you can drive a little farther?"

"If the truck can make it, I can."

"Good." The strain eased around his mouth. "Kel says we're only five miles out of town. He's rented a house on the outskirts of El Espanto. There we can rest, eat, get cleaned up. We're almost home."

Sarah had never felt farther from home in her entire life. "If you say so."

He raised his hand and brushed the back of his knuckles across her cheek. She understood the mute apology, but wished she understood what he was apologizing for. "Be patient with me, schoolmarm. I know you want to know about Luis and the others."

His gaze danced around her face, and she knew he was reading her aura. "I need to tell you about me. There are still some things . . ." He splayed his fingers, cupping her cheek before pushing them into the wispy curls behind her ear. Sarah leaned into the caress.

"What things?" she prompted, closing her eyes to savor the warmth of his rough palm on her skin.

"Just be patient. Please?" He pressed the pad of his thumb against the pout of her lower lip. He stroked it across her mouth, beseeching her. Her eyes shot open and she lifted her chin, granting him permission. He kissed her deeply, reverently, and all too quickly to satiate her wounded heart.

Then he pulled away without another word and walked around to climb into the passenger side of the truck. Sarah stood there a moment longer, nursing the sting on her lips with her tongue, and fortifying her courage. Maybe during this week with Hawk she *had* picked up a few of his talents for observation.

She might never understand men.

But she understood fear.

And she wondered just what it took to make a man like Hawk afraid.

Chapter Twelve

"You know the unwritten rule." Sarah recognized the odd inflections of Rafe Del Rio's voice through the open doorway. "Nobody goes into Tenebrosa alone. I couldn't believe it when Brodie called and said you'd come down here. Hell, the name of the capital, El Espanto, means *terror*."

Terror?

Sarah tucked herself into the shadows of the deserted hallway. With the staff retired for the night, she'd encountered no one on her way to the kitchen for a glass of water. The single light shining from the library downstairs caught her attention. At first she thought someone had left it on by mistake, so she went to turn it off.

But the sound of hushed masculine voices turned her conservation effort into unintentional eavesdropping.

"What did you hope to accomplish with a

bunch of kids tagging along that we couldn't do?" asked Rafe.

"I didn't come here to find Jonathan," answered Hawk. His softly modulated tones tightened with the barest hint of what Sarah thought to be his well-controlled temper.

"This place has too many ghosts for any of us. You more than most." Kel was talking now, his cultured voice laced with a touch of cynicism. A few moments of silence passed. Sarah caught her breath and inhaled the rich tang of tobacco smoke. "So why did you come here?"

"To pay an old debt."

"Nobody blames you for the colonel's disappearance."

Sarah leaned closer to the door frame to hear Hawk's response. "I do."

"Does Sarah know what you're planning?" Kel's question hung in the air like the aroma of their cigars.

"She's been through enough," said Hawk. "I'm counting on you to see her and the girls safely home."

"You know we will," answered Rafe.

Hawk wasn't going home with them? Planning what? Sarah pressed her hand over her stomach to quell the rise of panic and impending loss inside her. *No!* she cried in her mind. *Don't abandon me. Not yet. You said you needed time. Hawk, please, just give me more time. . . .*

The sound of chair legs scraping across the wooden floor halted her silent plea. She flattened her back against the wall, but knew, too late, that she'd been discovered.

"Sarah?"

When Hawk spoke her name from the doorway, she couldn't very well deny her presence. She didn't think she'd made a sound, but it wouldn't have mattered anyway. He simply knew she was there.

She pulled the white cotton robe more tightly around her, holding it together with a fist at her neck. She stepped into the light spilling out around Hawk's silhouette. From this angle, she couldn't see the expression on his face, only the distinctive outline of his long, sleek hair falling to his broad shoulders.

Not sure if he was angry or not, she simply apologized. "I saw the light and heard voices."

"Sarah, come in." Kel issued the invitation, not Hawk. But Hawk turned politely and she brushed past him, not touching him, but close enough to inhale the damp, clean scent of his freshly washed hair, close enough for every responding pore of her body to prick into a sea of goose bumps.

Rafe stood at the window, with a long-neck bottle of beer dangling between his fingers. Kel tapped his cigar into an ashtray and stood, adjusting his balance on his feet. Hawk stayed behind her.

Kel gestured to the seat across the desk from him. "Can I get you anything?"

"No, thanks. I wanted a glass of water. I didn't mean to intrude."

"You're not." Despite her refusal, he opened a bottle of water and handed it to her. Years of practicing good manners made her sit in the wicker chair and take a few sips.

Only then did Kel resume his seat. "Is everything to your liking? The girls are fine?"

Sarah fingered the collar of her robe. It

matched the lace-trimmed cotton gown she wore beneath. Without knowing sizes or clothing tastes, Kel had arranged for nightclothes and daywear for each of his guests. This simple button-front chemise was probably the most feminine thing she'd ever worn to bed, and it fit her like a dream.

"The girls are out for the count. Even Lynnette gave up on her journal and fell asleep an hour ago. You've been more than generous."

"Kel's the master scrounger." Rafe pushed away from the window and plopped down in the seat beside her, lifting his bottle in a toast. "If you need anything, he can make it happen."

"I'd like to repay you somehow."

Kel shook his head and picked up his cigar again. "Think of it as a favor to a friend."

She followed his upward glance and discovered Hawk standing right behind her chair. He pulled the bottle from her hand and set it on the desk. Then he tugged on that same hand and pulled her to her feet. "I think I'll walk Sarah back to her room."

Tension sizzled through her hand where he touched her, like an electric current leaping from his fingers to hers. The voltaic bolt zipped through her veins and lighted deep in her belly. She caught her breath, startled by the thrilling surprise of her body's reaction to his touch and the soft, firm promise in his voice. Embarrassed by the overwhelming rush of sensation that heated her cheeks, she tried to pull away and excuse herself, but Hawk tightened his fingers around hers.

"Good night, gentlemen," he said.

Both men stood, acknowledging Hawk and nodding to Sarah.

Julie Miller

She stumbled through thanking her host and rescuer. "Good night, Rafe. Mr. Murphy."

Rafe's grin creased his mouth into a well-worn smile. " 'Night, Sarah."

"It's Kel, ma'am," her host corrected, with neither a frown nor a smile. "Good night."

With her hand snared firmly in his grasp, she padded noiselessly down the hall at Hawk's side. His gallant gesture touched her, filled her with a sense of security and importance. Unless there was a "tutoring session" or audience involved, Walter had never once walked her to her door or escorted her to her car when they parted for the evening. That Hawk would claim the right and make the effort to do so warmed the wounded part of her, and made her final good-night feel that much more precious.

Once he seemed sure of her willingness to hold on to him, he softened his grip. Sarah relaxed, too, smiling beside his shoulder. "Is there something going on I should know about? It sounded like a pretty heavy discussion when I came in."

She felt the tension crackling around him and wished she could withdraw the question. He slowed on the stairs, but squeezed her hand reassuringly, silently asking for time to work through whatever was troubling him. She'd grant him anything so long as he didn't push her away.

At the top of the staircase he spoke again. "We're negotiating with the local authorities whether to return the treasures to the tomb or donate them to the national museum."

"They have to go back to the tomb," insisted Sarah in a flash of insight that preceded her own conscious agreement.

She halted beside Hawk, confused by the

surety of her decision, but knowing with absolute rightness that the treasures of Meczaquatl should be restored to their intended resting place. Hawk looked down at her, the brilliant light shining through the midnight color of his eyes evident even in the shadows on the landing.

"Yes," he whispered. With just the tip of his index finger, he traced a semicircle around her brow and cheekbone. "Are you sure there's not a little bit of psychic in you?"

He looked so proud, so relieved by her words. But just as quickly, just as profoundly, a mask shuttered his eyes and snuffed out the light. He withdrew his hand, leaving a chill where he had touched her.

"Hawk?"

With the swiftness of a panther, he pulled her to her room, pushed her inside and closed the door behind him. She spun around to face him, wanting to question his abrupt actions. But the air in the room seemed suddenly alive, raw with danger and unpredictability. Caged with the wild animal, Sarah clutched the front of her robe and hugged herself. She trembled with fear. Not of Hawk, but of the demon inside that he worked so hard to master.

"What is it?" she asked, sensing his desperation, not knowing how to help him or ease his torment or even to save herself.

The lamp beside her bed cast a soft glow across the room, lighting him only up to his shoulders. With his back pressed to the door, she was transfixed by the powerful rise and fall of his chest as he breathed deeply to regain whatever control he had lost.

"Tell me you want me to stay."

261

He stepped into the light, letting her see the clarity in his gaze, letting her know the raspy-throated request came from the man himself, fully aware of who and where he was, and not from a possessing spirit dulling his mind and actions.

He spread his arms to either side, opening his stance and presenting himself like an unarmed man. "Even if it's just to talk, or hold you, I promise I won't do anything you don't want—"

"I want you to stay."

She cut him off, making her point perfectly clear, understanding with equal clarity how much she wanted him and how desperately he needed her. She remembered his struggle with Prini's crown and understood how she had pulled him from its spell. He needed that kind of salvation from her now.

And she needed whatever he would offer. "I want you to stay," she repeated.

His nostrils flared in a ragged intake of breath. He pursed his lips and breathed out on one long, languid whisper of air. But though his body relaxed, the coiled tension never left his eyes. She fell into the darkness there, struggled to catch her breath in the clear black pools of night. Like a hunter, he had snared her, and she was powerless to escape.

She didn't want to try.

Frightened of what would happen next, and even more frightened that it wouldn't happen, Sarah couldn't speak. Her chin quivered as she searched for the right words to ask him to be with her, to love her, to complete the promise of what he had shown her the night before.

This last night in Tenebrosa might be *their* last night. Her last chance . . . her *only* chance to be with the man she loved. Her only chance to create a memory more precious than any other. This one night when the man she loved wanted to be with her. Wanted her.

This time, he saw her request. Reaching out, he cupped her face gently between his hands and tilted her mouth up to his. "I want it, too," he whispered in the instant before his lips touched hers.

Rising on tiptoe, Sarah leaned into the kiss, curling her fingers around his forearms for balance. He tunneled his fingers into her hair and cradled the back of her head, pulling her beneath the volatile exploration of his tongue. He traced the seam of her lips and then plunged inside, staking a claim she'd waited her whole life to surrender.

He tasted of something dark and dangerous, warmed with the sweet tang of finely aged rum. She stroked her tongue along his, and a feral call rumbled deep in his throat. The sound vibrated down along her spine and spread along the fraying tendrils of her nerve endings. It took her a few moments to recognize the soft, mewling sounds answering in her own throat.

Even with her limited experience, she understood the chained beast in him fighting to free himself. She breathed in through her nose, willing her mind to catch up to the primitive staccato of her heartbeat. He wanted something from her, needed something more . . . if she could only know what to give him. He slid his hands down her neck, the rough pads of his fingers soothing the pulse point at the base of her throat.

And then his healing lips were there, and she forgot all her thoughts. It was all she could do to feel, to keep up with the web of sensations unraveling deep inside her. He slid his hands up and over the delicate ridge of her collarbone, beneath her robe to her shoulders. Her fingers scurried along his sleeve, not knowing where to hold on, where to touch him.

Turning her, he slipped the robe off her arms and backed her against the door. She dug her fingers into his wrists for balance as he pinned her there, his mouth finding hers again and driving her into the smooth, unyielding wood at her back. His lips followed the path of his hand, tasting her neck, sipping at the pounding warmth of her pulse, pushing aside the nightgown and supping at the smooth, round strength of her shoulder.

Sarah angled her body to urge him to explore further, to learn where else he might place his lips. As she turned, her hips brushed his, catching the robe between them where it fell. The hard, solid column of his thighs yielded as little to her soft curves as the door at her back.

A spark of an unpleasant memory flared in her mind, but she quickly snuffed it out. This was Hawk loving her, wanting her, and she knew she couldn't bear to stop him.

But beyond conscious thought, she twisted her hips, squirming away from the sensation of being trapped. She brushed against the masculine evidence of his desire, heard him moan a sweet native word against her skin. She tried to think of the things he had said, the words of praise she wanted to believe.

Her hands, which had clung to him for support, now flattened across his shoulders. He reclaimed her lips, and she focused on the sleek power of his addictive mouth, losing herself in the magical beauty of his kiss. But then he shifted his body closer and rubbed his denim-clad leg against the juncture of her thighs.

Her body throbbed in one pounding pulse beat. The shock of her reaction to that one intimate touch froze her for an instant.

An instant too long.

A wave of cooling air whispered across her body. Did Hawk pull away? Or had she pushed him?

She curled her hand into a fist as she reached out, grasping nothing but air. Hawk turned his back to her, shoving his fingers through his hair and stalking across the room to the window.

"Did I do something wrong?" She barely recognized the throaty timbre of her own voice.

"Don't ever say that." His sharp words bounced off the windowpane. His shoulders heaved in a cleansing breath before he turned to face her. "Did it feel wrong to you?"

His shaman eyes pinned her across the room. Even with him blending into the shadows, she knew she couldn't hide the truth from him. "No. Not wrong. Just . . . new."

"I'm sorry if I scared you, if I went too fast. If I reminded you of . . . him." He hitched his shoulders in an uncharacteristic shrug. His unexpected show of doubt touched a responding chord in her. This proud man's hesitancy made him more human, made her more powerful.

Walter had denigrated her, taken her uncertainties and used them as leverage to raise himself above her. Hawk embraced his doubts and her own with honesty, and for the first time Sarah realized that she shouldn't be ashamed of her shyness. She should be accepting of it. She should accept herself, just as Hawk accepted her. Just as she accepted him.

"You didn't scare me," she offered by way of apology, moving to the middle of the room in a literal attempt to meet him halfway.

The hard lines around his mouth softened. "I want this to be right for you. I want to make this night as perfect as a man can make it for his woman."

His woman?

His words alone rekindled a spark in that most primitive part of her. The heat of it blossomed and spiraled through her, warming her with its energy, restoring that fragile scrap of ego held together by hopes and dreams and sheer will.

"If I'm with you, it will be perfect."

"Those are powerful words to say to a man, schoolmarm."

"I've never said them to anyone else."

At last he joined her at the foot of the bed, standing inches away, but not yet touching her. Instead, his hands hovered in the air around her, as though tracing her outline like an invisible sculpture. Could this man caress her aura? Could he touch the energy field surrounding her and make it feel like the stroke of fingers against her skin?

As profound as his touch, she felt his comforting embrace deep in her heart. "I don't want to say or do anything that makes you uncomfortable, that makes you doubt yourself."

"You're the counselor. What kind of therapy would you prescribe for me?"

Hawk's hands stopped in midair. His eyes lit

with surprise. "Miss Mack, I do believe you're flirting with me."

Sarah licked her lips, nervous about the idea taking shape as she spoke. Hawk's gaze darted to the movement of her tongue, and suddenly her whole mouth went dry.

"Well, counselor?" she prompted.

Hawk dropped his hands and cleared his throat, apparently craving a drink, or something more, just as she did. "I'd let you lead us through this. You would need to be the one in control of how we proceed. That way, you could recognize any feelings of panic and alter the progression of things."

"Like this?" She brushed the strands of hair that had fallen across his forehead back into place. "I could do anything, and you'd go along with it?"

His gaze zeroed in on hers, dancing with wry amusement. "Whatever you want."

This rangy, hungry, male jungle cat was hers to command. Feeling empowered by his willingness to play, and thrilled by the danger of it, she closed her eyes for a moment and let her imagination come to life. "I like it when you're not wearing your shirt." She stumbled over the first words, getting used to the idea of taking charge. "You have a very nice"—she swallowed hard—"chest."

"Look at me, Sarah. Don't be afraid of me."

She opened her eyes and noticed the tinge of color in his cheeks. Had she embarrassed him with the compliment? Could anything she said possibly have that kind of effect on a man? "I'm not. It's just . . . no one's ever asked what I wanted. It's hard to put it into words."

"Just speak from the heart. I'll listen to whatever you have to say. And I'll listen even when you don't have the words to say it."

Hawk's vow settled over her like a blessing, easing her doubts.

"You're nothing like Walter," she whispered, wanting to give back some of the reassurance he had given her. "He was never this patient with me."

"That's his loss," he said, the brackets of strain fading at the corners of his mouth. "So tell me, schoolmarm. What *do* you want?"

With the generous gift of Hawk's healing words, Sarah's shy heart grew bolder. "Would you take off your shirt?"

"No."

"No?" Her initial shock abated at the subtle hint of a smile on his lips.

She'd never seen that boyish sparkle in his eyes before. The breadth of his shoulders and the careworn lines on his face reminded her that he was a man in his prime, strong, earthy, a force of nature to be reckoned with. But his willingness to play this game with her humanized him, made him approachable. This was a man she could trust.

He crossed his arms in the time-honored stance of a dare being made. His powerful biceps strained the lightweight denim he wore. "You take it off me."

Sucking in a fortifying breath, Sarah rose to the challenge. She started at the top, undoing the first two buttons with clinical, perfunctory efficiency. Then she ran into the roadblock of his forearms across his middle.

"A little help?" She touched his wrist and glanced up. Watching her with the same keen intensity of a big cat in the circus cage with its trainer, he lowered his arms to his sides.

Hampered by a sudden shallowness of breath, she fumbled with the third button, her fingers stiff and unsure as she pushed it through the hole. When she reached the fourth button, his shirt veed open, revealing an inviting strip of coppery skin and that oblong black stone he wore around his neck.

She brushed against the stone, felt the heat it had absorbed from his skin. The escaping warmth should have thawed her fingers. Instead it only slowed her progress. With all the awkward anticipation of a child trying to unwrap a gift without tearing the paper, she slowly undid the fifth and sixth buttons.

By now she had reached the belt on his jeans. Her hands hovered in the air in front of the buckle; she wanted that next step, but not quite yet. What should she do? What had Walter said a man liked?

Hawk's rough palm cupped her cheek and turned her face up to his. "Whatever *you* want."

With that husky reminder, Sarah banished all thoughts of the blond, careless egomaniac who had crippled her so. She absorbed Hawk's strength—his gentle touch, his beautiful voice, his compelling eyes—and let it become her own.

She trailed her gaze over his prominent cheekbones, across the rock-solid dimension of his jaw, and down the tanned cords of his throat, stopping at the point where her hands rested on his shirtfront. Then, enjoying her journey of discovery, she pushed the material to either side, grazing her hands across his shoulders and down over the swells and shallows of his powerful arms as she removed his shirt.

She marveled in the glory of the man before her, simply filling her gaze and storing in her memory the sculpted perfection of healthy living and Mother Nature's handiwork. Her fingers tingled to share the delight of her eyes. Equally aware of his body's utter stillness and the unblinking scrutiny of the midnight gaze that followed her every move, Sarah spread her fingers over the flat, sinewed planes of his upper chest.

The sizzling electricity she had felt earlier scorched her palms. She pressed with her fingertips, holding on, unwilling to break the contact. The heat of it seeped into her wrists and spread up her arms, firing her pulse and melting her lingering misgivings into mush. She dragged her hands over the swell of muscle, brushed across his flat, bronze nipples and stopped, feeling the quiver of skin beneath her sensitized palms.

"You like that?" she said softly, afraid of breaking the beautiful serenity that surrounded them in this private, intimate world.

His answering moan emboldened her. She stroked him again. The swift rise and fall of his chest matched the pace of her own breathing.

Pulling her hands lower, she ran them across the spare form of his rib cage and out onto his sides, where she encountered a thin mound of gauze and adhesive tape. The rough textures of plastic and cotton disrupted the smooth connection between them. In a rush of concern, she pulled away, angling around to check the first-aid work.

"I didn't hurt you, did I?" She smoothed the ends of the tape on his skin. "I don't want anything to—"

"God, woman, don't stop!"

He seized her wrists and brought her palms back to his chest, covering her hands with his to hold her there. "I've been stitched and doctored," he said, the wild look in his eyes rendering her speechless. "There are other parts of me that need tending. Take pity on a man, and don't stop your therapy now."

The husky plea in that sinfully sexy request blurred the questions in her mind. Her therapy? Or his? Did it matter?

She wanted this man in every way a woman could want. His body, heart, soul, faith and trust. Maybe for just this one night. And, she hoped, for all her tomorrows.

But for now, it didn't matter. She simply needed him. Needed him . . .

A willing captive, she leaned forward and pressed her lips to the swell of his pectoral muscle between their hands. She kissed the indentation near the vee of his necklace. Then she closed her mouth over one flat, male nipple. She felt his hands tighten on hers, heard him catch his breath. She kissed him again, flicked her tongue around the hardening bud.

She pressed her nose into his chest, inhaling his woodsy scent, kissing him again. His hands left hers and moved to her shoulders. Sarah clung to him, learning the feel of his shape, learning the taste of his skin, losing herself in her love for him.

"So beautiful," she whispered, moving her lips up his neck and discovering the hollow beneath his chin. "Hawk?"

"Hmm?" His response rumbled through the skin beneath her lips. His large hands kneaded her shoulders, caressed her back, tried to mind his promise to let her lead them through this.

"Will you kiss me? I love the way you kiss me."

"Yes, ma'am," he said in a growl, and like a man triumphant, he cupped her face and pulled her beneath his mouth.

He caught her hard against him, pulling her up onto her toes, burying his fingers in her hair. He swept his tongue around her lips, swirled it into her mouth, then staked his possession with a swift, hungry surge. She clutched at his dark hair, stretching herself along the length of his body. She reveled in the claim of his lips and the urgency of his hands.

She felt beautiful. Desirable. Perfect.

In Hawk's hands, she felt perfect.

Those same hands pressed near the neckline of her gown. "May I?" He lifted his mouth for only an instant, trapping her *yes* in her throat.

She nodded, and with far more skilled hands than hers had been, he unbuttoned the gown and let it pool at her feet. The cooling breeze from the ceiling fan raised goose bumps along her spine. But in seconds Hawk was there. His long fingers nearly spanned her back, warming her, branding her, pulling her closer.

Her soft breasts flattened against his hard chest. Standing skin to skin like this, she felt the blood in her veins boiling. He slid his hands downward and cupped her bottom through her cotton panties. He reclaimed her mouth and asked for her body as he pulled her up to him. She felt the tight rasp of his jeans between her thighs, and a startling rush of heat flooded her feminine core and weakened her knees.

"Tell me you want me this way, Sarah." His plea was little more than a ragged breath against her mouth. "Tell me you want me, or tell me to stop."

"Don't . . . " She squeezed his shoulders and snatched at the midnight fall of hair between her fingers. "Don't stop."

Like a warrior's cry of freedom, Sarah's hungry request sang through Hawk's veins and freed his spirit to soar far beyond the realm of his earthly existence. His body thrummed with the need to become one with this woman, to bond their bodies and spirits in one perfect union.

He scooped her up into his arms and carried her to the bed. She nipped at the base of his chin again and he nearly stumbled, his normally sure-footed steps thwarted by the fertile earth-woman's call of her innocent seduction. With her bewitching hands and tempting lips and hungry eyes, she had quickly transformed him from a patient tutor into a primitive beast, intent on claiming his mate and bonding with her for life.

However short that life might be.

Squeezing his eyes shut, he forced the unwelcome future from his thoughts and concentrated on the insatiable curiosity of her fingers. Her every touch was a healing caress, a passionate promise, an undeniable request.

He set her beside the bed, humbled by her disappointed gasp when he moved away from her. He leaned down and laid claim to her swollen mouth, knowing he would regret the reddened marks of his passion the next morning, but unable to resist when she wound her fingers into his hair and demanded more from his kiss.

He spread his hands on her hips, fighting the urge to pull her closer. "It's okay," he reassured her, twisting his fingers around the elastic at her waist and kneeling to pull her panties off her.

The thatch of toffee brown curls at his eye level

proved a tempting sight, but this was all so new to Sarah, he wouldn't risk frightening her by introducing her to every pleasure he wanted to teach her. Willing his passions back down to a controllable level, he closed his eyes and breathed deeply.

Without looking at her again, he stood and turned and shed the remainder of his clothes and his sicun. He reached to shut off the light, sensing that the cover of darkness would alleviate some of an inexperienced woman's natural fears.

A soft hand on his back startled him. "Don't. I want to see you."

When Hawk straightened and faced her, she stood with one arm across her breasts and the other crossing down low over her abdomen. Hawk's heart flip-flopped with a swell of compassion and the overpowering need to protect and nurture this beautiful woman whose shy ways bespoke her fragile pride and giving heart.

"Do I frighten you?" he asked.

"A little." He would always treasure her honesty, her ability to reveal her true courage no matter what the personal cost. "But I want to see you."

He watched her gaze flutter from his eyes down to the unmistakable proof of his desire. The stain of color on her cheeks heightened the darkening green flecks of need in her golden eyes.

Feeling potent, feeling humble, feeling loved, Hawk stepped closer, locked his gaze with hers and reached for her hand. He pulled it down to her side, revealing her breasts to his hungry longing. The soft glow of the lamp warmed the creamy perfection of the small globes, and highlighted the peachy areolas that begged for his attention.

He reached for her other hand and exposed all of her to his gaze. "You're as beautiful as the good earth herself," he whispered, the praise filling his heart and spilling over into his embittered soul. "I'll always remember you this way, my brave, beautiful Sarah."

Then he leaned down and kissed her reverently, reigniting her passion, worshiping her with his love. She opened beneath him, the sweet welcome of her tender mouth making a mockery of his restraint.

He folded her into his arms and sank onto the bed. He lay back, carrying her on top of him. Her legs parted naturally and he felt the damp heat of her against his thigh. He pulled her farther, until a peachy, sweet breast hovered above his lips, ripe for plucking. He lowered her to his mouth, moistening the tip, and then laving the pebbling bud until her breathy moans vibrated through him. He treated himself to the other breast, showering it with his attentions, falling desperately close to the edge of his control when she tugged at his hair and clutched him to her.

"Hawk . . . " She breathed his name. He felt her legs clench involuntarily about his hips and knew she hovered as close to the brink as he.

"Easy, schoolmarm." The name rolled off his lips as intimate and tender as an endearment.

He rolled over, tucking her beneath him. He cradled her head on the pillows and stretched her arms above her, capturing her hands in one of his. Then he reached down lower, skimming the feminine flare of her hip and finding her delicate center. They both held their breath as he touched her there and found her ready.

Hawk breathed a silent question, waiting for

some word, dreading that she would push him away again. Her tawny gaze held his as she raised her lips to kiss him. "I want this. I want you."

With a shiny golden aura framing her face like a halo, he guided himself to her. He sank into her with one sure stroke. Her hot welcome sheathed him. He gritted his teeth and waited until he felt her relax. Then, helpless to deny himself any longer, he moved within her. He settled on top of her, letting her hips take his weight. He stretched his hand up and held hers, matching the length and spread of her fingers. Briefly, he noted the erotic contrasts in size and color and sex between them, until she blanked out all conscious thought by wrapping her long, elegant fingers around his knuckles and pulling against him in counterpoint to the growing power of his thrusts.

He buried his face against her neck, questioning the hot tears that brushed his cheek, wondering if they were Sarah's or his own. Their bodies fell into a pagan rhythm as old and as everlasting as time itself. Hawk gave himself over to the strength of her spirit guide, and let the great bear carry them both beyond their conscious selves, trusting his own sharp-eyed hawk to guide them back home.

She cried out his name as he surged into her, and when she shattered beneath him, he thanked the spirits for showing him heaven.

Chapter Thirteen

"Where are you going?"

Hawk froze with the laces of his black leather boot in his hands. He exhaled a slow funnel of air and finished tying off the boot beneath his jungle fatigues before responding to the drowsy, husky pitch of Sarah's query.

"Good morning."

"It isn't morning yet, is it?" He heard a rustle from the bed and then the lamp came on. "The sun isn't even up."

Hawk's forced smile grew genuine. Sarah made an adorably rumpled figure early in the morning. He caught a glimpse of one firm breast before she pulled the wrinkled white sheet up to her neck and held it there with her fist. With the other hand she pushed that untamed mass of caramel-colored hair away from her face. The fluid, sensual ease of her movements belied the unfocused haze in her golden eyes.

The memory of those silky tresses tumbling through his fingers teased his palms, and his body sparked with awareness as he recalled how she'd curled that lithe, lovely body into his chest and fallen asleep after the second time they'd made love.

"What time is it?" she asked, nonplussed by his lack of a response. He drank in the sight of her, imprinting this memory alongside every waking moment of the night before, knowing these final hours with Sarah had become the finest moments of his life.

Half of him had wanted to be gone before she woke. Before he had to face the heart-rending task of telling her good-bye.

But the better half of him knew she needed this time with him. As brave and fearless as his she-bear could be, he knew all her doubts couldn't be erased in one night of glorious loving. As much as he had wanted her, he had tried to give her a gift the previous night. The gift of self-assurance. The knowledge that the Walter Kensits of this world had no grasp of real beauty, but that he, at least, could see her for the rare treasure she was, and honor her. He hoped that in some small way he had helped her to believe in herself. He wouldn't take that newly seeded belief away from her by abandoning her without an explanation.

In that, at least, he would not fail Sarah.

He knelt on the bed and tucked a wayward curl behind her ear. He cupped her jaw, memorizing the soft scrunch of her hair beneath his fingertips, stroking the velvety smoothness of her cheek with his thumb. With her eyes half-open and filled with longing, he gave in to his own need and kissed her.

Gently at first, he simply touched his lips to hers. But then her sweet mouth parted and he pushed inside, taking his fill of her, begging her forgiveness, bidding farewell to his most cherished dream.

She responded eagerly, generously, just as she had the night before. But when he pulled away to snatch a ragged breath, he read the confusion in her now wide-awake eyes.

"How are you feeling?" he asked, deliberately ignoring her unspoken questions.

She had braced her hand on his chest and he felt the subtle pressure of her fingertips. She'd done that from her first kiss, shyly hanging on to him, wanting to hold him close. Whether done consciously or not, that tiny little gesture made him feel welcome, wanted. Her eloquent fingers reached deep into his soul and pulled him closer to her heart.

But, as if acknowledging that the way her touch transformed him meant he should be denied that gift, she pulled away. With deceiving interest in the task, she straightened the twisted cord of his necklace.

"I'm . . . fine."

Fine. So cool. So detached. Sarah normally spoke from the heart. He wondered what she'd really wanted to say. *Wonderful. Perfect.* Those were words he would have chosen to describe their night together. But then, with what he was about to do, he couldn't really expect her to say the same.

So he pretended her answer was sufficient. "That's good."

She slipped her hand down to hold the spirit sicun that hung in the middle of his chest. The oblong obsidian stone fit snugly inside her palm. "How are you feeling?"

"I'm . . . fine, too," he answered. The lie caught in his throat and he felt ashamed.

But Hawk wrapped both his hands around hers, absorbing the strength of her spirit. He closed his eyes and felt the power of the lifestone creeping through her into him.

A good portent, to his way of thinking. One person could not own another person's spirit, but when the power of two became one, the harmony between them became a force more powerful than any on earth. If only he could cling to that harmony. If only he had the right to make her his forever.

He had shared only a week with Sarah—a lifetime too short, in his opinion. But the strength he had gained from this gentle woman would sustain him this day. As in his vision so many months before, he knew her spirit would sustain him throughout eternity.

"You're leaving me, aren't you?"

He opened his eyes and saw the telltale frown marring the beauty of her mouth. He didn't bother trying to deny her instincts. She'd proven more than once to have some sort of mystical connection to him.

Hawk stood and picked up the olive green T-shirt off the dressing-table chair. He shoved his arms and head into it, and tucked it into his waistband with spare, deliberate movements. "I have some unfinished business."

"Returning the artifacts?" she asked. "Won't the authorities handle that?"

"Not the artifacts, Sarah."

He unfolded the bloodstained, shredded remains of his survival vest and methodically transferred items from it into a new camouflage flak vest Rafe had brought up to the room. Waterproof matches. A snakebite kit. A packet of herbs and powders to burn as a sacrifice. His knife.

"What's so important you have to leave before sunup?" He ignored the cautious accusation in her voice. "Is it what you three were talking about last night?"

"Partly. I was making arrangements for you and the girls."

"Arrangements?"

Hawk tore through the pockets of the old vest, searching for the strands of hair he'd taken from Sarah's braid.

"Damn." He must have lost them on the trail after he'd been shot. He had hoped to keep them as a reminder of . . .

The touch of her fingers on his arm scorched him with guilt. He jerked away, half-mad with sorrow that he alone could fulfill this duty.

"Why do you have to leave us?"

She stood before him like a goddess. The sheet was draped carelessly over her breasts and hips, where she clutched it, but he could tell her delectable backside was bared to the predawn jungle coming awake outside their window.

Hawk breathed in deeply, tamping down, but not erasing, the desperation growing inside him. "Because *he's* coming."

"Who's coming?"

He didn't answer. He didn't move until he saw the light dawn in her eyes.

"That thing that killed Luis and the others?"

Hawk crossed to the mirror at the dresser and tied a black cotton headband up on his forehead against his hairline. "That *thing* is the spirit of King Meczaquatl. When Salazar and the others opened the tomb, they woke him. His treasure's been stolen, his peace and honor have been violated. He's a vengeful energy who can no longer find his rest."

Sarah materialized beside him in the mirror. "So he killed them because they invaded his tomb?"

"Sounds crazy, doesn't it?" he taunted her, half wishing she'd agree, half hoping she'd say something cruel so he could justify having to leave her.

"No," she whispered, her focus turned somewhere inside. "Not after what I've seen."

Her fingers drifted to the fading bruises at her throat. "He was using you to get rid of me that night, in the tomb."

Then she lifted her gaze to his, her eyes bright with the same knowledge that dulled his. "You're going to lure him back. Call him to you. You said you could channel to the other side. . . ."

"He can't be trusted, Sarah. He has no idea who his enemies are now. Who knows where he'd see a threat? An innocent villager? One of your students? You? I can't allow anyone else to get hurt."

"*You* can't . . . ?" She wrapped her fingers around his forearm again. "Won't he try to kill you, too?"

"I'm a soldier." He covered her hand and willed her to understand what he must do. "I know the risks. It has to be done."

"Get someone else." Her voice rose a pitch.

"I'm the only one who can do this. I'm the only one that demon answers to."

"But you can't!" She tugged at his arm, her protest a cherished benediction to his doomed soul. "At the tomb you weren't the one in control. And when you touched Prini's crown, you weren't yourself anymore. You said you needed my help to pull free."

"Damn, the crown." He wiped a hand across his eyes. "I'll have to stop and get that, too. Restore everything the way it was."

"You can't!"

"Sarah. Schoolmarm." He turned to face the real woman. He should have left an hour ago. He shouldn't have subjected her to this pointless argument as her final memory of him. "I have to do this."

"Then I'm going with you."

"Absolutely not!"

"You need my help."

"No, I don't!"

"What happens if you can't pull yourself from the king's spell once you've got him back in the tomb? If he possesses you, how do you know you'll be able to pull free? What if he decides to use you to hurt more people?"

"It won't happen, Sarah."

"How do you know?"

"I'm not coming home from this mission."

The dead silence of her shock filled the room and hollowed out his soul.

Hawk finished preparing his gear, unable to bear the wounded look of betrayal in Sarah's eyes. He could try to explain how the only way to guarantee that Meczaquatl would return to his rest for all eternity was for Hawk to bury himself in that tomb with him. He would become one with that demon and carry him over to the other side. He'd try to show him that his peace lay in the spirit world and not on this earthly plane.

But if Meczaquatl chose not to stay . . .

He paused when he was packed, tried to meet Sarah's gaze, but she refused. Bereft of even that tiny contact, Hawk slowly straightened. "I think I finally understand what may have happened to Jonathan Ramsey."

"Your friend that disappeared here?"

At least she would still listen. Hawk breathed a bit easier. "There are powerful, inexplicable forces at work on this island. The extra sensitivity I've experienced here leads me to think this is some sort of pathway to the spirit world.

"If Meczaquatl is so willing to channel through me, maybe I can take advantage of his, uh . . . connections . . . and find out something about Jonathan."

"He must have been a very special man."

Hawk didn't know if he could put into words the unique friendship he shared with the men of his recon/rescue unit. "The best."

Sarah huddled behind the sheet. "So you make contact with your friend and you save us all from a vengeful spirit. And if you can't get back, we lose you without an explanation, too."

If Meczaquatl wouldn't relese him, then, with the demon trapped in his body, Hawk would commit himself to the land of the spirits. And he'd watch his beautiful world with Sarah turn to shards of ice, and crumble away into nothingness beneath his feet.

If she could only forgive him . . .

A light tapping drew him from his loathsome thoughts. Before he could reach the door, Sarah had flung it open. Rafe stood outside, dressed in similar military gear, his usual glib repartee momentarily stilled.

"Sarah?"

"Sarah!" Remembering her seminakedness, Hawk snapped into action, wrapping the sheet around her in a makeshift toga and pulling it tight.

But that didn't dissuade his buddy from flirting with his woman. "Aren't you a pretty sight in the morning."

Sarah grabbed Rafe's arm and pulled him into the room, overlooking the compliment that punched Hawk in the gut with a jealous fist.

"Rafe! You can't go without me."

Hawk looked over the top of her head at his longtime friend, warning him off.

Rafe smiled at Sarah, dismissing her request and turning to Hawk. "Kel has some last-minute instructions he needs to go over with you."

"I'm ready."

Hawk shrugged into his vest, expecting to follow Rafe downstairs. But Sarah wouldn't let go. "He's linked so strongly to Meczaquatl that we don't know if he can pull free on his own. I've helped him twice. There's no guarantee that you or anyone else can help him, but we know that I can!"

For a shy woman who struggled to find words sometimes, she seemed to have an amazingly succinct, persuasive effect on Rafe. Hawk closed his hands over her shoulders to pull her away. But she twisted free and tugged at Rafe's shirt.

"If you're any kind of friend, you won't let him go without me. Promise me, Rafe. Don't let him leave this house."

Rafe looked from Sarah to Hawk, all traces of

humor absent from his eyes. "She makes sense, Shadow Man. There's no guarantee that I can call you back. And I sure as hell ain't lookin' forward to blowing that place up with you inside just to destroy that thing."

Her shoulders flinched when she heard their alternate plan. But Hawk recognized the quick return of determined steel in her posture. "He knows I'm the only sure chance he has to come home. You want him to come home, right?"

Hawk sighed wearily, knowing Kel would be a harder sell than Rafe, but conceding that Sarah would not be beaten on this. Against his better judgment, he made a reluctant truce with his friend.

"You'll stay with the girls? Get them and Sarah home safely if anything happens to me?" Hawk demanded that one concession.

"They'll be as safe as my own nieces." Rafe winked at Sarah, then looked at Hawk. For all his devilish sense of humor and irreverent attitude, Hawk knew Rafe like a brother, and relied on the bonds of trust forged in battle and shared grief. "I give you my word."

Hawk nodded his approval.

Sarah apparently shared that same trust. She turned and hurried to the adjoining bathroom.

"Give me twenty minutes."

She was ready in fifteen.

And they'd been on the road for five hours, going back into the dark heart of the jungle that had sealed her fate and changed her life forever.

Sarah stared out the truck's side window, resigned to sharing Hawk's brooding silence. What could she say, anyway?

I love you?

Her love could never be enough. *She* could never be enough.

I'll always remember you like this, he had said the night before. Sarah knew a good-bye when she heard one. She'd heard too many of them in her life. Through her tears she had poured out her love for this man, knowing it wasn't enough to keep him. She had surrendered her body to his healing touch, and accepted the fleeting gift of his desire, knowing neither his kindness nor his passion could ever be enough for her.

But she could not deny him his life. No longer the meek, clueless schoolmarm who had started this journey so long ago, Sarah rose to the challenge with her eyes open. She made a conscious choice to accept this danger, to put her feelings aside and leave her sheltered world to help Hawk face that vengeful resurrected spirit. Hawk had inspired in her a passion for honor, and a calling to do what was right—no matter what the personal sacrifice.

She held the power necessary for his survival. And she would not deny him her help.

He'd saved her life. He'd saved her soul from the clutches of second-guessing and self-doubt.

She could do no less for him.

They stopped only once. And when she climbed back up the embankment with Queen Prini's crown tucked safely in her backpack, Hawk thanked her. Then he apologized.

"Forgive me someday," he said beseechingly. "For putting you through this."

He kissed her then. Briefly. Hotly. With a sense of predestined sorrow that left her numb inside.

When they reached Las Lagumas, Sarah

climbed out of the truck, chilled by the effect of being frozen in time. Everything stood much as they had left it those few short days ago. Shattered bits of the radio were strewn among the charred remnants of her clothes in the fire pit. The door to the mess tent swung open on its hinges.

And through the trees, the moss-shrouded basalt pyramid of Meczaquatl's tomb rose like a black mountain against the low-hanging sky.

"Let's unload everything," said Hawk. "Then you can fix yourself something to eat while I start the ceremony."

"Aren't you eating dinner?"

He stared at her from the bleak depths of his eyes, and she wondered if he thought taking in food now seemed pointless to him.

"I've fasted all day in preparation for this. But you can bring me some water when you're done."

Relieved that his refusal of sustenance had more to do with ceremony than fatalism, Sarah set aside her misgivings, picked up a small crate, and followed him up the steps and into the tomb.

"I feel him. He knows I'm here."

Sarah huddled in her blanket at the tomb's entrance, chilled by the ominous certainty in Hawk's voice. The only light inside the chamber came from the fire near Hawk. Through the pungent haze that rose from the fire and filled the air, she saw him clutch his spirit stone at his chest.

He'd removed his clothes at sundown and lit the fire. He wrapped a blanket around his hips, and, facing the open wall of Meczaquatl's burial chamber, he sat down cross-legged before the growing blaze. Cautioning Sarah to stay back, close to their source of fresh air, he tossed a handful of powder into the flames and chanted something in his native Pawnee language. The flames burned blue, red-orange, then pure white. The smoke changed colors, too, as it filled the chamber and made the air heavy with a tangy scent.

Awed by the simple ceremony, Sarah watched with the rapt fascination of a scholar, respecting Hawk's unique mysticism while filling her heart with a powerful, protective prayer of her own. Hawk continued to chant, tipping back his head and inhaling the smoky fog like an aphrodisiac. He sat like that for nearly half an hour, until the cloud began to dissipate. Then he bowed his head and fell into a silence broken only by the atmospheric rumblings of the gathering storm.

"He's coming."

Sarah pressed herself into the wall, finding small comfort in the cold stones at her back. At Hawk's request, she maintained a silent vigil. He'd invited her to observe, but not to interfere. If Meczaquatl perceived her as a threat in any way, then he might turn Hawk against her, or even possess her himself and force her to fling herself down the stone steps, or stop her heart, causing her death as he had with Salazar and his men.

Hawk *wanted* Meczaquatl's spirit inside him. He wanted to conquer the demon's will with his own, and guide the restless spirit back to his rightful resting place.

Hawk jerked his head up. His midnight eyes scanned the darkness. A subarctic shiver rippled along Sarah's spine. Some sixth sense kicked in, a feeling of being watched. She slowly turned and glanced over her shoulder.

A chimera of light hovered in the passageway,

its sparkling shots of color winking on and off in the air beside her.

"Stay perfectly still," Hawk warned her. "Come here, you bastard."

The glacial challenge in Hawk's voice snared the miasma's attention. It floated across the room, its prismatic colors fading as it moved. It lingered around the fire a few moments, recoiled, paused, then slowly blended itself into the hanging mist.

The flames of the fire grew hotter, whiter. A searing flash blinded Sarah's eyes.

When her vision had recovered and she'd adjusted to the comparative darkness once more, she saw Hawk writhing on the floor. The blanket entwined with his legs, capturing him instead of covering him. Centuries-old dust and dirt stained the sweat on his skin. His eyes were squeezed shut, his face a twisted expression of agony.

"Hawk?" She mouthed his name, tortured by the anguish he must be experiencing.

His body stiffened and his eyes snapped open, wide, glazed, a wild light splitting the darkness there.

"Hawk?" She called to him again, then shrank back and hugged herself tightly. She blinked back the sudden tears that stung her own eyes, and fell silent as he had asked.

Wherever Hawk was now, he couldn't hear her anyway.

Hawk circled around again, the impermeable mists spinning around him in opposition to his reeling equilibrium. He clutched at his head, planting his feet in the quagmire that seeped up to his ankles.

When the retching dizziness in his stomach had calmed and he could focus his eyes, he realized he was not alone.

Bathed in a brightness that shone from a nameless point above him, Hawk stood in a circle of light. Beyond the blinding circle a creeping growth of dark green leaves and ebony shadows, hung with the heavy mists of death, surrounded him.

His nightmare place.

The jungles of Tenebrosa.

Haunting him from this world into the next.

He blinked away from the swirling shadows and anchored his gaze in the light. With him stood a smaller man, bronze skinned, dark haired, his shoulders set with a royal carriage, his sharp eyes primed for battle.

"Meczaquatl." The slurred name tripped over his swollen tongue.

"You seek Me." The words rang clearly in Hawk's ears. "As I seek you."

Hawk bowed his head, humbled by the power of this great leader. "I am a man of peace."

"You are a warrior. Like Me."

"Only if I have to be." Vague shapes outlined themselves in the mists surrounding them. A silent warning pricked at Hawk's neck. His limbs were leaden extensions of his body. He concentrated, willing control back into his arms and legs and mind. He stood straight, his thoughts and words clearing. "You don't belong in my world. The men who raided your temple—"

"They do not honor My name!"

A gold-tipped staff of polished teak appeared in the king's hand. With grim, quick eyes, he studied the weapon. "You have returned what is Mine."

"Those men did not honor your immortal slum-

ber. They were common thieves. Greedy bastards who did not respect your name, your right to lie in state, the treasures of your kingdom."

"I can take back what is Mine. It is of petty meaning." The circumference of light widened. Solid forms stepped from the mist. Warriors. Men like the king, armed with staffs and spears, bowing down and taking their place at the king's right hand.

"I mean you no harm," said Hawk.

"He will make a fine prize." Meczaquatl ignored Hawk's entreaty. Six more warriors circled Hawk, closing in on him.

"The men who dishonored you are dead," Hawk urged. His head throbbed with the effort to remember his purpose.

"They do not honor My wishes! They must be punished."

"No!"

He felt a weight around his neck and looked down. A golden breastplate, like those the king's men wore, weighted him down in the mire.

"They defiled her!" cried the king. "I took her as a slave and made her My queen. And they keep her from Me!"

A staff of teak appeared in Hawk's hand. The light expanded and he could make out the forms of slave girls kneeling low to the ground, each carrying trinkets of gold and jewels to lay at Meczaquatl's feet. The king waved his staff above the treasures, offering them to Hawk.

He finally understood. "I don't belong here."

"You have fought for what is Mine."

"I fought to save those I love," Hawk protested.

"You have come to My world. You will make a worthy vessel."

"*I am leaving your world!*" shouted Hawk, trying to remember his own home. A pair of tawny eyes floated through his vision, cherished, yet forgotten as quickly as he recognized them. "*You're staying here. I have shown you the way home.*"

"*Silence him!*"

Hundreds of hands touched Hawk's shoulders, pulling him down. The muscles in his legs melted like molasses beneath him. He tried to fight off the warriors, but his hands grew numb. He swatted at his attackers, his fingers slicing through the mist of their bodies.

"*No!*" he shouted, his mind turning to mush. He must concentrate on his purpose. He must remember to go back.

Alone.

"*I will punish the infidels for keeping My queen from Me!*"

Hawk felt himself sinking. The light surrounding him stretched farther into the mist, transforming the nightmare jungle into a gruesome reality. He felt the humidity of it in his pores, smelled the damp stench of it in his nostrils.

"*No.*" His protest sounded weak, even to his own ears. "*I can't stay here.*"

Other faces took shape. Faces from the king's time. Fallen comrades from his own time. A black-haired marine in shaggy green Vietnam fatigues from a time in-between.

"*Father?*"

Hawk had stopped reaching out now. He fought only to keep his eyes open.

"*You don't belong here, son.*"

"*But I have to stop him. . . .*" The protest gurgled in his throat.

293

Another face materialized. A criminal. He'd tracked that face down to Tenebrosa.

A muffled roar growled through his consciousness. But the sound died in the mist, and the recognition escaped him.

He heard the bellowing call of a wild animal from across a distance, so far away it sounded like the last remnant of an echo. He turned toward the dying sound.

A familiar uniformed man stepped from the mist. He reached for Hawk with a broad, capable hand. "You don't belong here, my friend. Nobody could have stopped what happened that day on Tenebrosa. Not even you, Shadow Man."

"Jonathan?" Hawk tried to latch on, but his fingers had grown too weak. "Wait! I don't understand." He felt himself slipping.

"It's all right, my friend. I need you back home. You and Brodie and the others, I need you to take care of my girls."

"I will. I promise . . . "

"Seize him. Now!"

King Meczaquatl stepped into the hottest part of the light as Hawk slipped away into the darkness. He felt the hands on him again. Pulling him up this time.

But it was too far, and he was too weak.

The hands left him and he started to fall.

He heard the roar again, a distant imagining through the cotton inside his head. But he recognized the sound this time.

The call of a bear.

He tried to answer, but the mists swallowed his voice.

He felt the broad, hard pads of the bear's paws on

his chest, bearing down with a heavy weight. He felt its long claws digging into his skin.

The bear's golden brown fur danced through his vision. It bellowed again, closer this time, calling to him. He felt its warm breath on his face.

He tried to breathe in its reviving warmth, but the pressure on his chest vanished. He reached out, but found nothing but mist and darkness in his grasp, and he began to sink.

"No." He reached for the bear again, calling to it, willing its great power to guide him back home.

But other hands reached for him now. The king's hands. Warriors' hands. Pulling him down to them. Trapping his soul in the murky pit of mist and darkness.

A blinding light exploded around him, inside him. A circlet of gold inlaid with precious jewels swam before his eyes.

"Take it!" someone shouted. His ears unstopped. His vision spun in a dizzying eddy. "Give him back to me!"

The claws snatched at him again, digging into his chest, tossing aside his armor.

"You've had your true love!" The voice was a woman's, faintly familiar. "Give me mine! I love him! Give him back!"

Something pressed against his mouth. Soft. Hard. Urgent. Breathing life into his body. Giving him strength.

The pressure eased. "Hawk, I love you. Don't let him win. Fight him. Come back to me!"

Something brushed across his face, across his shoulders, down his arms. He felt the pressure at his mouth again, felt hot, moist pinpricks dotting *his cheeks. An odd warmth swelled inside him and radiated through his limbs.*

The faces of his father and Jonathan and Meczaquatl shimmered across his vision. Ten clutching talons dug into his flesh, and the circle of light shrank.

"No! He must stay!" Meczaquatl shook his staff. But even now his image grew faint. The swirling mists picked up speed, swallowing up the image of his father.

A dark-haired beauty he did not recognize came into focus.

Jonathan vanished.

"Wait. . . . " Hawk called weakly, but his friend did not return.

The pressure at his mouth distracted him again. He tilted his head, seeking its source, and a warmth pressed the underside of his jaw. He curled his fingers into fists and savored the rush of blood pumping into his hands. Blindly he reached out, needing an anchor to hold on to. His fingers brushed against soft brown fur. He dug in and held on, turning his mouth to the hot, beckoning warmth that had grazed his chin.

"No!" Meczaquatl's icy grip clutched Hawk's shoulder and he fell back, his breath frozen in his chest. "He must stay. I need him!"

"I need him!" A tawny gaze whispered into his mind. The Kodiak's eyes. No. Something much more precious.

"Husband, come to me." The dark-eyed princess spoke. Meczaquatl released him. Hawk collapsed. His eyes drifted shut and he plunged into the pit.

But something halted his fall. His shoulders jerked in their sockets. Something hard and rough rasped along his back.

"Damn you, Virgil Echohawk! Don't leave me!" a woman's voice, soft and husky, cried in his ear.

Virgil.

The name stabbed through his foggy subconscious.

Meczaquatl touched the woman in Hawk's vision. Gold sparkled in her raven hair. The gold circlet. Prini's crown.

"My queen," spoke the king, every trace of the vengeful despot fading into gentle disbelief.

"We are together now, my husband. Come rest beside me."

Hawk wanted to laugh but found no breath in his lungs. The damn king was out of control because they'd kept him from his woman.

His woman.

"Virgil!"

The mists vanished along with the haunting jungle ghosts, leaving Hawk suspended in a weightless, freezing darkness.

"No . . . " He reached out, seeking the Kodiak. The she-bear. No. Seeking the woman.

What Hawk saw and what he thought got jumbled up inside his mind. He had to find the way out before he was caught here forever. He had to find the path back to the living world. But he was so lost, so turned around. The man who'd earned his living blazing trails and helping others find their way couldn't find his own way home.

"Save me!"

The darkness swallowed him up, and Hawk's vision went black.

His body jerked. He sucked in a breath. His lungs ached as if expanding for the first time in eons. He crashed down hard and felt his body slipping.

Something warm and wet splashed on his face. And then he was falling.

"No!" he screamed, tucking himself into a ball to help his body absorb the jolts and jerks of his descent. He slammed to a stop against something soft.

"No." He clutched at the soft form beneath his body, holding tight and anchoring himself to its pervading warmth. "Save me."

"I'm here, Virgil." The same voice that had called to him in his vision whispered in his ear. He latched on to the sound and tried to follow it. "He's gone and you're here with me."

Then he felt kisses on his face and the tender ministrations of eloquent hands on his body. Real hands. Flesh-and-blood hands. Touching him. Healing him. Making him feel alive again.

"Save me," he said softly. He moved his own hands, discovering the shape of the creature—the woman—he held, the imprint of some distant paradise waking a memory that would never die.

He clung to her warmth like a dying spirit seeks the light. While the rain poured over them, he undressed her with urgent care. He bared her body to the clouds and the night, then covered her with himself. He needed her under him, around him, with him. He needed her affirmation of life after spinning too close to death himself.

He knew her at the last moment, too late for caution, too late for kind words.

He dug his fingers into the solid reassurance of muddy earth on either side of her head and levered himself above her. He saw her tears and the beckoning welcome of her shy smile. Then he buried himself inside her loving, healing warmth.

"Save me, schoolmarm." He swept her into his arms and took what she offered, needing her, using her in a way for which he could never forgive himself, and loving her more than he ever dreamed possible. "Save me."

Chapter Fourteen

"Rafe, quit flirtin' with my little girl."

The deep bass voice rumbled through the corridor of Kansas City's St. Luke's Hospital.

Hawk was only marginally aware of the man making faces and little cooing noises beside him. He looked through the glass of the hospital nursery at the same pink-hatted infant Rafe did, but his thoughts were more than a hundred miles away in Marysville, Kansas.

He scarcely noticed when Brodie Maxwell clapped his hand on Rafe's shoulder, pushed him aside, and took his proud place at the window. The big man blew a kiss and whispered in a falsetto voice, "Daddy's here. You can't see men like Rafe until you're forty-two years old."

Rafe defended himself with a smile. "I don't know, Brodie, with those big, beautiful eyes, Katie's pretty hard to resist."

Hawk thought of beautiful green-gold eyes, an unmistakable color that had first drawn his attention to Sarah McCormick.

"You won't get any argument from me," said Brodie. He nudged Hawk in the arm, forcing him to bring his attention back to the baby. "She's a beauty, isn't she?"

Hawk ignored the painful longing that ached in his gut and focused on the legitimate happiness he felt for his old friend. "It's a good thing she takes after BJ, and not you."

The three men laughed, and for a few brief moments Hawk let himself enjoy the relaxed familiarity among friends.

"Don't tell me one little girl who's not even a day old can turn seasoned soldiers like yourselves into a bunch of marshmallows." Kel Murphy limped up to the nursery, shrugged off the teasing comebacks from Rafe and Brodie, then proceeded to wave at Katherine Claire Maxwell through the window.

Hawk's heart skipped a beat, wondering what news Kel had brought with him. But he could sense the mournful calm that settled over the four of them. Even Rafe grew subdued at the reflection of four seasoned warriors, gone their separate ways, but reunited in times of trouble and times of joy. Except their team wasn't complete. It would never be complete until they were joined by their missing leader.

"I saw him." Hawk finally broke the reverent silence. "On the other side, I saw Jonathan's spirit. He gave me an order."

"That sounds about right," said Rafe.

"Yeah." Hawk tried to smile at the shared memory of their commander, but couldn't quite make it happen. "He said to take care of his girls."

"Emma and Kerry are just fine." Brodie reassured him about Jonathan's wife and daughter. "They're with BJ now in the visitation room if you want to check on them."

"Maybe I should." Hawk pulled back from the window.

Kel shoved his hands deep into his pockets and shrugged his shoulders. "You've got other problems to think about right now."

"What do you mean?" Hawk's radar clicked into alert mode. "You got Sarah and the girls back to Marysville, didn't you?"

"The flight was fine. They got into town last night, no problem," Kel reassured him. "But I think she wanted some different company on that plane."

"She doesn't need me," Hawk asserted, feeling the resolution in his bones that Sarah was better off without him. "Not after what I did to her."

He turned and found Rafe and Brodie standing directly behind him. Backing him up? Or creating a blockade to keep him from running?

Rafe frowned. "She's crazy about you."

"Do you know the town is setting up a hearing as to whether to keep her on as a teacher or not? Word is she may even get her teaching certificate revoked for endangering those teenagers." Kel spoke again, and Hawk felt buffeted from all sides, not unlike his time in the pits of hell, or wherever Meczaquatl had taken him.

He whirled around. "She didn't do anything wrong."

"Don't tell me." Kel's dry voice cut through all of Hawk's good intentions. "If you think she can handle it, fine."

"She can handle anything!" Hawk's need to defend Sarah against any slight thundered through his veins, touched on his temper and nicked at his conscience.

"If you say so." Kel dismissed the issue with a shrug of his shoulders. He tilted his head to look around him at Rafe. "Hey, loverboy, why don't I give you a ride to the airport?"

"Sure." Rafe shook hands with Brodie and smiled. "Listen, if you ever need a babysitter, call me. You know I'm the best."

"You live three hours away," reminded Brodie.

"So I'm flexible." Rafe spread his arms wide to emphasize his point. "Take care, buddy. My best to BJ."

"Brodie." Kel shook hands, too. "Katie has a good man for a father."

"Thanks," said Brodie. Hawk felt their focus shift toward him. "And thanks for stepping in to help."

"No problem. It's nice to feel useful every now and then."

Hawk took Kel's hand and traded a curt goodbye. Rafe held on to his hand a moment longer. "Don't leave her hanging, Hawk."

When Kel and Rafe left, Hawk closed his eyes and breathed in deeply through his nose and out through his mouth, trying to regain control of his peaceful center. He'd done Sarah a terrible injustice. He'd failed her, just as he'd feared—just as he'd known—he would.

Brodie's broad hand on his shoulder pulled him from his thoughts. "So what are you doing here when your heart's somewhere else?"

"She doesn't need me." Hawk repeated aloud

303

the mantra that had played through his head since climbing on the plane that had carried him out of Tenebrosa. "I can only hurt her."

"I know you. You'd never hurt somebody you love."

Love? The word struck him in the heart like a cruel curse. Hawk faced Brodie. He wanted his friend to understand, and he himself needed to hear again why he had to let Sarah go.

"I used her, Brodie. She opened up her heart and I took . . . "

He choked on his own self-loathing. "I took what she offered and gave nothing back. I didn't listen to what she felt; I didn't pay attention to her needs."

"You were coming out of a trance then, weren't you? Like one of your vision quests? Would she hold you responsible for your actions?"

"She had a fiancé once who treated her the same way. He used her for his own selfish purposes, and it wounded her. He robbed her of every shred of confidence she had in herself." He shook his head at the tragedy he'd seen in Sarah's spirit when they first met. The mother bear's ripped-out heart turned out to be Sarah's shattered self-image.

His pain turned into a begruding smile as he thought of the amazing strength he'd discovered in her, shaky at times, but never defeated. "I was no different. I used her all along. I used her gentle touches and beautiful eyes and incredible courage to heal me. And in the end I destroyed any good I might have done her. No, she doesn't need me."

"Did you ask her?" Brodie played Devil's advocate. Hawk hated him for it. His will was already weak enough. "One thing I've learned from loving BJ is that you've got to speak what you feel. Give her credit for knowing her own heart. And knowing what she can and can't handle. She may surprise you."

"Even if she forgives me, it wouldn't matter." Hawk squeezed the railing in front of the window, looking at the perfect, normal little babies on the other side, damning his powers for damning him. "I'm a Shadow Man. I'm weird. Different. A lady like her shouldn't have to deal with a creature like me."

Brodie crossed his massive arms in front of him. "From what Rafe and Kel said, it sounds to me like she handled you pretty well."

"She shouldn't have to." Hawk imagined that delicate slip of sensual femininity dwarfed by his friend's stature. "She's fragile, Brodie. I've put her through enough already."

"Hell, Hawk. She survived a week on Tenebrosa with you. She followed you to the land of the dead and brought you back. Just how tough do you want the lady to be?"

Brodie's fighting words sank in, and Hawk finally realized the delusion his guilt had created. Had he been just as quick as Kensit to judge Sarah's limitations? To deem his Sarah fragile?

Feminine? Yes. Shy? Working on it. Delicate? In the most incredibly sexy way.

But fragile?

His she-bear?

"Besides"—Brodie interrupted his thoughts, not knowing Hawk had already made up his mind to ask Sarah to forgive him, to accept him, to take him as he was, shaman and all—"if she's in trouble, you owe her."

Julie Miller

* * *

Hawk slipped into the back of the Marysville High School auditorium, the overwhelming sense of déjà vu blending with a mixture of anticipation and dread. It hadn't taken long for the lynch mob to form. As in that fateful town meeting so many weeks ago, the lines were drawn, with the people in the audience debating the issue as vigorously as their elected officials.

He spotted Sarah at once, sitting at a table up front, facing the mayor, superintendent and town council, who sat on an elevated platform above her. He slid his gaze over her, noted the coppery wisps of doubt in her aura, but took heart in the brave blue courage he saw surrounding her.

"This is a kangaroo court, Walter," he heard her say. "If the parents don't hold me liable, why should you?"

"It's a question of decency, Sarah." Hawk thought of his twelve-inch survival knife, locked in the toolbox of his pickup. He rubbed his palms together, quelling the urge to carve Kensit up into tiny pieces in the midst of these uncivilized proceedings. "Up until this incident, your reputation has been impeccable. But to hear that you've engaged in such reckless, inappropriate behavior makes me wonder if you're still competent enough to teach our children."

"Reckless?" Sarah challenged him, rising to her feet. Kensit leaned back in his chair. "Mr. Echohawk and I righted a wrong that has been plaguing Las Lagumas and other historical sites for centuries. We saved lives. I call that being responsible, not reckless."

Her shoulders stiffened like steel, and Hawk smiled, knowing Kensit had no chance to win this

306

argument now. "Inappropriate? The only thing inappropriate down there was Luis Salazar and his band of criminals. His nephew was cleared of any charges by the state. Even they recognize an evil man taking advantage of a good program. Would you like to see my citation from the governor of Tenebrosa?"

A tall, reedy, white-haired woman stood up in the audience. Hawk had never hit a lady, but if Mrs. String Bean said one word against Sarah . . . "Think of the publicity for our school system. We have an international hero on our staff."

Mrs. Plumpy stood up beside her. "Could we put that citation on display in the school trophy case?"

Hawk was in the midst of revising his opinion of the town's busybodies when five familiar figures stood up in unison from the front row. They circled their beloved Sarah, standing as straight and poised as their favorite role model.

Denise addressed the council in a loud, clear voice. "We're here today because of Miss Mack. We learned a lot on our trip. Not just about history and geography, but about us, and what we can accomplish if we believe in ourselves. She taught us that we can be more than who we think we are."

The room hushed and Denise continued. "Our schools are facing enough trouble with overcrowding and violence and budget cuts. Don't take away our best teachers, too."

Kensit's aura glowed with frustration. He shot his fingers through his hair, mussing its moussed perfection. "Young lady, you're missing the point. . . . "

"*You're* missing the point, Walter." The mayor

frowned and pounded his gavel on the table. "I'm dismissing these ridiculous charges." The superintendent nodded his approval. "Thank you for teaching all three of my kids, Sarah. We're glad to have you back. Now all of you, go home."

Hawk rose to his feet with the rest of the crowd. Twenty-four endless hours had passed since Brodie Maxwell had knocked some down-to-earth sense into his unearthly brain. He had made the drive home in record time, but had stopped to clean up and grab a minimum amount of sleep so he could face Sarah like a civilized gentleman, and not the jungle predator he'd turned himself into the past week.

But now that she was so close, she seemed that much farther away. Swimming upstream against the crowd of people filing toward the door, Hawk had to stop repeatedly to accept congratulations from people who'd never spoken to him before, or to answer questions about taking on new clients and expanding his practice.

Welcome. Acceptance. Hawk read the sincerity of the people who spoke to him, thanked the Great Spirit for it, then secretly applauded Sarah for her role in his newfound inclusion into Marysville.

Over the heads of well-wishers, Hawk saw the throng of townsfolk pressing toward Sarah to congratulate her. He worried what effect the stress of meeting all these people might have on her. But then he relaxed. Shyness might make all this attention a little daunting, but she wasn't one to back down from a challenge.

"Hawk!" A high, excited chorus of voices snagged his attention, and he was engulfed in a flurry of hugs from five of his favorite young ladies.

"We wondered when you'd get here," said Lyndsay. "Miss Mack was pretty down on the way home."

"But that plane was so cool!" Lynnette bubbled with excitement. "Mr. Murphy had a butler who served us pop and Twinkies. Do you know he writes books? He told me to write about Tenebrosa and send it to him to read. Isn't that cool?"

Colleen chided her enthusiastic friend. "He called our parents to meet us, and then explained everything that happened. He told the truth in a nice way and nobody got in trouble."

"Until Mr. Kensit showed up." Quiet Andrea joined the fray.

"He's such a jerk," said Denise. "We're glad she found you."

Hawk tried to agree, but he was no match for five teenage girls.

"You're going to marry her, right?" questioned Lynnette.

"Of course he's going to," answered Lyndsay. "People in love do that."

Giving up with a smile and a wave, Hawk moved on past, letting the girls enjoy their moment in the spotlight. A few more steps put him behind Sarah, but before he could call to her, Kensit broke through the crowd on the other side. He cornered her against the table.

The need to protect her raged through Hawk's blood. But obeying the wisdom of patience, he stood back. Curling his hands into fists, Hawk held his ground and watched Sarah fight her own battle. Kensit bent his head to Sarah's ear, close enough for his breath to stir the tendrils of her hair.

"I've never seen you like this. So sure of yourself. It's damned appealing. Let me take you to dinner, to apologize for any misunderstanding between us." Kensit's hand drifted to Sarah's hip. Her hand was there just as quickly, removing it.

"Go back to your bimbo, Walter." Hawk winced at her cutting tone. "Maybe she's too dumb to see through your two-faced charm. I'm not."

"It's that Indian, isn't it?" Blondie's mouth dropped open; he seemed dumbfounded, too caught up in his own ego to accept any blame himself. "He's not the right kind of man for you."

"He's the only man for me." She pushed at Kensit's chest, forcing him back a step. "Leave me alone, Walter. You're invading my personal space."

Kensit shook his head. "My God, Sarah. What would your father say?"

"That it's about time I stood up for what I want."

Grumbling under his breath, Kensit stalked off. Hawk smiled, his pride in Sarah too strong to hide. The power of his emotion must have alerted that latent sixth sense of hers. Her slender shoulders relaxed with a sigh and she turned to face him.

Her shy half smile rocked him back on his heels. "I wondered when you'd be coming home."

Home. On Sarah's lips, the word sounded pretty close to heaven.

Suddenly he felt as awkward and shy as Sarah had once been. He looked from side to side, watching the gatherings of friends and colleagues lingering in the auditorium. "You want to run off to a tropical island somewhere?" he asked.

Sarah laughed, the weight of dread lifting from her heart. Walter's groundless threats to take her job away had sapped her waning strength. But the real fear in her heart had come from the uncertainty of whether she'd see Hawk again. True, they lived in the same small town. But she was an expert at blending into a crowd and remaining anonymous. She had no doubt Hawk could slip in and out of her world unseen, too.

"Been there. Done that." She tried to keep the desperate question she wanted to ask out of her voice. "But I'd settle for a walk to my car."

"Yes, ma'am."

The summer air was cool on her bare arms, but Hawk's large hand burned her skin at the small of her back. He guided her through the night as unerringly as he had guided her through the jungle. He made her feel safe. Cherished. Loved.

She prayed she could do the same for him.

When they reached her car, Sarah turned to face him. The soft amber glow of the streetlight reflected off the blue highlights in his inky black hair. The light warmed the coppery skin across his regal nose and cheekbones. But his darker-than-midnight eyes glowed with a light of their own.

"Sarah—"

"Hawk—"

They laughed together, and Sarah took heart in knowing he might be experiencing the same set of nerves she did. "You go ahead."

"No, ladies first," he insisted.

Lifting her chin, Sarah reached down deep into

her heart and did the bravest thing she'd ever done. "I love you, Hawk."

He shifted on his black-booted feet, and she put her hand on his chest, hastening to stop him from interrupting her.

"I didn't say all those things at the tomb just to keep you in the land of the living. I didn't want to lose you." She frowned at the arrogance of her statement and corrected herself. "I didn't want to lose the chance to be with you."

"Sarah—"

She pressed her fingers over his lips to silence him. He held himself perfectly still, a docile brute fighting his instinct to take action. She wondered if he'd ever forgive himself for strangling her while under Meczaquatl's influence. She wondered if she could make him see that she had already forgiven him.

"When you . . . " Her breath came in shallow gasps as she remembered Hawk's tortured wails as he fought to bring himself back to the living. She pushed the nightmare from her mind and concentrated on the living, breathing, fully cognizant man in front of her. "When I pulled you from the tomb, and you made love to me, right there on the jungle floor, I felt beautiful."

"I'm sorry I—"

"Don't you dare apologize!" She brushed her fingers across his jaw now, petting him, soothing him. "You needed me, Hawk. Only me. I've never been that important to anyone in my whole life. You weren't using me. I was giving myself to you. My body, my heart, my strength . . . I wanted to give you whatever you needed."

She cupped his jaw and met the full force of his

obsidian gaze. "I still want to give you that. Everything. If you want me."

"If I want . . . ?"

He gathered her into his arms then. His mouth claimed hers in a searing kiss that left her pulse pounding all the way down to her toes. She wrapped her arms around his neck and held on, feeling whole at last, locked in this man's arms.

When he ended the kiss, he still held her, running his hands up and down her arms, along her back, over her hips, and then back up again to frame her face. The light in his eyes glittered with hope, and the faintest sheen of tears glazed the tips of his sooty lashes.

"I thought I'd destroyed everything between us." She smiled through her own tears, and Hawk knew they were shed in happiness, not sorrow, this time. "At the estate house, I couldn't tell you I loved you because I didn't want to raise your hopes, not knowing if I'd make it back or not. I didn't want to hurt you the way Kensit did. But then, at the tomb, I was so desperate for you, I just took, and I didn't care, and I thought—I worried—that was the same way Kensit had used you."

He stroked her with every catch of his breath, beating himself inside, even as he apologized. Finally Sarah caught his hands. She pressed a kiss inside one palm, then rested her cheek on its callused pillow.

"You were never like Walter. You never could be. You love me." Sarah went still as her courage wavered. "You do love me, don't you?"

Protecting herself instinctively, she released him and backed toward her car. But with a devil-

313

ish smile, Hawk followed her. At the last moment, he reached for her and turned. With her snug in his arms, he leaned against the car and pulled her right off her feet.

Every solid inch of chest and thighs and man imprinted itself along the length of her body like a caress.

"Yes. I love you. I loved you when I cut your hair. I loved you when you stood up to Salazar. I loved you when you saved my soul. And I'll love you forever, if you can stand being married to a big, crazy Indian who sees things he shouldn't, and knows things he doesn't always want to." He punctuated every sentence with a kiss, igniting a feverish combination of touch and words and love.

Sarah wound her fingers into his midnight hair, nibbled on the sensitive hollow beneath his chin, and gave back some of his own seductive medicine. "Well, know this, Virgil Echohawk, gifted man who uses his powers to help others in need. I love you. I want you. I want to be your wife."

Some time later, tangled in the flowered sheets of her four-poster bed and Hawk's arms, sure of his love and sure of herself, Sarah snuggled closer. She traced circles along the sculpted contours of his sinfully beautiful chest and hummed a tuneless little song of contentment.

"I'd like to invite my mother, and my father's uncle, Otis Peace Hands," said Hawk. "Brodie, Rafe and Kel, of course."

Sarah flicked her finger over one taut male nipple and his breath hissed. He caught her hand and spread it flat on top of his heart. "Witch," he teased. "I'm trying to plan a wedding here as soon as possible." He pressed a kiss to her forehead and hugged her to his side. "I'm afraid I'm going to tarnish your reputation because I won't be able to stay away."

She harrumphed like a scolded little girl and levered herself so that the top half of her body rested on top of his. "I'm thirty-four years old. It's about time my reputation lost a little of its luster."

Hearing him laugh helped her understand just how deeply she had touched this man. The trail of her fingers led her to the sicun resting on his chest. She lifted it reverently, continually amazed by its vibrant, radiating warmth. "This is your spirit stone, right?"

He nodded, capturing the stone and her hand together in his grasp. "My father led me on the quest to find it when I was thirteen. It resonates with the power of my soul, protecting me, sometimes increasing the strength of my perception.

"I think I figured out the end of my vision, schoolmarm." He closed his arms around her. Sarah nestled her head beneath his chin, keenly aware of the warmth of his sicun, his soul, vibrating through her. "I saved you, and you saved me. Together we can conquer anything. In this world or the next."

Sarah sought his lips to thank him, and to pledge her love on their journey together. She had found the adventure she had sought in the loving heart and honorable soul of her Shadow Man.

And he had found the courage and will to come home to Sarah's heart.

STRANGER ON THE MOUNTAIN

Linda O. Johnston

The mountain lion disappeared from Eskaway Mountain over a hundred years ago; according to legend, the cat disappeared when an Indian princess lost her only love to cruel fate. According to myth, love will not come to her descendants until the mountain lion returns. Dawn Perry has lived all her life at the foot of Eskaway Mountain, and although she has not been lucky in love, she refuses to believe in myths and legends—or in the mountain lion that lately the townsfolk claim to have seen. So when she finds herself drawn to newcomer Jonah Campion, she takes to the mountain trails to clear her head and close her heart. Only she isn't alone, for watching her with gold-green eyes is the stranger on the mountain.

___52301-9 $4.99 US/$5.99 CAN

JAGUAR EYES

Casey Claybourne

Daniel Heywood ventures into the wilds of the Amazon, determined to leave his mark on science. Wounded by Indians shortly into his journey, he is rescued by a beautiful woman with the longest legs he's ever seen. As she nurses him back to health, Daniel realizes he has stumbled upon an undiscovered civilization. But he cannot explain the way his heart skips a beat when he looks into the captivating beauty's gold-green eyes. When she returns with him to England, she wonders if she is really the object of his affections—or a subject in his experiment. The answer lies in Daniel's willingness to leave convention behind for a love as lush as the Amazon jungle.

___52284-5 $5.50 US/$6.50 CAN